Cats in the Cradle of Civilization

C. L. Kraemer

Published by Rogue Phoenix Press
Copyright © 2014
ISBN 978-1-62420-128-8

Credits

Cover Artist: Designs by Ms G
Editor: Christine Young

Dedication

To my sister, Shawneen, whose patience and outstanding editing skills helped keep this book in line. As always to my husband…

Chapter One

Glenda Nagel grabbed her attaché bag and walked to the front door. Her hand on the knob, she surveyed the house trying to spy her three roommates. Scat, the calico stray that had shown up on her doorstep one night, lay stretched across the sofa, eyes closed, soaking in the morning sun. I Ching, the brown, Seal Point Siamese given to her by her ex-fiancé, and Pandora, the Blue Persian she'd bought from the breeder, sat on the window seat regally surveying the front yard.

"You guys behave, and don't tear up the house."

Three sets of furry ears barely twitched.

She locked her front door and opened the garage to enter her silver Lexus. Today was a special day. She would be driving over the hill to Los Angeles, the Getty Museum to be exact, to meet the new Antiquities Director. She could only hope he wouldn't be another of the insufferably stuffy, lost-in-the-past geeks the museum seemed prone to hire. As contributing editor of the museum's magazine, *Archaeology in Today's World*, Glenda had grown to appreciate the past, especially the Egyptian era. She could relate to a civilization that worshipped cats. Her own female felines considered they should be the object of worship, and wasted no breath in letting her know their feelings.

The sleek, silver car undulated down the winding driveway of her Juniper Hills home. She stopped at the end and admired the Antelope Valley spread out below her. The contract she'd penned with the Getty Museum agreed she would live in the desert researching and sending her work over the internet on her home computer, as long as she was available to drive in three times a week to steer the magazine in the right direction.

Glenda had grown up in Los Angeles. After earning her journalism degree at UCLA, and working as a part-time stringer on the LA Times during school and full-time for several years after, the opportunity with the museum turned out to be a godsend. The idea of living in the Los Angeles area, however, did *not* enthrall her. When she inherited the desert home from her grandparents, she'd moved from her tiny apartment in Pasadena to the cabin in Juniper Hills. Within three years, she'd remodeled and added to the original building. It suited Glenda and her three furry roommates.

Her trip to the city this morning had been, blessedly, uneventful and quick. She parked the Lexus before a sign that bore her name, and made her way through the bowels of the museum's administration building. Walking past the Egyptian wing, she noted a lithe, dark man speaking animatedly with the museum director.

Must be the new Antiquities Director--at least I can hope. She smiled as she unlocked the back door to her office. Her in-box overflowed with mail and articles for the issue of the magazine currently in the layout stage. She sat her attaché bag on the floor and picked up her phone.

"Amunet? Fine, and you? Excellent. What's on my agenda today? Okay. We're running a little behind on the next issue, so unless the building is burning down, or the Museum Director appears at my door, I don't want to be disturbed until the meeting with the new antiquities department head. Have you seen him? Good looking? Well, we can always hope. Buzz me when it's time."

She hung up the phone and attacked the inbox, quickly separating junk and wait-until-later items, from those needing immediate attention. One hour later, Glenda found herself deeply immersed in an article by a new freelancer she'd recently hired. The writer had journeyed to a town called Ta'izz, in a remote mountain area of Yemen, tracking a rumor regarding a reputed tomb bearing a single sarcophagus said to be the remains of an obscure, Egyptian child-Princess.

Very often, callers, claiming to have discovered *new* Egyptian rulers, would contact her office--repeatedly. Usually, they turned out to be scam artists searching for quick fame and fortune trying to pawn off bad replications of recently discovered artifacts. To date, this particular writer's articles for the magazine were scrupulous in the accuracy of their information. What had captured Glenda's attention about this specific article were the accompanying photographs. Difficult, at best, to snap undetected due to the security surrounding most tombs, the pictures showed concise details of the young Princess' death chamber. A petite, brilliantly painted sarcophagus rested in the center of one photo. The next picture zoomed in on a small statuette cradled in the arm of the tiny mummified body: carved ivory with emerald eyes, exquisite detailing, and about four inches in height, it was a perfect likeness of Bastet, the cat goddess. Other images featured the young Princess' life detailed in hieroglyphics on the walls and a playroom for her to use in the next life. The writer concluded if verified, this could be one of the biggest finds since Tutankhamen.

Glenda retrieved a close up shot of the glyphs on the sarcophagus's exterior from the desk. Using her magnifying glass, she copied the pictographs to a pink sticky note she'd study later at home. She recognized one or two of the glyphs as death threats. She wanted to see what curse this little Princess was passing to those who defiled her final resting place.

Quickly slipping the note and writer's article into her briefcase, Glenda flinched when her intercom buzzed.

"Yes?"

Amunet's lyrical, accent-tinged voice announced, "It is time for your meeting, Ms. Glenda."

"Thank you."

Glenda retrieved a small notebook and pen, and headed to the Director's office.

Chapter Two

Lifting the lid of the innocuous, wooden box sitting in the middle of his desk, Dabir Omar Ben Rashid Yacoub Riyadh allowed a smile to transform his bronzed features. His ebony eyes glinted as they slid appreciatively over the form resting on straw packing. Unconsciously, his tanned finger reached to stroke the artifact. He stopped, hand poised in midair, as his mind flashed to the photo of the hieroglyphics painted over the doorway of the vault posted on the internet at the Cairo museum's site. There was a warning regarding misery and eating one's self. Omar Riyadh didn't put much stock in the curses carved on crypts thousands of years ago, but recent scientific studies of the germs entombed made him cautious, nonetheless. He reached into the desk drawer to his right, and removed a pair of surgical gloves from the opened container. Slipping his hands into the milliliter thin second skin, he lightly ran a finger over the relic resting inside the box.

Gingerly, he picked up the detailed piece, jumping at the buzz of his intercom. As he felt the artifact slip from his fingers, he cursed. Inspection of the new object d'art assured him no damage had come to it. He punched the button on his intercom.

"What?" he growled.

Sharp, snapping sounds assaulted his ears. "Uhm, Mr. Riyadh?"

"Yes?"

The popping sounds filled the air. "Uh, Dr. Burkhardt and Ms. Nagel are here."

"I'll be out in a moment; tell them to have a seat." *I must speak to Miss Showers regarding her office demeanor. This gum popping will have to cease.*

Omar reclosed the lid of the small box and slid the package into his bottom drawer, surgical gloves resting on the top. Bits of straw littered his desk. He looked around his office and, spying the large shipping crate sent to him by his cousin Feneku, hastily ripped open the top pulling out a clay vase, and setting it on the spot where the little treasure had sat.

He stood and straightened his tie, then opened the door to face the Director and Miss Nagel.

Karl Burkardt, Getty Museum Director, made the formal introductions.

"Glenda Nagel, let me introduce Dr. Dabir Omar Ben Rashid Yacoub Riyadh, our new Egyptian Antiquities Director. Dr. Riyadh comes to us after many years working in the Egyptian antiquities system and on several important digs in the Valley of the Kings. His last post was in the Cairo Museum.

"Dr. Dabir Omar Ben Rashid Yacoub Riyadh, allow me to introduce you to Glenda Nagel, contributing Editor to the Museum's publication, *Archaeology in Today's World.*"

Omar extended his hand.

"Please... just call me Omar. All the other stuff has meaning only in my country. Omar is much simpler. I am pleased to make your acquaintance." He wrapped a velvety smooth, copper colored hand around Glenda's squeezing gently and gazing intensely into her turquoise eyes.

Glenda's hand tingled. Her heart skipped a beat, and breath suspended in her lungs. Slipping her appendage from Omar's, she replied, "My pleasure".

Director Burkhardt launched into Glenda's achievements droning on endlessly about her taking on the dying magazine and reviving the publication.

She felt herself flushing at the lavish compliments the Director was heaping on her.

"Please, Director Burkhardt..." Glenda dropped her gaze to the floor.

"It is well deserved, young lady. You've helped to breathe new life into this institution. As much as we would like to function without the public's help, we do need them. Your efforts have paved the way to a successful partnership."

He continued, "Now, Omar. The reason I've brought Glenda here today is, she'll be in need of your expertise, on occasion, to guarantee the information we impart to the public is correct. Please extend her all the resources at your disposal." He glanced at his watch. "If you two don't mind, I've a meeting with the Budget Committee. Can you carry this without my help?"

Both nodded.

"Good. Then, I expect to see our magazine, as well as our visitor numbers, thrive."

Turning on a heel, Director Burkhardt exited leaving the magazine editor and new antiquities director glancing nervously at each other.

Omar motioned for Glenda to take a seat.

"Please feel free to contact me at any time." He pulled a business card from the holder on his desk and scribbled something on the back. "This is my home phone. Should you have a question that arises after business hours, do not hesitate to call." He shoved the card past the vase to Glenda.

Taking the card, Glenda eyed the clay vase on the desk.

"This isn't authentic ancient Egyptian, is it?" She leaned toward the vessel and squint her eyes to take in the details.

Omar loosed a deep, baritone laugh.

Glenda felt her skin rise in goose bumps at the pleasant sound washing over her ears.

"Yes and no. All the authentic *antiquities*, we store in a room in the basement with monitored temperature and humidity control. We wouldn't want something the desert has preserved for thousands of years destroyed by today's harmful pollution.

"This," Omar picked up the vase, "is my cousin's handiwork and he is from Egypt. He sent it to show me what he has been creating for the tourist business he runs; in case someone decides to try to pass it off as an antiquity." Omar smiled as he replaced the vase. "His heart was in a good place."

Glenda ran a slender finger over the smoothness of the vase's surface.

"This is quite lovely. Your cousin is a talented artisan."

Omar nodded. "That, he is. I have told him he should come to America and start a pottery factory, but he loves Egypt too much to leave. He sells enough goods to own two Mercedes, and put his five children through college."

The two chuckled as Glenda continued to admire the simple designs on the pottery.

"Miss Nagel?"

"Hmmm?"

"You have a question?"

"What? Oh, yes. I wanted to ask if you could direct me where to start research to verify a story one of my freelancers recently sent."

"I'll try. Can you relate what your writer has so far?"

"Well, according to his source, there was a little known Princess named, Kia, who fled to Yemen to be concealed from the sadistic Pharaoh to whom she was promised in marriage. Rumors had been leaking from unknown sources in the palace that his former queens had met Ra under suspicious circumstances. Kia's protector, and nursemaid, hired a boat for the two to flee down the Red Sea where they landed on the Yemen shores at a place known today as Al-Hudaydah. The nursemaid's family had been slowly migrating from there to the town of Ta'izz, so the pair trekked to Ta'izz. Things went well for a while. The little Princess adapted, as most children are wont to do, and seemed to be thriving in her new home. As the story goes, she contracted some unknown illness a couple months after arriving, and died very quickly. Writings, recently uncovered, indicate the Pharaoh had located the whereabouts of his young fiancé and, in a fit of rage, ordered her death along with all who had defied him by stealing her away. To keep the image of himself as a divine entity, he buried the Princess in a royal tomb telling all she succumbed to forces from the underworld. He would have saved her had she been by his side but, unable to move with enough speed, he arrived too late. He gave no one the tomb's location.

"Now, mind you, all of this had been hearsay passed from generation to generation until this point. My freelancer also sent these photos."

Glenda handed pictures taken in the tomb to Omar.

He thumbed through each pausing on the last shot.

She watched his eyes scrutinize the details.

Handing them back to Glenda, a slight smile crossed his face. "These could have been taken at any tomb in the Egypt, Saudi Arabia area; there are so many. I have heard the story you tell me. It is similar to your American fable of the Lost Dutchman's Goldmine; everyone has been told the story, and is certain they know the true location. I'll be happy to start the search in my library to see if I can, at least, verify the Princess existed. When do you need the information?"

Glenda gathered the photos and stood up. "You don't need to do this, Dr."

Omar, grinning broadly, waved a hand in the air. "It is no problem. It will help me to get my bearings here, *and* help a fellow employee."

She blushed, "Thank you. If I need the writer to redo the story, I'll have to get it back to him by the end of the week. Will that be enough time?"

Omar nodded.

"Thank you, Dr. Riyadh. I appreciate the time you're lending to this. I'll leave my number with your secretary if you need to get in touch."

She walked into the outer room. Nodding at the Director's secretary, she left. The new director was good looking, all right. He sent sparks up her spine, but something just didn't sit well with her. Glenda shook her head as she entered her office.

"Any messages, Amunet?"

The young woman behind the computer screen looked up. "No. How did the meeting go? Is he handsome?"

"I think I can honestly say he is the most handsome man I've ever met."

Amunet raised her eyebrows. "He can't be *that* good looking."

Glenda stopped and turned to her assistant. "Compared to Dr. Riyadh, Brad Pitt is homely."

"Wow."

"That's an understatement. I'll be in my office pulling out my hair. Buzz me only if the building's on fire. On second thought, don't. If everything goes up in flames, I won't have to worry about it." Glenda flashed a grin and closed her door. The magazine deadline was looming, and she needed a lead story with undisputable facts.

Chapter Three

Omar's phone rang. He noted the extension number of the director shown on the display.

"Omar Riyadh, here. How can I help you, Director?"

"Sorry, Omar. I've been distracted with this bloody budget thing. Always hated the money end of this job; anyway, I forgot to mention we will be having some international visitors this afternoon. I believe they mentioned they'd arrive around 3:30 or 4:00 p.m. Couple of chaps from Interpol coming to see you. Not sure what it's about, but offer them as much assistance as they need, will you?"

"Certainly, Director. I'm at their disposal. Is that all?"

"For now. If I think of anything else, I'll ring you." Director Burkhardt's years at Oxford always showed when he allowed the stress of the job to creep up on him.

Omar replaced the phone to its cradle, his brow furrowed in deep thought. *Why is Interpol here?* Opening the desk drawer, he withdrew the tattered wooden box, placed it in the center of his desk, and removed the lid. He re-gloved and admired the simplicity of the artifact's lines. Hieroglyphs he'd not noticed the first time caught his attention, and he retrieved his magnifying glass to read the inscription.

Bastet, daughter of Re, guardian of the Princess Kia. He who removes this from the Princess shall be consumed by his flesh.

Omar sat up and stared at the ivory cat headed figure holding the delicate sistrum. He would need research for further affirmation of this find. *The editor woman, Nagel, that's it, Glenda Nagel, has an informant, a freelancer, who seems to have stumbled on the location of this tomb. I need to see that article before she prints it in her magazine and sets the world searching for my little Princess.*

The intercom buzzed. Omar grit his teeth. He gingerly placed the artifact in its holder and answered.

"Yes, Miss Showers?"

The pop of gum answered him. "Dr. Riyadh?"

Omar closed his eyes and drew a deep breath before answering. "Yes?"

Snapping. "I got a phone call for you from some real official sounding guys."

Silence.

Omar sighed. "Yes, Miss Showers? What is the message?"

Snap, pop. "Oh, yeah," she giggled. "They said they'll be here promptly at four o'clock, and they expect you to be ready to talk with them. They said they were from Internet or something."

"That's Interpol, Miss Showers. Thank you." He started to hang up the phone when he remembered his wish to discuss office procedure with the young docent.

"Miss Showers?" A click in his ear told him he was too late. He dialed her extension, waited, and when there was no answer, opened the door between the offices.

He stared at the young woman with the spiked, blue-streaked, blonde hair chomping on her gum, and conversing into her cellphone.

"Miss Showers!"

His deep voice rattled against the office window. The startled young docent dropped her phone uttering a swear word in the process. Omar stared at the young woman.

"As of this moment, you will stop the chewing of your gum while you work in this office. Turn off your cellphone. Get rid of the blue in your hair, or I'll have you replaced." His towering form leaned toward her over the edge of the desk. "Do I make myself clear?"

April batted her blue eyes at him and popped her gum loudly. "You can't replace me, I'm a volunteer." She flashed him an insincere smile.

"Do not tell me what I can, and cannot, do in my own office. Tomorrow morning, I expect those changes to be made or, by noon, you will be walking out the front door of the museum." He spun around toward his office.

"You can't!" April was whining. "I need this for my art degree."

Omar pivoted to face the young secretary. "Then I suggest you make the necessary changes, or you'll be looking for your work experience elsewhere. Am I clear?"

She picked up her cellphone and glared at the director. "I'm talking to Mr. Burkhardt about this."

"You do that. In the meantime, get rid of the gum. I'm going out for a while. Take messages and finish the typing I asked you to do *two days ago*. I'll return by four o'clock to meet my visitors." Omar closed his door. His eye was drawn to the wooden box open on his desk.

Damn! I don't want this in the office when the inspectors from Interpol show up. What to do? He could just return the box to his drawer, but he knew himself. His face would give him away. The treasure would have to be spirited out of his office for further study later. Hurriedly slipping on one glove, he picked up the statuette and dropped it into the first secure location he could. He closed the shipping crate and shoved it into his coat closet securing the door.

He dialed the Museum Director's office.

"Director's office." The voice at the other end was crisp--efficient.

"Yes, this is Dr. Riyadh. The director told me I would be able to call him if I needed assistance. I find myself needing the office number of Miss Nagel."

Omar heard paper rustling.

"She's located in room 116."

"Than…" The phone had gone dead.

He shrugged and, grabbing his keys and the vase, closed his door striding past his pouting secretary and in the direction of Glenda Nagel's office.

The ringing of his cellphone echoed off the polished floors and elegantly painted walls of the museum. Omar glanced at the read out screen and breathed out a small groan.

"Yes. A problem has arisen. Interpol. I've got it handled. It'll be close enough for me to reach at any given moment, but this is not the time to act. I'll contact you."

Reaching the door with Glenda's name and title stenciled on the outside, Omar brushed invisible dust off the jacket of his Armani suit and, putting on his most winning smile, entered the office.

Amunet glanced up and involuntarily gasped. Her exotic, dark eyes widened, and her mouth gaped slightly at the presence standing before her.

"May, may I help you?" Her cheeks tinged ruby.

"Yes, I'd like to speak with Miss Nagel." He leaned toward Amunet.

The intoxicating aroma of his spicy aftershave gently tickled her nose.

"She told me not to disturb her even if the place was on fire."

Omar smiled widely. "Tell her there is a raving Persian out here who will not accept no for an answer, and he's threatening to place a horrible curse on you and all your relatives."

Amunet smiled as she picked up the phone.

"That doctor is here, and won't take no for an answer. He's," she glanced up at Omar and smiled, "threatening to put a horrible curse on me and all my family if you don't see him. It would mean I wouldn't be able to work. Yes, ma'am." She nodded in the direction of the door.

"She says to come on in, but you can't say anything about the mess."

Omar bowed slightly and clicked his heels together. "I am in your debt for life." He went through the door to Glenda's office.

Amunet fanned herself. "Woo, he *is* good looking."

~ * ~

Omar walked into an office overwhelmed with paper. Glenda was removing a skewered stack of items from a chair to the top of a filing cabinet. She indicated he should sit.

"What is so important you would curse my secretary's family if you didn't get in to see me?" Glenda leaned back in her chair.

"I am hoping you will agree to have lunch with me. I brought this vase to you as a token, in anticipation of our working together." Omar placed a vase on Glenda's desk.

She started to protest.

Omar held up his hand. "My cousin will be pleased you find his work worthy of admiration."

"Thank you for the lovely gift. It is a fine piece of artwork. I am, however, going to have to turn down the lunch invitation. I have a deadline to meet and, without verification of the Princess Kia information, I'm trying to decide which story will be my lead. Maybe another time?"

Omar clutched his chest. "I am wounded, but will ask again. I understand having a deadline. It is the same with a new exhibition. Time becomes a fleeting bird." He stood and extended his hand to Glenda. "Someday soon?"

The brilliant white smile against his honey brown skin stopped her breath mid-throat. She gave a little cough and smiling shook his extended hand.

"Until that time." He vanished through the door.

Glenda sucked air into her lungs. The unique scent of his aftershave lingered in the air of her office. Mingled with the dust, and smell of paper, it made for an unusual essence. Glenda found herself staring absently into space.

"I have *got* to get myself together. The deadline isn't getting any further away. I'll put the destruction of centuries-old temples by the Afghani Mujahadeen in the lead. That ought to shake some of these conservatives out of their apathy."

Glenda found herself drawn to the vase Omar had presented her. It was quite lovely in its simplicity. His cousin had a real talent with pottery. She glanced around her office, and deduced the vase would probably get broken if she left it.

I'll take it home. I'm sure I can find somewhere to display it.

Finding more distractions in her office than at home, she packed the vase into her briefcase and grabbed the list she'd made for her secretary. A brief explanation to Amunet, and Glenda pushed her way out of the museum. She stood for a moment in the overcast, smoggy courtyard debating whether she should turn around and finish her work at the museum or finish at home. The appearance of goose bumps on her arms, and a chill that was quickly finding its way to her bones convinced her she could finish the layout of the magazine in the sunshine and warmth of the desert just as easily as in her office in the valley. A smile formed on her lips. *Being your own boss has its advantages.*

Chapter Four

She entered the freeway, amazed at the amount of traffic filling the lanes at two in the afternoon. The crush of cars thinned the closer she got to the freeway turnoff leading her from the Los Angeles basin to the desert. Glenda relaxed with each passing mile. The vase pulled at her to touch its surface. Her hand stroked the smooth, graceful lines finding no imperfections beneath her fingers. Egyptian hieroglyphics, intended to impress tourists as authentic, lined the top and bottom of the earthen jug. She fought the overwhelming urge to pick it up and cradle it in her arms. Glenda shook her head. *Where did that come from?*

Focusing on the road ahead of her, she exited the indicated off ramp to Sierra Highway which would lead her home to Juniper Hills. Forty-five minutes later, she was turning into the driveway, three pair of feline eyes trying *not* to look interested gazing her direction. Glenda parked the car in the garage and entered the house. She dropped her briefcase on the dining room table and turned at the thunder of furry paws.

Scat wound her way in and through Glenda's legs complaining loudly. I Ching delicately jumped from the window seat. Stalking through the living room, she planted herself directly in front of Glenda and proceeded to yowl.

"I know, I know. But ladies, someone in this household has to work so you can lounge around all day. Since you didn't volunteer, I guess it has to be me. Let me put my stuff down somewhere, and we'll sit and talk."

Pandora had been lying on her back in the window seat, paws dangling mid-air. Glenda, vase clutched in one hand, strolled to the window seat, and leaned over to scratch Pandora's exposed belly. She bent and reached her hand down barely connecting with the silken fur, when Pandora flipped herself upright. She arched her back and hissed at Glenda.

"Pandora!" Glenda snatched her hand back before impaling herself with the claws the cat was swiping at her. "What is your problem?"

She backed away from the couch, still clutching the vase. Glenda wandered to her office and set the pottery on the edge of her desk. She eyed the clay vessel.

"It really is a pretty little thing."

Moving around the desk, she sat in the chair and pushed out a sigh.

"I need to get busy." She fired up her computer, shoving paperwork to one side. Glancing up, she caught movement from the edge of the desk and her hand shot out to catch the little vase as it slid off the corner toward the floor.

"Whew, that was close." She searched the desktop and decided the best home for the vessel was between the calendar and in box. The computer monitor lit up displaying the Giza pyramids screen saver she'd installed. Glenda navigated the system to her email. She noted messages from the usual litany of advertisers, good and bad, and three messages she wanted to open. The first two were a couple of her copy editors checking in. They mentioned it was getting close to the time for them to receive their pages of the month's layout. Glenda replied and assured them they'd be seeing the drafts within the next eight hours.

The address of the third message was Egyptian. She was intrigued. Opening her drawer, she grabbed a pencil. She needed a sticky note and began to search under the mountain of papers residing on her desk. She picked up one pile then another and when she'd located the yellow pad, looked up to see the vase tumbling to the floor.

"Damn it." She jumped up, darting around the corner of her desk, and dove to the floor her hands outstretched. The little vase settled itself in her palms. She dropped her forehead to the carpet.

"Why are you so determined to crash on the floor?" She started at the growl behind her.

Pandora, eyes large and luminescent, was growling deep in her throat and stalking toward Glenda. She pulled back her lips and, snarling, emitted a dangerous yeowl that increased in volume and intensity the closer she got to Glenda.

Pulling herself from the floor, Glenda stomped a foot at the crouching cat.

"Knock it *off*. Stop acting so schizoid!" She clutched the container to her chest.

"Where am I going to put you? I want to be able to see you but not in a hundred pieces." She turned the vase, noting the primitive hieroglyphics painted on the side. "Are you embarrassed at the poor attempt to fool tourists?"

This is ridiculous. I'm talking to a clay pot. I need to get this month's issue done and out of here. It's making me crazy.

Scat and I Ching poked their heads around the doorsill. Scat's little voice whispered a meow, nearly drowned out by the characteristic howl of the Siamese.

"Now what, ladies?" Glenda leaned against the desk. The little stray tip toed in the room carefully avoiding Pandora who was stomping her furry paws in circle eights in front of Glenda. I Ching swayed in behind the little cat yeowling with each step.

"I suppose you guys think it's time to eat? Give me a minute then we'll all go to the kitchen and I'll feed you."

Glenda placed the urn in the center of the desk, and wrote the email address down on the yellow sticky note.

"Happy now?"

Two sets of fur-encased eyes squeezed shut. Pandora still pacing in front of the desk, growled menacingly with each step.

"If after you've eaten, your attitude doesn't change, young lady, you'll be visiting your carrying case for the evening. I don't have time for this." Glenda shook a finger at the cat.

She toted the vase to the kitchen and set it on the counter as she filled cat bowls with food and water. Scat pounced on the dish, her tail swishing furiously, daring anyone to invade her space. I Ching sauntered to her dish and with the delicacy of a debutante, took out one piece of food at a time, for all the world looking as though she were counting how many times it took to chew. Pandora ignored the food. Her eyes fixed on the vase.

Finished with the food ritual, Glenda leaned against the counter and stared out the front window. The serenity of the scene quieted an unease that had crept over her since this morning. She picked up the clay pot rolling it from one hand to the other, the feel of the clay cool and smooth against her fingers.

Realizing she was carrying the vase around the house with her, Glenda moved to the fireplace mantel. As she raised the vase, Pandora, who'd been shadowing her every move, jumped to the window seat and launched herself at Glenda.

"What the hell are you doing?" Glenda shoved the vase on the mantelshelf and sidestepped the furry missile.

Pandora's fur, down the center of her blue-gray arched back, stood straight up. Her deep emerald eyes were mere slits in the hit-by-a-frying-pan face that distinguished her as a purebred Persian. She continued to emit low guttural growls.

"Enough!" Glenda backed herself into the kitchen to set the teakettle to heating.

The gray cat paced in front of the fireplace, a low growling punctuating the flicking of her tail.

Enough is enough. Glenda retrieved the spray bottle and aimed it at the Persian.

"Pandora!"

Normally, just the sight of the bottle sent the cats scurrying, but Pandora seemed determined to be contrary. Glenda let fly a stream of water leaving a large wet spot on the silken gray fur. Grudgingly, the cat ceased her pacing and began the laborious task of ridding her fur of the unwanted liquid.

Glenda grabbed her tea and the squirt bottle in one hand, and, picking up her briefcase, moved back to her office. She bobbled the squirt bottle and tea mug capturing the one corner that had mysteriously escaped the paperwork piles residing on the rest of the wooden surface, and, with enviable skill, guided the tea mug and bottle safely down. She plunked the attaché in the center, and attacked the paperwork spilling out. Splintering sounds of pottery hitting terra cotta tiles evoked a scream from Glenda and brought her running into the living room. Pandora hunkered down over the broken vase growling lowly, her eyes blinking furiously, and tail swishing. She reached out a paw and pushed at a large piece of pottery in the middle of the broken shards.

"Shame on you!"

Glenda stomped into the kitchen. Dustpan and broom in hand, she marched to the fireplace hearth to clean up the pieces of the shattered vase. She muttered as she began sweeping. As Glenda reached to clear away the piece of pottery the cat was toying with, Pandora arched her back and spat.

"That is *quite* enough." Glenda swooped down, grasping the cat by the back of the neck, and rendered her motionless. "You will stay in your carrier for the rest of the night. What has gotten into you?" She deposited Pandora unceremoniously in her carrying case.

"Until you get a change of attitude, Miss Thing, you will remain here."

She bent to finish the task of cleaning when a flash of color caught her attention. Leaning closer, she realized she was seeing a form in the pieces of broken pottery. She delicately brushed away the dust and bits of vase.

"Oh, wow." Before her lay a four-inch statuette of Bastet, cat goddess; small emerald eyes from within an ivory body staring up at her, and clutching a sistrum in her hand. "Wait a minute." Glenda ran to her office and returned with a photo. She knelt and compared the picture to the item lying on her hearth.

"This looks identical to the one in the picture Nasim Shabouh sent me. This little statuette is either a very good imitation, or I need to warn the new antiquities director about the merchandise his cousin is selling." Sweeping the small artifact into the dustpan, she put the broom on the floor. Carrying pan and picture to her office, she settled both on her desk. Reaching in her drawer, she removed a pair of thin, white cotton gloves which she donned. Experience had taught her prevention was worth your life when dealing with artifacts-real or presumed real. Reverently, she picked the statuette out of the dustpan with one gloved appendage and, with the other, grabbed the jeweler's glass which resided on her desk. She moved the picture to the center of the desk. Turning on her lamp, she secured the jeweler's glass in her eye and began to inspect the little cat goddess currently resting in her palm against the pictorial fact. It never ceased to amaze Glenda at the talent exhibited by some of the forgers whose work she'd viewed. There'd been a show of forgery handiwork her first week on the job. She'd made a point to spend time in the small gallery studying the works; recognizing antiquities meant also being able to recognize the forgeries. She reached for the phone.

Until I can verify whether this is or is not genuine, I shouldn't involve Omar. If it's real, he probably doesn't know about it.

Glenda slid open her bottom drawer and pulled out a shoebox. Rummaging through the items tossed randomly inside, she concluded this was nothing more than a catchall and she had enough of those scattered around the house. She opened the top drawer and grabbed several pairs of the thin, cotton gloves to line the box. The tiny cat fit snuggly. Lid secured, she replaced the container in the bottom drawer, which she slid shut. She leaned back in her chair and pondered her next move.

Should she contact the director? Surely, he'd come across this situation in his tenure at the Cairo museum. Or should she wait until… what? It wasn't as if the statuette would glow blue if it was a fake. How was she going to handle this load dumped on her?

And what about her cat? Pandora, normally a sweet-tempered, docile cat, acted so irrationally Glenda was prone to believe the artifact was authentic.

Weren't cats more sensitive to smells than people?

She swung the chair around and e-mailed her freelancer about the article he'd sent and the figurine he'd photographed.

> *Mr. Shabouh--were there any inscriptions on the little statuette? Any unique forms, or etchings, to identify it as the real deal and not a reproduction?*

Glenda pushed the send button. She pulled up the magazine layout and began to work on getting the month's issue ready for print. A looming deadline waited for no one.

Chapter Five

Omar pulled a cloth from his bottom drawer and quickly dusted desk and the coffee table in his sitting area. This ritual he performed before every gathering in his office. The motion helped quiet his mind and gave him time to organize how he wanted to direct the progress of the meeting. Today, there was a twofold reason for his ritual. He, of course, wanted to make sure his office was clean to receive guests, but more to the point, he wanted to remove evidence of the items his cousin had sent him. He'd dealt with Interpol agents before and knew they were sharp--very sharp. Anything remotely out of place would capture their attention and could bring a barrage of unwanted questions and possible investigation. Omar could not afford to attract attention. As he placed the cloth back into his bottom drawer, his intercom buzzed. He glanced at his watch. It was precisely 4:00 p.m.

"Yes?"

There was a hesitation. "The people from… Interpol are here to see you, sir."

"Thank you. Send them in, Miss Showers."

"Yes, sir."

Omar smirked. Apparently, Miss Showers needed this job more than she needed her attitude. He rose and rounded the end of his desk to greet the two visitors entering his office. The first was a younger man; Omar figured him to be in his late twenties, dressed in an inexpensive, business suit with the dark complexion that hinted to Omar he might be Middle Eastern. Following the young man was a smaller figure. Omar gasped when she stepped from behind the young man.

"You! I thought you were an exchange student!" Omar stumbled backwards, grabbing the desk.

The blonde, wearing an expensive, tailor-made black suit smirked and replied in Egyptian.

"I was. Only, it was ten years before you took the position at the Antiquities Museum in Riyadh. I was undecided about the direction I wanted to take in my career, so I applied for an internship at the museum."

Omar leaned against his desk.

"So what is the real reason you were at my museum all those years ago, Lydia?"

"My family encouraged my interest in archaeology. I'm not sure if it was the fact I actually applied myself to studying or if it was being thousands of miles away, but they helped me secure the job in Cairo.

"After the time I spent learning the culture and experiencing the kindness of the Egyptian people, I found the blatant stealing of the country's heritage infuriated me. I know the theft of ancient artifacts goes back to the original tomb raiders, but I wanted the peoples of Persia, my friends, to know their history would remain in their own countries.

"Outsiders securing priceless articles to hide away in private collections for their own viewing are wrong. I felt the need to do everything in my power to stop the flow. So, I applied at the FBI academy then emigrated to Interpol.

"Sorry," she smiled, "time to get off my soap box and make introductions. I'm Lydia Thompson, as you know, and this," Lydia nodded to her companion, "is Nasim Shabouh. Nasim, I would like to introduce you to Dr. Dabir Omar Ben Rashid Yacoub Riyadh, former director of Antiquities at Ar-Riyadh Museum of Saudi Arabia, and current director of Antiquities at the Getty Museum in California. Dr. Riyadh is a specialist in little-known royalty of the Late Period, his specialty being the Second Persian era of 343 to 332 BC. There is no one with more knowledge of that time period than Dr. Riyadh."

Omar felt heat tinge his cheeks and extended a hand. "Lydia always did have a penchant for exaggeration. I am pleased to make your acquaintance. Shabouh--do you have relatives in Cairo?" He peered into Nasim's eyes.

The young agent didn't falter as he shook the director's hand. "Probably cousins many times removed. *My* family is from Aswan."

"Please; let's sit while we talk. Would either of you care for coffee?"

The two agents declined the offer as they positioned themselves on the burgundy leather couch. Omar noted Nasim casting an eye over the room. He hesitated at a spot in front of Omar's desk.

Lydia pulled a small notebook from her purse and flipped it open.

"Dr. Riyadh, at the request of the Yemen government, we are investigating the recent theft of a newly discovered burial spot in the southern mountains of Yemen. What we've been able to ascertain so far is the occupant of the tomb was a young princess, not widely known, who appears to have been murdered due to her refusal to become the Pharaoh's who-knows-what-number bride. She was an ardent Bastet worshipper. There were literally hundreds of cat mummies in the tomb, and they buried her with a small ivory and emerald figurine of the cat goddess in her arms.

"When the Yemenese archaeologists arrived to catalogue and document the tomb's treasures, they noted a large number of small items were missing. The only reason they were aware of the theft is the amateur archaeologist who stumbled upon the burial site had the good sense to bring a camera and extra film. He took numerous photos of everything he came across; the walls, furniture, sarcophagus, and cat mummies, everything down to the small figurine held in the little princess' arms, which he mailed to the government's archaeology division.

"We're hoping you'll be able to assist us by keeping your eyes and ears open to acquisitions offered to the museum which might appear too good to be true."

Omar shifted in his chair, the leather quietly protesting. He glanced at the young man, but found no emotion visible in his deep brown eyes. They relentlessly scanned the room.

Omar cleared his throat. "I recall the story of a young princess whose name, I believe, was Kia. She was smuggled away from the palace by her nursemaid and taken to Ta'izz to be hidden. Unfortunately, the Pharaoh's reach was farther than the range of the boat which spirited the young girl away. He placed a price on her head. The one who brought back her favorite cat, her finger, and the body of her nursemaid would receive a handsome reward of a home on the Nile and servants. I believe you will find the ring finger of the princess' hand is missing. The Pharaoh did not wish her to be able to marry in the afterlife so he removed the appropriate finger."

Omar observed Lydia shoot Nasim a quick look. Nasim nodded his head.

"So you are aware of the Princess. Excellent. May we count on your cooperation in this matter?" Lydia stood up. Nasim and Omar followed her lead.

Reaching out to shake their hands, Omar answered. "Yes. Please be assured I will contact you if I hear of anything."

He accepted the business card Lydia extended to him, and escorted the pair to the hallway. Shutting the door, he strode to his office, instructing April as he passed, "Absolutely no calls. No exceptions. Do you understand, Miss Showers?"

"Yes, sir."

Omar slammed his door and leaned against the frame. He stared absently at the floor in front of his desk until his brain registered the light spot.

"Damn it!" He bent over and picked up a single curled bit of straw. Tossing the bit into the wastebasket, he moved to the chair behind his desk, and picked up the phone.

"Yes. Is Miss Nagel in? Oh, she's not? Hmmmm. I believe I left some of my research papers in her office. May I come down and see if they're on her desk? No, thanks for the offer, but it won't take long. I'll just poke in my head. Great. I'll be there in about five minutes. Thank you, Amunet."

Omar used the exit off the conference room adjoining his office. He sprinted, his soft Italian loafers sliding on the highly polished marble hallway, to the doorway of Glenda's office. Stopping for a moment to catch his breath, he strolled inside.

"Amunet. May I go in?" He offered his most genuine smile.

"Sure." She returned his smile, and nodded at the doorway.

As Omar opened the inner door, he heard the tapping of keys on the computer behind him.

Good. She won't be worrying about how long this is taking.

Omar checked the desktop then, with the expedience of a professional, he searched the entire office for the vase he had given the magazine editor.

Curses. It's not here. She must have taken it with her.

He exited her office and slowed his pace in front of the secretary.

"Amunet?"

"Yes, director?"

"Omar, please. Did Miss Nagel take home her vase?"

Amunet placed her hand over her mouth and giggled behind her fingers. "Yes. She figured it was safer in her houseful of cats than it was here in the office."

Forcing himself to smile, Omar remarked, "My cousin will be pleased she has taken such pains to care for the little vase".

He started out the door and turning said to Amunet, "I was unable to locate my research material. I think, though, I may have it stored on my computer. Thank you for allowing me to check the office." With a wave of his hand, Omar left the office. He quickly covered the hallway with long, determined strides returning to his desk.

If she has taken the vase home then I must find a way to get inside her house. The buyer will be expecting to see the figurine before depositing the broker's fee in my account. Somehow, I must arrange a dinner invitation. Once inside, I'm sure I can find a way to retrieve the statuette without detection. The young editor is such a trusting soul...

The ringing of a phone interrupted Omar's contemplation. Automatically, he reached for the instrument on his desk, intending to read his secretary the riot act, when he realized none of the lines were lit. The second ring sounded from the top drawer of his desk. He slid it open, and answered his cell.

"What? You will have to find patience, my friend. The article has slipped through my possession, momentarily." He held the phone away from his ear at the explosive ranting directed from the other end. "As I said, it is but a momentary delay. I will have the piece within the week. At that time, I will contact you. Do not call me again, or I will locate another to handle its disposal. Goodbye."

Omar propped his chin up with the palms of his hands and rubbed his eyes with his fingers. He needed to get an invitation to the editor's house, but how?

~ * ~

Lydia turned to Nasim. "What's the matter with you? I've never seen you act so suspicious of anyone we're investigating. What's going on?"

Nasim stared unseeing out the passenger side window. His mind was churning with dozens of scenarios. Should he tell his partner the truth about what this investigation meant to him? Could she grasp the concept of generational honor and the loss therein? Her interest, while admirable, was an outsider's view. Nasim pulled in a deep breath. He missed his family most at times like these when feelings ran so deep words weren't necessary.

He'd have to rely on his instincts about his partner, and they were telling him Lydia could be trusted. Nasim was drowning in the need to talk to someone.

"What I'm about to tell you does not leave this vehicle. Agreed?"

"Agreed. Just tell me what's going on."

"Do you remember me telling you the reason I got involved in chasing these history thieves was a personal one?"

28

Lydia nodded. She signaled a turn and headed the company vehicle in a westerly direction.

"There has been a Shabouh in the royal palace tending to the preparation of the tombs since the Early Dynastic Period. It has only been in the last twenty years we have moved away from our rightful place. A move precipitated by an act so heinous it is not spoken of in my family to this day. My father, Kansbar, and his brother Gazsi, were entrusted with the family occupation. In times past, they would have been gathering household and recreational items to be buried with the Pharaoh when he died. In today's world, they were keepers of the archaeological warehouses in Riyadh and Cairo. My father was in Cairo, where I grew up, and my uncle was Warehouse Master in Riyadh."

Lydia's brow wrinkled. "You said you were from Aswan."

"My family lives there now but twenty years ago, you will recall, there was a huge theft from the Museum warehouse in Riyadh. It made all the papers because of the immense value of the items stolen. Someone anonymously phoned in a tip that the Warehouse Master, my uncle, was working with an accomplice to empty the Museum's surplus items for his own personal gain. The investigators found several $100,000 deposits made to my uncle's bank account. He showed up at work driving a new Mercedes and, suddenly, his sons were attending colleges in America. There was no logical explanation for his unexpected wealth. He was tried and convicted on testimony from an individual whose voice was electronically altered, his face hidden behind a protective wall in the courtroom. Before my uncle's execution, my father went to see him and asked how he could shame the family this way. Uncle Gazsi told my father he'd been helping the Museum Director, Omar Riyadh. He knew nothing of the deposits because Laleh, my aunt, always handled the money. He was driving the Mercedes because Dr. Riyadh had asked him to take care of it while he was away on a new dig inspection. He didn't know the Dr. had put it in his name.

"He had my aunt bring the letters to my father, which stated my cousins had won scholarships to the various American colleges. The letters were forgeries and a bank account with unlimited funds in the name of Uncle Gazsi was the source of the college payments. My uncle, of course, knew nothing of the account.

"All of the information discovered by my father pointed to Dr. Omar Riyadh as being the actual thief of the antiquities, but the authorities felt they had their man in my uncle. They wouldn't prosecute an honored citizen like Dr. Riyadh.

"Because of the stigma attached to the name Shabouh, my father was asked to resign his position. I was eleven when he died in shame. Seeing Dr. Riyadh today brought back many unhappy memories.

"I *will* find who is stealing these items from the Ta'izz dig. I can only hope the thief is Riyadh."

Nasim couldn't recall when they'd reached the ocean but the sun glinting off the turquoise tinged surface snatched his breath away. He sat and stared at the waves thundering against the beach. The pale blue sky streaked with white cloud streamers belying the fury and power of the sea mirrored the turmoil bubbling beneath Nasim's composed exterior.

"Wow. This is amazing." Nasim turned to Lydia. "Thanks. This is just what I needed."

A tender smile crossed her face. "Me, too. Thank you for trusting me enough to confide in me."

Nasim nodded, his eyes drawn to the rhythm of the ocean.

The two agents sat quietly allowing the sound of crashing waves to wash away their stress. Lydia glanced at her watch.

"As much as I would love to sit here all day and watch the waves, we really need to get back to the office and file a report for the boss. Ready?"

"Yes. I want to follow up on a lead I'm pursuing. There may be a way into the viper's nest without getting bitten. Let's go."

The white four-door sedan pulled out of the parking space, and entered the stream of traffic heading toward downtown Los Angeles.

~ * ~

Glenda checked her e-mail, again. "Darn it. I wish he'd get back to me. This is going to drive me crazy until I find out."

She stood up and wandered into the kitchen. Setting the kettle to boil, Glenda ambled into the living room and gazed out the window at the open expanse of desert. I Ching, her Siamese, was sitting on the sill majestically surveying the front yard, her slender chocolate tail swishing languidly from side to side. Scat, the calico stray, crouched on the window seat, and attacked each time the chocolate tail came near. Glenda frowned. *What's Pandora up to?*

"Pandora?" she called.

A muffled yeowling could be heard.

Glenda frowned. "Where--? Duh!" She rolled her eyes at herself. Opening the door to the laundry room brought forth a loud, complaining oww. She bent down, and peered into the emerald eyes.

"Will you behave if I let you out?"

A quiet mew and loud purring were the answer she received. She opened the door of the carrier, and stepped aside to let the cat emerge. One dark paw touched the tile floor, hesitantly, then another. Pandora slowly serpentined her way out of the plastic prison. She wound her silky body around Glenda's legs, purring loudly, and emitting sounds with each step that sounded like "out, out, out".

Glenda ran her hand over the soft fur. "Yes, you're out, but if you start behaving like you were earlier, I'll put you *out* for the coyotes."

The smoky face turned up, eyes squeezed shut, and Pandora let loose a loud, "Rowwr." She walked past Glenda toward the front room. As Glenda straightened up, she heard the computer in her office announce, "You've got mail."

"About time." Fixing herself a cup of tea, she padded back to her office. "Hope it's from Nasim and not Amunet with more work."

Seeing the anticipated e-mail address, Glenda opened the reply and read.

~ * ~

Nasim pressed the Enter button on his computer. His printer chunked out pages, and when finished, he pulled them from the tray, stapling them in order. Sliding them to the side of his desk, he hesitated, reaching his hand to the silver framed picture. He traced a finger over the image of the two dark-skinned men, arms wrapped around each other, broad sparkling smiles emitting from the sun-darkened faces.

"I will restore the name of Shabouh to a place of honor among the annals of the pharaohs, I promise."

Nasim leaned over to flip off his computer. In the upper right hand corner, the blinking mail messenger caught his attention. He opened the e-mail portion of his computer to find a message from the inside contact he'd made at the museum.

"Let's see what we have here." He read the attached message. "Well, well. Seems I just got lucky. She wants a way to verify the authenticity of a small figurine resembling the statuette held by the young Princess Kia in the photo I sent her. Hmmmm. Let's see now."

He opened a drawer and rummaged through a manila file folder. Retrieving a lined tablet with hand written notes, he flipped through the pages until he came to the one bearing drawings across the top. He murmured as he read the scribbling on the page. He began to type.

> On the bottom of the statuette will be three hieroglyphs; one that looks like a torch, one that resembles an egg with a half egg over the top, and the third is a woman kneeling. All three of these figures will be on the authentic statuette. A forgery will have one or two, but not all three of the hieroglyphics. If you need anything further, please feel free to contact me.

Nasim sent the reply, filed the tablet, and shut down his computer. *Let's see where this takes us.*

~ * ~

Glenda slid open her desk drawer, wiggling her hand into the cotton glove, and carefully picked up the statuette. She held the figurine in her hand as she read the e-mail sent by her freelancer and, when she'd finished, turned the small cat goddess on her head.

"Sorry, Bastet. Let's see--there's the torch, the two eggs, and the woman kneeling. OH--MY--GOD." Glenda's hand began to shake. Her fingers began to tingle and she gently placed the little ivory goddess on her desk. She stood and paced.

"This is insane. I work around stuff older than this all the time. Why is this making me so crazy?" She stopped and pushed the figurine with her gloved finger. "Because this has come to *my* house." She stood for a moment, finger to chin, thinking. The distinct growl of her Persian captured her attention. She turned to find Pandora crouched in a stalking position, eyes wide and fixed on the top of her desk.

"Stop it!" Glenda stomped her foot. The cat ceased its forward motion, but started a mournful yowling. Another stomp of the foot sent the Persian scurrying out of the room. Why was her cat being so--psycho? Glenda picked up the figurine and examined the back of the statuette. Pain from inflammation in her wrist shot through her fingers; Bastet slid toward the floor. She reacted, bringing her knees up, and catching the artifact in her lap. Sweat beaded on her upper lip. *If I would have broken this...* She couldn't contemplate the consequences. *Then again, who would know? Surely, the new director isn't aware of the stolen artifact in his cousin's vase, is he?*

Gingerly, she lifted the statuette from her lap, and secured it in her desk drawer. *I really need to get in touch with my freelancer, and see how much information he has about this. I don't want to make a rash move before I have all the facts.* She shook her head as she removed the glove and stood up. *This is like a bad B-rated Egyptian mummy movie. Trouble is--unlike a movie; I can't get up and walk out.*

Chapter Six

Omar picked up his phone and called the Museum Director's office. The crisp, clipped accent of an Oxford voice answered.

"Yes?"

"Is the Director available? This is Dr. Riyadh. It is *imperative* I speak with him immediately." Omar hoped the slight sense of urgency would move the impenetrable Audrey Cooper. He'd been warned of the Director's no-nonsense secretary. A formidable outer wall often bolstered a soft interior. Audrey Cooper was that wall.

"I'm very sorry, Dr. Riyadh, but the Director just left for the day. You might catch him on his way out to the car park. I could take a message and relay it to him."

"Thank you, Miss Cooper, but I'll try to catch him."

"As you wish, Dr. Riyadh."

Omar bolted through his conference room, and took a short cut through the museum's grounds to the employee parking area. He spotted the Director at his Cadillac juggling his briefcase, and trying to retrieve his keys from his pocket. A quick sprint brought Omar to his side.

"Dr. Burkhardt," he huffed. Omar leaned against the burgundy four-door vehicle setting off the alarm.

The director quickly extinguished the offending sound, and placing his briefcase in the back seat, turned to face Omar.

"What's the problem, Dr. Riyadh?"

"I wish to enlist your assistance, sir."

The director raised an eyebrow.

"I would very much like to see your high desert."

The raised eyebrow had not moved.

"It is a piece I am preparing for a journal back in Egypt. I have compared the desert of my home to your desert here, and really need to see the landscape to properly formulate my conclusion. I understand the Museum's magazine editor lives in this high desert."

Dr. Burkhardt nodded his surprise fading.

"If you would be so kind as to broker a visit with the editor, I will be able to conclude my article with authority. The sooner the better as I, too, have a deadline. The completed piece must be in the magazine's offices by this Friday."

Dr. Burkhardt removed a phone from his pocket, and punched in a number.

"Glenda, Karl here. I'm hoping you can give me a hand with a bit of a problem that has arisen. Great. Remember the new Antiquities Director I introduced to you?

"Well, Dr. Riyadh is authoring an article for a periodical back in Egypt, and requires some first-hand research of the Antelope Valley. Will this interrupt *your* deadline or work schedule? Good. I thought you'd understand. Would you be able to host him at your place, tomorrow? He's facing a close deadline. May I give him your phone number so he can get directions? Thank you, Glenda."

Snapping the phone shut, the director pulled out a business card. He wrote a number on the back and handed it to Omar.

"Will this help?"

"More than you know, Dr. Burkhardt. Thank you for your intervention. Drive safely, sir."

Omar walked to his office, a smug smile distorting his handsome features. *Within forty-eight hours, I will be ten million reasons closer to retirement.*

~ * ~

Glenda dunked the teabag one more time before squeezing out the flavor. One spoonful of sugar, and it was ready for consumption. She wrapped her hands around the mug and moved into the living room. Thoughts raced around her brain as she plunked down on the window seat. I Ching emitted a small yowl of protest at Glenda invading her sunspot.

"Get over it, your royal highness." Glenda drew her knees up, cup to chest, and stared out at the fading sunlight bathing the desert scene.

The Siamese's hair rose all over her sleek body; she turned azure eyes rimmed in black on Glenda, and hissed. Backing away from the window, I Ching swiped a claw-extended paw, and bolted toward the back of the house.

"What is the problem with you cats?" Glenda stretched her legs out on the seat's cushion. *The statuette.* "No way." *What else could it be?* She jumped when the ringing of the house phone stopped her inner argument.

She carried her mug to the kitchen with her while she answered the old fashioned wall phone. Glancing at the clock on the stove, she realized it was past six.

"Hello? Dr. Burkhardt. How nice of you to call. Is anything wrong? Good. How can I help you? No, there won't be any problem with Dr. Riyadh visiting tomorrow. Any particular reason? No, just wondering if I should plan an excursion to town to get groceries. Just research; I see. No, this won't interrupt my work schedule. By tomorrow evening, I should have next month's layout of the magazine ready for editing. I can e-mail that to my copy editors for proofing. Sure; just have him call me when he gets over the Highway 14 pass, so I can give him more explicit directions. No problem, sir. Have a great evening."

Glenda stuck her mug in the microwave to heat up the remainder of her tea. Why would the Antiquities Director want to visit the Antelope Valley? There weren't any recent Native American digs she could recall and, being from Egypt, surely he'd seen enough deserts to last him a lifetime. *Oh stop being silly. Dr. Burkhardt said he was researching an article for a magazine back in the Middle East. I'll just have to wait until he arrives.*

~ * ~

Omar flipped open his phone and keyed in the number. A deep, gruff voice answered.

"What?"

"I need you, and an associate, to perform a service for me tomorrow evening."

"You know what the fee will be."

"Yes. It will be in your bank account by 10:00 a.m. Are you familiar with the Antelope Valley?"

"I have someone who lives in the area."

"I'll leave details on your voice mail. The job is tomorrow evening around 1900 hours."

"They'll be ready."

The dead air of his phone signaled Omar his conversation had ended. He would never understand the rude habit of hanging up without saying goodbye; however, he would not allow this to color his mood. The little statuette would be back in his possession before the end of the week.

Chapter Seven

Glenda typed to her freelancer, her fingers flying over the keyboard in her haste.

> *Must meet you before tomorrow evening; situation changed; need verification I'm not losing my mind. Call me at 661-236-6696.*

She pushed the send button, and uttered a little prayer he was emailing her locally and not from the Middle East.

~ * ~

Nasim reached his government issued black sedan and patted his pockets to find the keys. Chuckling at himself, he realized he'd left them sitting on the edge of his desk. He returned to the building, flashing his badge for the security guard seated at the front door. He hummed quietly as the, otherwise vacant, elevator rose to his floor. The doors slid open on a quiet, nearly deserted office. On the few occasions he'd indulged himself and watched the TV programs about his agency, the fictional offices were bustling at all hours of the day and night. The truth wasn't nearly as exciting. By 5:30 most nights, one could fire a weapon, and not hit a soul. He guessed real life was too boring. Nasim nodded at a couple of agents moving toward the elevators carrying their briefcases. He worked his way through the cubicle maze to his desk, where he located his keys exactly where he'd left them. Grabbing them from the top of his in basket, Nasim turned to leave but hesitated. The hair on the back of his neck began to tingle and his palms itched. His senses were screaming at him. Experience in the field had taught him to trust these warnings implicitly. He sat at his desk, and allowed his auto-pilot to take over. His hands turned on the computer and maneuvered the path to the e-mail. A message from his museum contact had arrived in the few minutes since he'd closed down the tower.

He skimmed through the email.

"This changes the situation considerably." Something about the message bothered him; there was desperation to the few words printed on the page. If he came out from cover, he risked exposing the whole operation, however, any hesitation on his part and his quarry would have no qualms about killing his contact.

Nasim picked up the secure line, and entered the phone number attached to the end of the signature. His nerves buzzed with each ring, and he jumped when a voice answered.

"Yes. This is…"

"You have reached 236-6696. I am unable to come to the phone right now, but if you will leave your name and number after the beep, I will return your call as soon as possible. Thank you for calling."

There was a pause then the beep, and Nasim began, "This is Nasim Shabouh, and…" Before he could say anything more, he heard the click of the receiver lifting from its cradle.

"Nasim?"

The female voice was a velvety contralto.

Nasim gasped in surprise. "Yes. This is Nasim. May I correctly assume I am speaking with Glenda Nagel, editor of the Getty Museum magazine, *Archaeology in Today's World*?"

A moment of suspended silence was followed by a quiet giggle. "Yes, you may. Am I correct in assuming I am speaking to the freelance writer I engaged over the internet?"

Nasim unconsciously cleared his throat. "Yes, ma'am, you may. I am Nasim Shabouh of Cairo, Egypt. You engaged my services, for the first time, about a year ago. I wrote an article for you about the continuing encroachment of the Nile upon the tombs of antiquity. Six months ago, I contacted you with information regarding the recent discovery of a sepulcher in the country of Yemen. Today, I am responding to a request for me to contact you. How may I be of service?"

Glenda hesitated. *I'm just being paranoid. The museum wouldn't hire anyone they hadn't checked out and cleared.*

"Miss Nagel?"

"Sorry, Mr. Shabouh, I'm not sure I've done the right thing in contacting you."

"I beg your pardon?"

"Well, I, uh, uh,…"

"Ms. Nagel?"

"Yes?"

"Do not negate any gut feelings you may have. As a freelance writer, my gut feelings have kept me out of the line of fire in many countries, *and*, as you saw by my portfolio, gotten me some terrific stories in the process. I can only guess from your previous notes you have stumbled across the statuette, or a very good facsimile, pictured with the little Princess. Am I right?"

Glenda felt her stomach roll. Goose bumps raised on her arms. It was her turn to clear her throat. She croaked out, "Yes."

Nasim continued. "But you have a great deal of hesitation, even though you have identified the article as being genuine. May I ask how this came to be in your possession?"

Glenda worried her lower lip. *What if I tell him the truth and he's one of the – bad guys?*

40

"Ms Nagel? I won't be able to help you at all if I don't have all the facts." Nasim realized he would have to share part of his experience to alleviate her doubts.

"I have a personal stake to clear my family's reputation which is very important to my relatives living in the Middle East." Nasim was about to end the call when he heard the distinct sound of a deep sigh.

"I met the newly appointed Antiquities Director for the first time today. When I entered the Director's office with the head of the museum, he was examining a clay pot. Dr. Omar Riyadh, the director, said his cousin had sent the item to him as an example of what he was producing to fool the tourists. I admired the artistry and said so. He acted as if the vase wasn't important and after introductions and small talk, we parted company.

"The Museum Director had asked Dr. Riyadh to assist me with my magazine articles about the Middle East from time to time and he willingly agreed. I'd returned to my office, and within 20 minutes, he was standing in front of my desk offering me the vase I'd admired as a gift. I was too flabbergasted to say no, and placed the vase on my desk. Due to my, uh, casual filing system and the maelstrom I call my office, I hesitated to leave the piece so brought it along when I came home."

Nasim interrupted. "About what time was that?"

Glenda hesitated. She barely knew the person on the other end of the phone, but her gut instinct was giving her a pass to confide in him. "Around 12:30. I remember he asked me to lunch, but I had to refuse because of my need to set up and organize the layout for this month's print run.

"It wasn't until I got home things started to get *really* crazy. I carried the vase in the house, and when I leaned to pet my Persian cat, she attempted to remove my arm with her unsheathed claws. That's not like her at all.

"I carried the urn to my office and tried placing the vessel on my desk. I *swear* it tried to jump to the floor—twice! The entire time my cat was growling, and acting very weird. When my other critters demanded dinner, I took the clay pot with me to the kitchen and set it on the counter. After I realized I'd been carrying the thing from room to room, I set it on the mantle over the fireplace which is designated as a no cat zone when I'm home. Who knows what they do when I'm gone?

"I hadn't turned halfway around when my Persian launched herself at the pottery knocking it off the mantle and shattering the clay vessel. After locking her in her cage, I started sweeping up the pieces. That's when I saw the ivory statuette of Bastet. The piece was wrapped in shavings and stuffed inside the vase."

Nasim felt excitement build in his stomach. *Hold on. It will be the magazine editor's word against the antiquities director. He will slip away again if I don't get indisputable proof.*

He cleared his throat. "I spent four years of college studying archaeology. My family has some background in the field, and I realized how foolish it would be not to take advantage of the history at my own back door. So when I examined the little statuette at the site, I knew if it were authentic, a curse would be printed along the bottom edge. There was. It said something along the lines of, 'the offender who defiles the tomb will be detested by his family, and he will eat himself.' The eating-himself part possibly refers to a flesh-eating virus. Contrary to what many modern people think, the ancient Egyptians were quite knowledgeable about diseases. Your cat may have been responding to ill smells closed into a crypt for thousands of years."

"Mr. Shabouh?"

"Yes?"

"Would you be able to come to my home and verify this statue is authentic? I've checked all the signs against the information you sent, and concluded it may be the real deal, but you've seen the original."

"I believe that would pose no problem. Your e-mail seemed to have an underlying urgency in its message. Is verifying the authenticity of the statue the only reason you wish me there?"

Glenda mulled over her answer. Should she be totally honest with this man; or hold back until she could look him in the eyes? His voice betrayed no subterfuge, but professional con men could lie without a hint of guilt. She decided to tell him part of the truth. Time would tell if she indulged it all.

"Shortly after my cat tried to attack me, I received a phone call from the Museum Director asking if I would host Dr. Riyadh for dinner tomorrow evening. He gave me some reason about the doctor desiring to see the desert, but my intuition tells me that's not the real explanation why he wishes to come to my home. Surely, there are enough deserts in Egypt for him to get his fill."

Nasim chuckled. "You are right; there are enough deserts. I think you are wise to be cautious. What time is he expected?"

"Six o'clock tomorrow evening."

"I will rearrange my work schedule, and be at your home around four in the afternoon. That will allow enough time to verify the statue's authenticity or not, and give me time to leave before your doctor arrives for dinner."

"Thank you, Mr. Shabouh."

"Ms. Nagel?"

"Yes?"

"Please call me Nasim."

"I will, Nasim, if you will call me Glenda."

"Consider it done."

Glenda gave him detailed directions to her home, and hung up the phone. She walked to the front room and settled on the couch to finish watching the sun paint the desert of the Antelope Valley in hues of reds and oranges.

With Scat curled against her feet, and I Ching draped over her shoulders, Glenda sat stroking Pandora until darkness blanketed the scene, and the amber and crystal lights of the twin cities of Palmdale and Lancaster twinkled across the valley.

Untangling herself from her three snoozing, furry roommates, she ambled to her office. Tomorrow was going to be busy; not much work on the magazine was going to get done, so she'd best crunch it out tonight. Sleep would have to wait for another time.

Chapter Eight

In the driveway of his home, Dr. Omar Riyadh stood beside his 2006 Mercedes SL two-seater searching for the keys. When he'd arrived in the United States, he'd indulged himself to this one small show of wealth-- because he deserved it. In his own country, circumstances had forced him to keep a low profile. The Shabouh incident had drawn unwanted attention to his museums, and any visible sign of wealth would immediately be the subject of public scrutiny.

Locating his keys in their habitual resting spot within his suit jacket, he opened the vehicle's door and slid into the luxurious interior. He pulled in a deep breath, reveling in the new-car-leather smell. *I need to compose myself. It will not do me any good to become careless. Those idiot Shabouh brothers allowed trust and carelessness to end their careers. I shall not.*

Maneuvering the Los Angeles freeways was child's play compared to the streets of Cairo at any time of the day. Dr. Riyadh easily slipped through the snarls of early morning traffic.

Arriving at the sparsely populated parking area, he briskly set off to his office. He felt his irritation rise as he was forced to unlock his office door. *Where is that daughter of a camel?* He was about to utter some unkind characterizations of her family, when he glanced at the clock on the wall and realized, he was two hours early. Sitting in his chair, he steepled his fingers

44

together over the desk. He drew a deep breath, holding it until he felt the tension leave his shoulders, whereupon he exhaled heavily.

"I mustn't allow this transaction to affect me this way." Gathering himself, he moved to his espresso maker, and brewed a steaming cup of Egyptian coffee. Holding the demi-cup between his hands, he allowed the bittersweet smell to waft over his senses. Two cups later, he undid the latches on his briefcase, and began assembling the information he was presenting the magazine editor this evening. There was enough fact to make her think he'd spent time researching, but most of what he was gifting her was disinformation. He hoped it would convince her the little statuette was a fake, and handing it over to him would be an excellent idea. The creak of the office door opening brought his head up from the work.

Before him stood a young woman with shiny, blonde hair, softly haloing her face. An expensive suit and matching silk blouse was accented by subtle makeup. She walked to his desk to place some papers in the middle, and jumped when she realized he was sitting behind it.

"Dr. Riyadh! I… I didn't see you there. You're awfully early, aren't you?"

Omar noted the chewing gum was gone, and she exuded the soft scent of baby powder.

"Miss Showers?" Omar's dark eyes could not hide his surprise.

"Actually, Dr. Riyadh, it's Avril Livingston. When I complained to my father about what you said to me yesterday, he agreed with you. In fact, he told me if I didn't make the changes, he'd cut off my college funds. You see, he's on the Board of Directors here."

Her chagrined expression brought up a deep chuckle from Omar. "Am I correct in guessing the board member you speak of is Alfred Windsor Livingston, multi-millionaire and philanthropist?"

Avril's resigned nod brought another chuckle.

"Well, Miss Livingston, I must say, I much prefer the new look. It brings respect to the office and yourself. I will be more inclined to send a positive report to your school when you return in the fall." Omar stood, coming from behind his desk to face his young docent. "It is always hard to let childhood slip through our fingers. But you are an attractive, young woman who needs to understand the working world and adapt. Be who you wish after working hours and on the weekends." He placed his hand on her shoulder, and guided her to the outer office.

"I have a very full schedule today. Please take messages. I will come out and retrieve them throughout the morning." Omar turned and shut his door. He connected to a blind phone number, and left a simple message. "Will have artifact by midnight. Meet me at the designated spot by two."

~ * ~

Omar pushed back his plate. It had been a discovery-by-mistake when he had found this Egyptian restaurant so close to work. The food reminded him of his favorite spot in Cairo, and stepping inside, took him away from this cursed cold city for a brief time. He smiled at the waiter, Musad, and left a hefty tip. He knew the young man was working his way through school and supporting his parents in the old country. *One has to support one's fellow countrymen.* The short drive to the office was uneventful, and would have been enjoyable had the smog not colored the air dingy brown; a likeness to Cairo he would be glad to eliminate. Strolling through the grounds to his office, he noted yet another section of the museum undergoing renovations. It seemed to be an unending process.

Avril wasn't in, having gone to lunch according to the small sign placed in the center of her desk, so he picked up his mail. He was perusing the offers of credit cards and subscriptions to magazines as he entered his office.

"About time."

The reed-thin, scratchy voice emitting from the black-suited figure seated in the darkened office made Omar's hair stand on end, and sent the mail tumbling to the floor.

"Who let you in?"

"It was simple enough to bypass the locks. You really should get that checked."

"I told you I would have the artifact by tonight."

"And I trust you will keep your word. In my business, however, it pays to be circumspect. I am simply following my gut, and my gut tells me you're about to screw up this deal."

Omar reached to the lamp on his desk, his nerves taut with the cloak-and-dagger atmosphere preferred by his visitor.

"I wouldn't do that."

Omar growled. "You wouldn't but I would. This is *my* office, and I prefer to work in the light. Your visit is unwarranted, *and* interrupts my workday. I will state this once more for your benefit--you *will* have the artifact by two a.m. at the latest. By three a.m., I will be checking my account in the Bahamas and better find the agreed upon sum safely inside."

Omar waited for a reply, but the silence continued to hang heavy in the air. He flicked on the light switch, and turned to face the chair where he'd identified the source of the scratching voice. The chair was empty. He looked around his office amazed the visitor could have left unnoticed. There were but two doors to his office, and he hadn't heard either of them open.

"Damn!" These were not the kind of people with whom one trifled. He, nor the authorities, had any concrete evidence of wrongdoing on their part; but the bodies of one too many lowlife characters, which had plotted to cross the organization, had been located in the desert by unfortunate hikers or dirt bikers.

Omar sat in his chair and wiped the beads of sweat from his forehead. His uncle had warned him not to do business with these American gangsters but, in his arrogance, he'd ignored the advice; and now, he was into this arrangement so deep that extrication was not an option. He rose and crossed to his espresso maker. A quick shot of pure, bitter coffee would clear his brain. Noises from the outer office signaled the return of his docent secretary. Using the intercom, he buzzed her.

"Miss Livingston?"

"Yes, Dr. Riyadh?"

"Please get Ms Nagel on the phone for me."

"Yes, Dr."

It was time to initiate phase two of his plan.

Chapter Nine

Nasim paced in his small apartment. He'd not been able to sleep the previous night and given up all hope of rest around four a.m. The object of his twenty-year search was within his grasp, but he'd have to be careful not to terrify Ms. Nagel. She was the key to his success.

He jumped when his phone rang. Glancing at the wall clock in the kitchen, he uttered an expletive. "Who would be bold enough to call my house at six in the morning?" As he picked up the phone, he felt the buzz of warning crawl up his arm.

"Yes?" he gruffed.

"Nasim?"

"Lydia? Why are you calling so early?" Nasim stopped in front of the one extravagance he'd allowed himself when he'd gotten this assignment-- the espresso maker. Automatically, he began to prepare himself a cup of the dense liquid.

"Lydia?"

His partner's voice was subdued so much he had to step away from the small kitchenette and into the living area of his apartment to hear her.

"Nasim," Lydia whispered, "I've just come back from my morning run. While standing on my back porch taking my heart rate, I heard noises in the house. I'm going to retrieve my hidden car key and come over to your place. Will that be all right?"

He felt the fingers of danger tickle down his back. "Of course. Shouldn't I call the Captain?"

Crunching sounds and rustling leaves rang in his ears. "No!" Lydia was still whispering, the reply producing a metallic echo. "I'm going to put down the phone for a minute. Don't hang up."

He heard the distinct click of a lock, and the roar of a motor. Distant shouts and several gunshots followed.

"Lydia! Lydia!" he was frantic, standing in the center of his apartment, shouting into the small phone in his hand. The noise of early morning traffic resounded in his ears, and the sound of the engine leveled to a monotone droning.

"Nasim?"

"Are you all right? I thought I heard gunshots." Panic crept into his voice.

"Yes, I'm fine. Two massive apes were coming out of my front door when I backed into the street. I got a good look at one of the thugs and could probably give a fairly good description of the second one. The second guy was the one who shot at the car. I don't think he hit anything, but I won't be able to tell until I stop and examine it more closely. Give me instructions on how to get to your place, again. I had them, but they're inside my house."

"Where are you now?" Upon learning her location, Nasim gave her step-by-step instructions on how to find his apartment complex in Pasadena. "Would you like a cup of espresso when you get here?"

"That would be great. They interrupted my morning routine, and, *that* really irritates me. I don't suppose I'd be able to shower and borrow some jeans and a shirt until we get to work, would I?"

"I'll find something for you to wear. I'm going to call the Captain, now."

"Probably a good idea."

After Lydia had hung up the phone, Nasim called the emergency number the Captain had given all his officers to use. Thinking he would leave a message, he was surprised when the senior officer answered.

"O'Sullivan here. Who's this and what's the emergency?"

Nasim stuttered. "Off... off... officer Shabouh here, sir. Sorry to disturb you so early, but my partner, Lydia Thompson, had her home broken into this morning. She's on her way to brief me before we come into the office and fill out the necessary reports. She heard the intruders prior to entering her home after her morning run. She says they took some shots at her, but she escaped in her vehicle unharmed. We'll relay the details to you within the next two hours, sir."

Liam O'Sullivan let go a string of swear words. "Hell of a way to start the morning. I expect to see the report *on my desk* before ten o'clock. Is that clear?"

"Yes, sir."

Nasim traveled about his apartment picking up clutter left in front of the couch and dirty dishes residing on the coffee table. He moved to the hall cupboard and pulled out a fresh towel and washcloth for his partner, which he laid in the bathroom. Rummaging in his closet, he dug to the rear and retrieved a pair of jeans he'd recently outgrown, noting they would fit his partner better than him. Thumbing through the shirts on hangers, Nasim located something he felt Lydia might find comfortable.

A light tapping announced his partner. He opened the door, and Lydia strode past him still dressed in her running shorts, FBI sweatshirt and running shoes. Her normally flawless hair was pulled into a ponytail, several wisps flying about her face. She started pacing around Nasim's living room.

"I can't believe those hairy knuckled thugs! What the hell did they think they would find in my house? I *hate* when my routine is interrupted."

Nasim had to stifle the urge to snicker. His American partner would not work well in Egypt. Chaos was the norm in most of the cases he'd had to investigate. He watched as Lydia finally plopped down on the couch and blew a stray tendril of honey colored hair out of her face.

"Lydia?"

She blew out a deep sigh. "Yeah?"

"What's this all about? Why would someone break into your home?"

"Do you remember the San Pedro dock case?"

Nasim shook his head.

A line formed between Lydia's eyes. "Oh, that's right. You were in the Middle East visiting family I think you said. Anyway, I volunteered to assist in a joint case with Customs and the Coast Guard. They were tracking a mainland China importing company. Seems several containers arrived at the docks in San Pedro carrying human cargo; upon transfer to a warehouse close by, the victims rested in overcrowded cages until the owners arrived to claim them.

"A crewmember on one of the ships tipped the agencies to the warehouse in return for political asylum. We got *very* lucky when one of the top members of the ring showed up to inspect his new merchandise.

"We subdued the outside entourage and snuck up on the hired guns and leader inside. They were so engrossed in arguing over price, we were able to walk right up behind and overpower them. I was saddled with hauling in this skanky, wheezy-voiced, slick mob wanna-be. He swore he'd *hunt you down and put your lights out*." Lydia used her fingers to emphasize the quotes. "I guess he finally made good on his threat."

"It makes me angry. I feel so… violated. Having someone enter your home, uninvited, well," Lydia turned the palms of her hands up and lifted her shoulders. "I guess I can relate to some of the vic's now. Would you mind if I showered? Maybe hot water will make me feel a little better."

"Not a problem. I've put a pair of jeans and a polo shirt on the vanity. I think they'll fit you. I'm afraid I don't have tennis shoes in your size."

"That's all right. I always have a pair of work shoes in my car. They'll look a little dressy with the jeans but, under the circumstances, I think the Captain will understand. Thanks, Nasim."

Lydia followed her partner down the hallway and into the bathroom. After a whirlwind tour of the small room, she peeled off her running clothes, and stepped into the steaming shower. Not one for makeup or complicated hairstyles, she completed her shower routine and was back in the living room within fifteen minutes sipping the strong Egyptian coffee her partner had prepared.

"I just don't understand. If they were going to 'put my lights out', why did they find it necessary to tear stuff up? I swear I heard the sound of breaking dishes. What did they think they'd find? It's not like we take paperwork or evidence home." Her cheeks burnished pink. "Well, we're not supposed to take paperwork home."

Nasim sitting in the wing backed chair opposite the couch chuckled. He was as guilty as Lydia of bringing home paperwork. Sometimes there weren't enough hours in the workday to get the reports typed on company time.

Working out of the Los Angeles office with one other partner before Lydia, Nasim had run into the wheezy-voiced, mob wanna-be, she mentioned. The man was more than a wanna-be. He was very dangerous and *very* connected. If, for some unbeknownst reason, he was part of the deal involving Dr. Riyadh, the situation had just taken a decidedly lethal downward turn.

He wasn't sure how much he should divulge to his partner. His vendetta against the Museum's new director could get him fired even though he'd stayed within the law; the fact remained, he was playing out a personal agenda on company time. He took a sip of his coffee and chose his words judiciously before voicing his thoughts.

"It could be other influences are entering the picture, Lydia. These knuckle draggers, as you call them, could be working under the assumption you know more than you're admitting. Maybe they think you've taken a piece of evidence into protective custody as we do with people." Nasim shrugged his shoulders.

Lydia pulled some of the hot, bitter liquid into her mouth allowing the flavor to roll over her tongue and waft through her nose before she spoke.

"That's ridiculous. We never take home evidence. There's something else going on here. I can feel it in my bones, but I can't quite put my finger on it. I think when we get into the office today; I'm going to go over every detail of this new case at the Getty Museum. Dr. Riyadh is just too glib with his answers. I really hate to use this word but... he's always seemed shifty, even when I was a student. I don't know how else to describe the feeling."

Nasim rose from his chair. He knew his partner was a good agent, but he hadn't counted on her being so perceptive of the situation. It was only a matter of time before she found out about the statuette of Bastet.

He looked at the clock on the kitchen stove. "Is that the time? We'd better get going."

Lydia glanced at her watch. "Whoa. You're right. You want to carpool?"

"No. I have a personal errand to run after work. I'll need my vehicle."

"Well, I need to get going so I can get started on the blasted paperwork this little morning stroll into the criminal world has created. This is *not* how I wanted to start my day--more paperwork. See you in the office. And Nasim?"

"Yes?"

"Thank you."

"Please, don't think of it. It's what partners do for each other."

"Thanks, anyway."

He watched as the form of Lydia bounded out to her car in his clothing.

"I must say, she looks better in my clothes than I do." Shaking his head, he finished his morning routine, and left for work.

~ * ~

Lydia slid behind the wheel of her car and rummaged in her briefcase. Pulling out her cell phone, she pushed the button and autodialed a number.

"Bob? This is your favorite cousin. I need you to start looking for a house for me. Yeah, again. Mine was broken into this morning by some overzealous Mafia wanna-be's. I need to find a safer neighborhood. Well, I'd like to be a bit closer to work but not enough to live in that crush of humanity. Try the hills. Something with a view, a hot tub and maybe a pool. Just take it out of my account. I'll get back to you in a day or two. Bye."

~ * ~

Nasim was feeling the push to pick up the pace with his investigation. Things were heating up, and, with the possible introduction of the "wheezy-voiced man", he didn't want to identify another partner on the coroner's slab.

Chapter Ten

Nasim's day had evaporated. Before he realized it, the time on his desk phone was flashing 12:00. *American TV programs don't show the viewer how many hours of paperwork hell is attached to the one hour of excitement made by discovery.* Nasim sighed heavily. *They'd probably cancel the show after the first night.*

He pulled the paper piles he'd been working on into the file folder and locked it away in his desk. He needed to swing by his apartment and change into something more appropriate for his visit to Ms. Nagel's home. His suit and dress shirt wouldn't work well if he was forced to depart in a hurry. Picking up the phone, he dialed his partner's cell number and drummed his fingers on the desk as he waited to leave a message.

"Lydia, as I said earlier, I have plans this evening. This meeting might put a different light on your attack."

Knowing his next statement would trigger warning bells inside her head, Nasim couldn't help but add, "If you do not hear from me within forty eight hours, call the number I have left on my desk calendar."

Nasim gave a cursory glance about his office space. He snatched up his briefcase and quickly left. While he broke no laws in driving to his apartment, he did shave ten minutes off his normal time. After a quick change out of his work clothes, he grabbed binoculars, and something to snack on as he bolted out of his place. He was running behind the schedule he'd set for himself but could make up the time on the freeway.

He'd not made the trip to the desert before today. As he'd told Ms. Nagel, Egypt had enough sand to suit anyone's taste. He maneuvered the concrete maze, per the instructions she'd given him, at heart stopping speeds. More than once, he'd glanced at his speedometer to find the needle pointing at 85 mph or more.

"Egyptians have much to learn from these California drivers," he muttered as he eased his speed to the legal limit.

His eardrums were feeling stretched to the limit and, as he glanced at the surrounding scenery, he realized why. The roadway was ascending quickly as the mountains converged together. The openness of the Los Angeles valley was giving way to rolling foothills that were becoming more barren the farther north he traveled. Feeling his stomach complain, he took the off-ramp in to a small community the highway sign named as Acton. He followed the signs to the McDonald's and opted to eat inside. After ordering his meal, he inquired about Juniper Hills and the curt answer he received from the young woman behind the counter told him, he wasn't the first to pose the question to her. She indicated his destination was just over the hill off the Pearblossom Highway. Sitting in his booth, the sun glinting off the windshields of the passing vehicles on the ribbon of concrete, Nasim felt a pang of homesickness. Until this point, he'd not allowed himself time to miss his homeland. Egypt was greener, lusher; however, the surrounding hills bore a great similarity to the area where he'd located the little princess' sarcophagus. If this Juniper Hills resembled what he saw here, he could understand Ms. Nagel's concern about the new museum director.

Why *would* someone wish to see more deserts? Why not go to northern California where there were rumored to be trees as tall as skyscrapers and as old as the cedars in his own country? Why the desert, indeed?

He deposited his trash within the brilliant orange-topped container realizing he should use the facilities before he drove any further.

Nasim continued his journey, refreshed and relieved. Climbing into his vehicle, he consulted the directions again. Ms. Nagel's detailed explanation should put him in her driveway within the hour. He realized, upon consulting his watch, he would be earlier than the appointed four o'clock meeting time. While Ms. Nagel's instructions appeared straightforward, experience had taught him to be careful. Not everything was so simple.

"Excellent. I will reconnoiter the area. No sense in being lax about this. Knowing how to get out is as important as knowing how to get in."

It was sooner than expected when he turned on the road where Glenda indicated she lived. Nasim glanced at the car's clock and discovered he was, indeed, an hour early. Driving down the road, he noted a For Sale sign next to a driveway a quarter mile up the road. He turned and cautiously drove the inclined, hard-packed, dirt driveway. Asphalt covered the last 100 yards into the triple car garage. Nasim scanned the two-story home with wraparound porch. The blinds were shuttered on all but the front windows. He left his vehicle and silently ascended the four steps to the porch. Far below the house, on a single black ribbon of highway, Nasim could make out tiny specks of movement indicating cars but no sound assaulted his ears. After the noise of LA, this quiet was a bit unnerving. There were no sounds from within the home. He approached the front door. One step to the side and he peeked through the slatted blinds observing no furnishings, and, with bravado he didn't honestly feel, firmly knocked. The sound echoed against bare walls. He tried the door, shocked to find the knob turning easily under his grip. Stepping into the tiled entry, he surveyed the empty room. Next to the entry was a petite, three-legged table upon which sat a plastic cardholder filled with business cards.

After I complete my surveillance, I shall call and let the sales person know the door is unlocked.

Nasim slipped a card into his jacket pocket. He moved with skill and stealth through the home's two stories, peering in closets and checking all the rooms. Assured no one was inside, he exited the way he had entered and proceeded to search the outer grounds. The building looked down upon Glenda Nagel's house. A pair of binoculars could bring everything on the back side of her home into clear focus. He would need to warn her without alarming her into rash action. He observed a primitive, two-rut lane next to

Ms. Nagel's home and the one where he stood. This was knowledge he might have to employ if Dr. Riyadh followed the course of action he'd used in Egypt against Nasim's father and uncle.

I doubt this leopard will change his spots.

Satisfied with his scrutiny of the area, Nasim used the paved portion of the driveway to turn himself around and reach his destination. He meandered his car up her winding driveway and parked in an area set to the west side. As he left his vehicle, he cursed himself for not bringing something to this meeting.

Where are my manners? I will have to beg her pardon for my boorish behavior. He brushed invisible lint from his jacket and lifted his hand to knock on the door when it opened.

"Mr. Shabouh?" Glenda extended a hand.

"Yes. Ms. Nagel?" Nasim returned the gesture.

~ * ~

Glenda felt the warmth of the young man's hand. The softness reminded her of an office worker, but she realized, as she stood holding the warm brown extremity in her own, old calluses underlying the softness testified to a lifetime of hard work. She blushed when she realized how long she'd stood with his hand in her own.

"Please come in. I hope you aren't allergic to cats. I have three of them around here somewhere." She waved him in to her living room and offered him a seat on the couch. "Would you like coffee or tea? I have Earl Grey."

"Tea would be lovely with one or two lumps of sugar."

Glenda giggled. "I don't have sugar cubes. How about teaspoons of sugar?"

Nasim nodded. "That would be just fine."

Glenda excused herself and set about preparing the beverage in the kitchen.

He laid his arm across the back of the sofa and gazed over the expansive view of the valley below. The afternoon sun caressed each plant and tree in his vision with bright sunlight. The clarity of the air generated the feeling he could reach through the window and touch the branches of the Joshua tree regally standing next to the front porch. Gone was the brown air, which constantly hung over the Los Angeles basin replaced by lucidity Nasim had not witnessed since his exploration of the little princess' burial chamber in Yemen.

To this point, the small country had escaped the crush of civilization in this century. That blessing provided them clean air and water. Nasim could only wonder how long it would take for them to fall victim to progress.

The clink of pottery on the wooden coffee table diverted his train of thought. Glenda had brought her own mug with her and sat in the overstuffed chair facing the fireplace.

"I hope your tea is to your liking," she blew lightly across the top of her cup.

"Thank you. Please forgive my bad manners. I was in such a hurry to arrive; I completely forgot to bring a gift to thank you for your hospitality." Nasim shook his head and sighed.

Glenda chuckled. "Mr. Shabouh…"

"Nasim, please."

"…Nasim. One of the many things I love about the Middle East is the detail still given to manners and century old customs. It was not necessary to bring a gift. I appreciate the thought, though. Now, if you can give me some piece of mind about this little statuette, I'll be forever in your debt. Let me retrieve it. If any of my fuzzy roommates appear, don't worry. They're friendly although a little standoffish with people they don't know." Glenda rose from her chair and disappeared into the back portion of the house.

Nasim gingerly tasted the hot liquid in his cup. The pungent aroma of Earl Grey drifted past his nose, and he ventured a sip. Hot liquid sizzled down his throat. He quickly placed the cup on the coaster and swore lowly in Arabic.

Something was tickling his ear, and he lifted his hand to brush away the feeling. He encountered silky fur. Turning, his nose nearly touched the moist, black nose of a large, bluish-gray Persian cat. Deep emerald green eyes dilated revealing the iridescence inside the black pupils. Nasim sat very still unconsciously rubbing the soft skin between his thumb and forefinger on his right hand. Two faded, pale puncture marks marred the tanned skin. He'd learned by hard experience a wagging tale wasn't always a friendly sign.

The cat leaned toward him, its nose wrinkling as it sniffed his essence. Lightly touching the end of his nose with its own, it pulled back, narrowed its eyes then began to laboriously clean its paws.

"Pandora!"

Nasim jumped. He'd been so intent on not upsetting the cat, he'd not heard Glenda enter from the back of the house. He jumped again when the cat yeowed in response.

"Get off the back of the couch." Glenda had a small cardboard box in one gloved hand and a set of gloves she placed in front of Nasim.

"I'm sorry these are so small, but I'd rather be safe than sorry when handling artifacts. These were all I had."

"Thank you. They'll be fine. Now, how is it I can be of assistance?"

Glenda set the box on the coffee table and lifted out the statuette. As she started to hand the little princess to Nasim, Pandora growled loudly and arched her back.

"Pandora! Stop! Nasim, if you'll just slide off the couch and stand by the mantle near the fireplace, I'll grab this monster." Glenda put the statuette back into the box and peeled the gloves from her hands, wagging her finger at her crouching, growling cat.

"Shame on you. I'm so sorry, Nasim. Every time I bring this out, she goes crazy. I don't know what comes over her. Normally, she's just a very spoiled, pampered cat that likes to sleep in the sun on the back of the couch. Since this artifact came into this house, she's been psycho. I'll put her in her carrier, again."

Nasim watched Glenda maneuver herself behind the hissing animal and pick it up by the scruff of the neck. All four paws went limp but the animal continued to growl. He heard Glenda quietly scolding all the way down the hallway. There was the scraping of metal against plastic, followed by plaintiff yeowling. Glenda appeared, once again, at her chair and indicated to Nasim he should sit on the couch.

"My other two cats are content to sleep in the back bedroom and stay away from all the action, but Pandora has always been a bit nosy. I'm really sorry for her behavior." Her cheeks colored as she pulled the statuette from the cardboard container.

"You might consider her behavior as a good sign." Nasim finished donning his gloves.

Glenda raised an eyebrow. "How so?"

Shrugging his shoulders, Nasim slid his hand under hers and relieved her of the small artifact. "Because the cat senses something unfamiliar about the item. If it were a fake, there would be no foreign smells associated with the statue. Your cat seems to be able to detect the smells from the sarcophagus. She might just have saved you from a very nasty skin infection."

"Then why haven't my other two reacted the same?" Glenda's forehead creased with worry.

"This one cat has decided to protect all of the family. She, apparently, will not allow the others close enough to be harmed." Nasim turned the tiny statuette over and closely scrutinized the base. "I believe what you have here is the original Bastet figurine from the little princess' resting place. See the markings on the bottom here?"

He pointed his gloved finger at the small indentations in the bottom.

"They are all that's necessary to authenticate this piece."

He set the small sculpture back in the container.

Glenda flopped back in her chair. "How is this possible? I thought all artifacts from a dig were cataloged and guarded until the time they were either shown in a museum or stored."

Nasim took off his gloves and laid them on the coffee table as he picked up his teacup and took a sip. With slow deliberate movements, he set his cup on the table and turned to face Glenda.

"In the majority of cases, your knowledge of procedure is correct. However…" he hesitated. The next few words out of his mouth would either infuriate his host or bring her to understand the gravity of the situation she was currently facing. He cleared his throat.

"…if you have the proper international credentials and enough *authority* behind you; one could smuggle the pyramids of Giza out of the country, and there would be no protest. Dr. Riyadh is such a person." Nasim hesitated to sip of his tea and gage the reaction of his host. She was sitting forward in her seat absorbing each word he spoke.

"I can't completely disclose how I come to be in possession of such information, but know this; you are in grave danger. If the director believes you have the statuette, he will stop at nothing to retrieve it. No one will be able to connect him directly to any accidents that may occur, but he will be the person directing the actions."

Glenda sat, mouth open, staring at the young man she had thought to be *just a freelance writer.* She snapped her mouth shut and scooted back in the chair. She had to decide if this young man was being overly dramatic or serious about what he had just divulged. She searched the handsome, dark face and found the ebony eyes staring at her to be guileless. The small lines around the corners showed his genuine concern for her safety.

"What am I to do now? He's on his way here to have dinner and *see*," she used her fingers to act as quote marks, "the California desert. How do I keep my cats from giving away the statuette? Pandora will go crazy if I let her out, but I wouldn't normally keep her in her carrier."

"You must try to preserve your wits. Any suspicious actions on your part might give him reason to assume you have the statue. Be as cordial as possible but beg off as soon as you can. Tell him you have a deadline and send him on his way. I'll be near, and, as soon as I see his auto drive toward the highway, I'll dash back here. You must be ready to depart quickly as soon as you hear me knock on the back door."

"Why? If he leaves then there's no reason to worry, is there?" Glenda bit the inside of her lower lip.

Nasim sighed. She was such a nice woman and, thankfully, so naïve.

"There is much to worry about. Dr. Riyadh will appear to be content with any explanation you give him about not having the statuette, but he will send others to search for it. They will not be gentle in their endeavors so you might wish to hide away any valuables you have. If you have a friend who would watch your cats, call them now and ask them to come over. Tell them your guest is extremely allergic, and you would like to have them out of the house."

Glenda shook her head. This was James Bond stuff from the movies.

"Then the little cat statuette is authentic?"

Nasim nodded as he watched several emotions cross his host's face. He hadn't wanted to scare her, but she needed to realize the kind of man Dr. Riyadh could be. His father and uncle had been too trusting and reverent of the authority the man's position wielded, and it had cost them their lives. Nasim would not allow that to happen to anyone else--if he could avoid it.

"Then, may I ask you to help me?" Glenda stood and gestured toward the back of the house.

"How may I be of assistance?" Nasim rose from the couch and followed her into a small room, which appeared to be her home office.

"I have some work I don't want destroyed and, of course, this month's magazine is on my computer. If we work quickly, we can put all of these items in your vehicle. While I wouldn't want any of my things destroyed, they are just… things. They can be replaced. I've got some boxes in here," she opened a sliding closet door and dragged out a stack of boxes which she placed in the center of the room, "we can load everything in to. Don't worry about wrapping it right now. Let's just get it loaded and in your car. I'm going to call LaVonne up the road to come down and get the cats. She'll take them with little or few questions asked."

The two moved efficiently through the house, Glenda making decisions as to what she could afford to lose and what was priceless to replace. The sweep yielded two boxes full of items which Nasim placed into the trunk of his vehicle. After a quick phone call to the neighbor, Glenda gathered up the protesting cats and placed them in their carriers.

Five minutes later, a dark green Cadillac Escalade rolled up the driveway. Nasim watched a plump, blonde woman struggle to climb from the driver's seat. She marched to the front door of the house and, knocking twice, entered.

She'd opened her mouth to announce herself, when she made a visual sweep of the room. She started at Nasim's presence.

He nodded. "Ma'am. Ms. Glenda will be out in just a moment."

Affecting a sniffle, he coughed lightly.

"It is a sad thing. I have glimpsed the cats, and they are such beautiful creatures. I was hoping it would not bother me, but…" he shrugged, sniffling and coughing again.

The blonde nodded her head at Nasim and clucked her tongue.

"It's such a pity. They're really quite wonderful, and Glenda's three, in particular, have such unique personalities. That's okay. My Alvin and I don't mind. Oh, here they are."

Glenda placed two cat carriers on the floor.

"LaVonne, I can't thank you enough. Let me go get Pandora. I don't know what her problem is today, but she's been a little turd. If she won't behave, let her sulk in her carrier."

Glenda went to the back of the house as the blonde took the other two cats in their carriers to the back of her SUV and placed them inside.

Glenda turned to Nasim, "I'll be right back."

She took the last carrier with the pouting Persian to the waiting car.

"I'll get them after my guest leaves, LaVonne. Thank you so much for taking them on such short notice." She slid the last transporter to the floor of the vehicle. Glenda closed the door and hugged the stocky woman.

"Don't bother. Just come over tomorrow before noon and pick them up. Although he would rather choke than admit it, my Alvin just loves your cats. They have such a good time at our house, and he spoils all of them rotten. Take your time, honey." LaVonne swung into the driver's seat and with a quick wave drove off with the furry cargo.

Glenda darted into the house, taking the front steps two at a time.

"What do we do now?"

Checking his watch, Nasim realized his extra time was running out.

"I have to leave before the director arrives. I think it would be best if you gave me the little cat statuette."

Glenda hesitated. "Give you the statuette?"

He nodded.

She moved to the coffee table and returned the lid to the cardboard shoebox before they exited the house. Nasim glanced at the road winding up the hill to the house for sale, noting, at the moment, it was empty.

Standing next to Nasim's vehicle, Glenda clutched the box.

"How can I be sure you won't steal and sell it?"

Nasim looked her in the eye. "You can't. It's sad but true. I can make you promises until the pharaohs rise again, but you shouldn't trust anyone."

"I have no choice." Glenda handed the box to him.

"I'll be very close. When the director leaves, I'll be at this very spot within a couple minutes. If you can put together a small overnight bag, I would. I have a friend, from where I work, who'll be happy to provide you a place to stay for the night. For just this one night, I believe you'd be wise not to be in your house."

Glenda shuddered. "This is like something out of a detective novel. I can't believe it's really happening."

"Please believe me. There is a huge business of thievery involving authentic Egyptian relics. Private collectors will pay any price to have something that is pristine and one of a kind. As far as they are concerned, there is no price too high as long as they don't know how it comes to them. Until later, Ms. Nagel."

Nasim got into his vehicle and drove away from the house. Glenda watched him turn right at the end of the driveway and disappear down the street. She went directly to her bedroom and put together an overnight bag. Then, she moved to the kitchen and began the process of cooking dinner. Dr. Burkhardt hadn't said anything about Dr. Riyadh coming to eat but good manners demanded she have something ready. His visit would coincide with the dinner hour--not preparing a meal was rude in any culture.

I just hope all of this is nothing more than smoke in the wind. I just can't believe Dr. Riyadh can be a thief.

She glanced toward the front room and realized the two cups and gloves were still sitting on the coffee table. With a quick survey of the house, she erased all signs Nasim had been inside. A spike of sunlight into her bedroom window made her look up at the vacant house on the next street. She noted a vehicle resembling Nasim's was parked out front. The light spiked into her eyes, again. He was keeping watch from a safe distance. The butterflies inhabiting her stomach settled down. A fleeting sense of safety stole over her. *He said he'd be close.* Now she believed him.

Chapter Eleven

The growing confirmation of Omar Riyadh's dread opened to a multi-shaded, tan vista of rock and sand. There were several small oases of green he assumed to be housing developments but, for the most part, Omar felt as though he'd just driven into the south side of Cairo. The only things missing were the ever-present pyramids. He nearly missed the exit he was to take for his overwhelming feeling of misery but maneuvered the Mercedes skillfully to the far right of the road and exited with little time to spare. The valley before him widened and, the sky, presenting a pale washed, clear blue backdrop, offered him an unobstructed view for miles in any direction he gazed.

"How depressingly like Egypt. Why would anyone choose to live here when they could have the excitement and greenery of the Los Angeles basin?" Omar shook his head as he continued to follow the directions given him by Ms Nagel. He soon found what small pockets of civilization that existed were thinning considerably as he was, once again, in desolate, barren desert. The road had narrowed to two lanes and passed through a settlement called Littlerock. He cursed as the single light in town turned red causing him to stop, but a glance at his console clock soothed his worrying when the realization struck he was early. There would be time to explore the area around Miss Nagel's home, after all.

When the directions led him up the road to Juniper Hills, he slowed his Mercedes so as not to miss the signs she'd noted to him. The extra time he thought he had disappeared because of his ignorance of the area. On his journey up the winding camel path that passed for a county road, he spotted a light colored truck parked conspicuously; he reflected that it might belong to his accomplices. He suspicions were confirmed when, as he passed, they flashed their headlights at his vehicle. He cursed the magazine editor and her penchant for privacy. He arrived with only five minutes to spare.

The house before him was attractive but not ostentatious. A well maintained yard surrounded the home and garage. Omar noted the narrow, dirt road that appeared to create one side of the property line and calculated the nearest house to be two acres away. A dangerous smile spread over his face.

This will be much easier than I anticipated. Tomorrow, I'll have a ticket to the Bahamas in hand, and no one will be the wiser. He stepped from his sedan, turning to retrieve the bottle of inexpensive wine he'd brought, and moved toward the front door.

~ * ~

Glenda watched the black Mercedes snake up the road toward her house. She knew the director had no idea how far she could see from this vantage point as she witnessed a pickup, parked a couple acres away, flash its headlights at his passing car. Her stomach rolled, and she found her palms were beginning to sweat.

"I can't do this."

Grabbing her cell, she dialed the number Nasim had given her.

"What's wrong?"

"Nothing yet. I don't think I can pull this off. There's a pickup down the road that signaled to him as he passed. What am I supposed to do if they break in while we're having dinner?" Glenda couldn't control the panic rising in her voice.

"Ms. Nagel, they won't enter the house while Dr. Riyadh is inside. If he succeeds in finding the statue, he'll make some excuse to use the phone and call them off. If not, when he passes on his way out, he'll probably flash his lights to signal them to go to work. Even if that occurs, the minute he leaves your driveway, I'll be at your back door to lead you away from here. Right now, you need to gather yourself together and act as if you have no knowledge of the statuette. As far as you know, this is a dinner so the director can become acquainted with the California desert. If it will make you feel more comfortable, put my number into your phone so all you need do is push the button to call me should trouble arise sooner than we expect."

"I have confidence in you, Glenda. Take a deep breath and give an Academy Award winning performance. I'll see you soon."

Glenda knew Nasim was right. To insure her safety, she needed to quit acting like a ninny and pull herself together. She took a deep breath, closed her eyes and willed the unruly butterflies in her stomach to settle down.

There was a knock at the front door.

"Showtime." Glenda eased a smile on her face.

She opened the door to find the smiling, handsome face of Dr. Riyadh gazing expectantly at her.

"This is incredible. It is so like home I keep expecting to see camels grazing nearby." His smile widened.

Glenda pulled in a breath and stepped out to the porch. "It is truly amazing, isn't it? This is the reason I don't want to live in the Valley. If you look that way," she pointed straight forward, "those mountain peaks you are seeing are nearly eighty miles away. And over there," she moved her hand slightly to the left, "those little white slashes on the hills are giant windmills at the pass above Mojave fifty miles away."

She watched as his eyes swept the scene before them hesitating on the light pickup which stood out against the tan landscape.

"It is indeed a beautiful sight to behold. But I must admit to you that, personally, I prefer the distractions of the city. I guess it must have been all those years in dusty digs in the middle of the desert miles from civilization as we know it." Omar chuckled.

Glenda realized the sound of his baritone voice washing over her ears was settling her nerves. *Be careful, girl. If Nasim is right, this man is an expert at deception.*

"Why don't we go inside?" Glenda led Dr. Riyadh into her home.

"Your home is very soothing, Miss Nagel. Oh yes. Lest I forget," he handed the wine to her.

"Please have a seat anywhere you wish. Just be aware you may leave with a multi-colored fur cover." She took the wine into the kitchen and searched the drawers for a corkscrew. Popping her head out, she watched the director casually investigate her living room.

"I'm sorry, director, but do you drink wine?"

Deep chuckling reverberated off the stone fireplace. "Yes, I do. My parents raised me in the Christian faith, but I have come to consider myself Agnostic by choice. My studies in the field have colored the upbringing my parents so carefully tended. I would love a glass of wine if that is what you're asking."

Glenda blushed and ducked into the kitchen. Her hand shook as she uncorked the Bordeaux and poured two glasses. Taking several deep breaths, she took the glasses into the living room.

"I wanted to be sure I didn't offend you. I know most of Persia is Muslim and not allowed to indulge in alcohol." She sat sideways on the love seat tucked in to the window nook.

"That is true, but, as I said, I've chosen to remain neutral on religion. So many of the countries back home are killing themselves over degrees of religious difference that soon, there will be no Persia about which to worry. I can only hope there are more like myself who see the reality of the situation. It is fine to worship a god but, as is evidenced by the pyramids themselves, many religions that are alive today will not be alive in two or three hundred years. We need to take a path of common sense. However, I'm afraid my country, as your own, has no more common sense than that of a doddering old man. Even the children think more clearly than we adults. It is a sad comment on our world."

"How true. Please, Dr. Riyadh, make yourself comfortable." Glenda swept a hand at the available seating.

"Omar, please." He moved to sit at the other end of the the love seat, their knees lightly brushing against each other. "You do have the best view from here. You spoke of fur?"

"Oh, yes. I have three cats, but they're at the vet today. I send them once a month to get bathed and their nails trimmed. I hope you're not allergic."

"No, not at all. I'm sure I'll survive a few cat hairs upon my clothing."

The aroma of cooked meat began to permeate the living room. Glenda took a sip on her wine and rose.

"I need to get busy in the kitchen. Please continue to enjoy the view. It'll be about fifteen minutes before we eat. I hope you like roast beef, rice pilaf, and green beans with slivered almonds?"

Omar turned his warm eyes toward her. "That sounds delightful. The smell is making my mouth water." He flashed a dazzling smile then turned to gaze over the view.

Glenda watched her hand shake as she blanched the almonds in butter.

I have to get a hold on myself. She straightened and busied herself finishing the preparations of the meal. The table was set with her grandmother's china. Glenda placed the roast beef on the gold-ringed platter and thinly sliced the meat. She put the rice in a serving dish and spooned the green beans into a matching bowl. After placing the dishes on the dining room table, she called her guest.

"Dr. Riyadh? Dinner is ready."

He lifted himself from his position on the small couch and carried his wine glass to the table where he placed it at the setting opposite Glenda's. He picked up the cream colored dish trimmed with a single gold ring.

"This is a lovely set of dishes. Heirloom?" He noted, eyebrows arched in question.

"Yes, my grandmother's. She'd been deployed to England during the Second World War as a nurse and discovered Wedgwood ceramics. Just before my grandfather had his heart attack, he surprised her with a trip back to her old Army post, and the Wedgwood factory, to pick out a set of dishes. She left them to me when she died.

"I don't often get the opportunity to use them but decided today was a special occasion and deserved the honor of using the set."

"They're exquisite in their simplicity." Omar noted. He watched as the editor carefully placed a serving of meat, rice and green beans on the plate then placed it in front of him.

"Is that enough?"

"Yes, thank you."

"Please start to eat. I would hate for everything to grow cold." Glenda spooned small servings on her dish and took a thin piece of meat upon her plate. She started to slice the meat into small bites as she spoke.

"My grandmother was an extraordinary woman. This cabin and the land surrounding it belonged to my grandparents. When grandfather became too ill to move around very much, she took on the project of adding two rooms. She built them herself from the floor up. She sold property they owned in Palmdale-proper to a developer, who paid a hefty price, and hired a full time nurse to care for grandpa until he passed away."

Omar was delighted with the meal. The meat was flavorful and juicy and melted in his mouth, the rice fluffy and light and the green beans had a delicate flavor he'd not experienced previously.

"May I interrupt for a moment?"

Glenda stopped.

"I must compliment you on the amazing meal, Miss Nagel. I can't remember when food has tasted so good. Thank you for inviting me to dinner."

Her cheeks colored a deep hue of pink. "Thank you, dir… Omar. I enjoy cooking. It's much more enjoyable cooking for two than for one."

He flashed a quick grin her way. "I agree. My ex-wife was a tremendous cook and mother. This reminds me of the good times past. I'm sorry--I interrupted. Please continue."

"Well, I'd been visiting for years with my parents and moved in when grandpa passed. I love this house, and this area, so it wasn't a burden to move here. In fact, I think moving here was a life saver."

Omar looked up. "How so?"

He finished his meat and eyed the roast on the platter.

Glenda noted his yearning look and automatically placed another slice of meat on his plate.

Omar broke into a wide grin. "Thank you."

"You're welcome. The party life of LA is *very* seductive."

Omar's eyes twinkled and he nodded his agreement as he continued to chew.

"I'd started to spend more time going out with my friends and neglecting my studies the last year of college. My grade point slipped from nearly perfect, 3.99, to 3.00. My parents told me if I slipped any further down the scale, they'd cut off my college funds. That's when Gram stepped in and suggested it might be a good idea if I came to live with her.

"I moved here, finished college with the highest grade point average I could, taking into account my lost quarter, and continued to get my Master's degree in journalism. I moved to the Los Angeles basin when the LA Times gave me a job but found myself fleeing to the Antelope Valley every chance I got. Then Gram died…"

"I'm so sorry."

"Thank you. Anyway, after Gram died, I found she'd left me the property. As soon as I was able, I moved, started remodeling, and this," she waved her hand around, "is what happened. My cats and I are very comfortable here. May I offer you more roast?"

Omar shook his head. "Thank you, no."

Glenda got up and removed both plates to the kitchen.

"Do you find the commute to the museum to be a chore?" Omar started to rise from the table.

"Let me get you coffee and dessert. I hope you won't mind but one of our local bakeries creates the most sumptuous, light éclairs. I picked up a few for after our meal."

"Eclairs? I love them." Omar sat back in his chair.

A moment later, after clearing the table of dinner foods, Glenda carried a tray with coffee accoutrements and a plate with two dessert treats on it. She placed the platter on the table and began to pour the coffee into the cups.

Her hand shook, showing in the stream of coffee entering the cups. She filled the two cups, and portioned out the dessert before sitting down.

"Miss Nagel?"

"Yes?"

"Are you all right?"

"Yes sir. Why do you ask?"

"Your hands are shaking. Do I scare you? I surely hope not. It's not my intention to frighten." A look of concern crossed his swarthy features.

I had better think fast. If he thinks I suspect him, I could be in big *trouble.*

"Well, you are a bit intimidating. After all, you've lived in the heart of the history that fascinates me. I can't imagine waking up every morning to the sight of the pyramids on the horizon. It's so overwhelming.

"The other issue is the lovely vase you gave me."

Glenda watched the director's face tense. He grasped the silver spoon and began to rapidly stir the cream in his coffee.

"Yes?"

"I'm afraid one of my cats knocked it over and broke it. It shattered when it hit the tile floor near the fireplace. I'm so sorry. I *really* liked the piece." Glenda allowed worry to etch over her features, pulling her mouth down at the corners.

"Please--not to worry. My cousin sent me a case of the vases. I would be happy to replace the broken one with a new one, if you wish. Out of curiosity, did you find anything else when the vase broke?" Deep brown eyes stared innocently.

"Anything else?"

"I was just wondering. He sometimes hides things in his vases to see if I really look at them, you know, like a dead scorpion or a replica scarab pin, things like that." He'd set the spoon on the table and took a sip from his cup.

"No. I tried to put all the pieces together and glue them, but they were beyond fixing. The only bits were of the vase."

"Oh. As I can see the sun beginning to lengthen the shadows, maybe you would be so kind as to take me on a tour of your property outside?"

Omar watched a shadow of worry cross Glenda's face. He brushed it aside attributing the look to her concern over the vase.

"You're right. The sun is going down. Now *would* be a good time to show you around," Glenda rose from her chair. "Director?"

"Remember to call me, Omar, Glenda." He placed his spoon on the trivet Glenda had set in the center of the table. "After you."

Glenda rose from her chair, automatically brushing imagined cat hair from her clothing. She opened the front door and waited until the director had passed through before closing the carved wooden entry with etched oval center window. She guided him to a path dotted with terra cotta hexagonal steps leading to the back of the property.

Omar covertly noted all the entrances to the house; how many windows were low enough to enter, how many doors, what landscaping blocked entry and so on. He wanted this operation to move smoothly and be undetectable. The longer it took the authorities to realize the property had been violated, the better it bode for him.

They rounded the corner of the house to an acre-large, tiered backyard exploding in desert foliage. There were wildflowers in bloom as well as small trees beginning to grow; ocotillo cacti stretched spiky, lightly greened arms to the sky and the thrum of humming birds visiting several feeders hanging from the back porch beam disturbed the otherwise silent scene.

Omar sucked in a breath.

"This is so different from your front yard. You've created a wonderful oasis here. I wouldn't have imagined such beauty in the desert."

Glenda felt heat rush to her cheeks. "I took the idea of the Hanging Gardens of Babylon and improvised plants of hearty desert varieties. I started working out here last year when my doctor told me to get a hobby that would provide me with down time. I'm sure you probably had to stop at the one light down in Littlerock?"

Omar bobbed his head in acknowledgement.

"Well, there's a nursery in town where the owners have the most amazing knowledge of horticulture. They were kind enough to take me by the hand and lead me step-by-step to creating this haven. They even came up and looked over the space I had planned to plant, making some excellent recommendations. When life gets too hectic, I come out here, turn on the fountain," she pointed to a tier of shell shaped bowls currently holding small puddles of water, "and just relax in my hammock. It's in the garage, right now. When the weather gets a little warmer, I'll bring it out."

Omar stood on the back porch and surveyed the area. There was a house a couple acres away but, squinting his eyes, he could see a For Sale sign planted out front. From his quick glance, it appeared empty. There'd be no snooping neighbors with which to contend. He turned to Glenda. "This is very peaceful. Shall we continue?"

She shot him a quick sideways look to find him feigning interest in the surrounding area.

"Of course. How could I be so insensitive? You still have to drive back to the city. The west side of the house is bordered with a dirt road, so it's really not very attractive. Since I don't have windows on that side of the garage, I don't worry about the view. We can go into the house through the laundry room door."

She led him through the back portion of the house entering the laundry room and moving down the hallway past the bedrooms into the kitchen area. They continued to the living room.

Omar made a show of glancing at his watch.

"Oh, dear. It *is* getting late. I should really be heading back to Los Angeles. Thank you for indulging my curiosity and providing such a delicious meal.

"Again, may I offer my assistance in your research? Feel free to ask any questions you may have at any time. Miss Nagel."

He bowed slightly from the waist and tipped his head as he lightly brushed a kiss over the back of her hand. "Until next time."

Striding down the steps, Omar held his back straight and restrained himself from bolting to his car. He was certain she'd found the statuette. Her nervousness had been bubbling just beneath the surface all evening. He'd just placed his foot on the brake to stop at the end of the driveway when his cellphone rang.

"Hello. Yes, I'm certain but wait until her lights have gone out or midnight, whichever comes first. I don't want her injured. You'll get your pay when I have the object in my hands. Call me when you've completed the task."

He flipped the phone closed and drove past the light pickup to Fort Tejon Road, his shoulders relaxing the closer he got to the freeway going south into Los Angeles. He allowed a smile to touch the corners of his mouth. *Life is good.*

Chapter Twelve

Nasim watched through binoculars as the Mercedes stopped at the end of the driveway. The figure inside the vehicle put something to his ear. Head and hand gestures indicated a conversation in progress. It appeared brief and the vehicle moved along the lane past the light pickup truck that flashed lights as the car passed. Nasim started when his cell rang.

"Hello?"

"Nasim?"

"Yes. I'm on my way. I'll be there momentarily."

He snapped off his phone and locked the front door behind him. A few steps to his vehicle, and he slowly piloted over the rutted lane to the back of Ms. Nagel's property. He noted the curtains move in the window of the back door before she appeared with her overnight bag in her hand.

Moving with the stealth of one of her cats, Glenda quickly covered the area between her door and his car. She slid her overnight bag to the floor behind the passenger seat, shutting the door with a soft click before entering the front.

"Can we please get the heck out of here?"

Nasim felt the fear emanating from her.

"You'll need to give me directions. Is there a way out which won't take us past that pickup?"

Glenda nodded. "Yes. Up the dirt road, turn left at the next paved spot. That will drop us into 106th street. We'll follow the street to 131th and go to Big Pines Highway. When we get to there, I'll give you further directions."

Nasim stopped the car.

"What are you doing?" She turned panicked eyes toward him.

"You drive."

"What!"

"You drive. You know this area better than I do. It only makes sense for *you* to get us out of here quickly and quietly."

Before Glenda could protest, Nasim had turned off the car and was opening her door. She shrugged her shoulders and traded places.

He's right. I'll be able to double back, take side streets, and use dirt roads he doesn't know. Once she settled into the driver's seat and restarted the car, they moved without lights to the paved street above her house. She was thankful for the dark government vehicle. The color would blend well with the evergreen creosote bushes of the Juniper Hills.

~ * ~

John watched the sleek Mercedes sports car glide past the light pickup truck.

"When we get paid for this job, I'm gonna buy me one of those."

Mike rolled his eyes to the side. "We're not getting paid enough for you to buy one of those." He regretted his comment the moment he saw the shadow slide over John's face.

"Not new, asshole. What did the great director have to say?"

The sneer on John's face made Mike shudder. John had never been particularly handsome but with each bar fight he instigated, his face seemed to get into the way of somebody's fist leaving another *badge of courage* as John called them. Usually, his nose got broken, and his eyes got blackened. Today, his nose pointed slightly left of his eyes, which were a deep purple and blue; Zorro without the mask.

"He wants us to wait until the lights go out or midnight, whichever comes first. He said he didn't want the woman hurt."

79

John turned up the corner of his lip. "Of course. He wants her for himself. Have you seen the bitch? She is *hot*. My boss sent me up here to help put in her backyard about a year ago."

A lascivious grin spread across his battered face.

"She'd look really good *under* me."

Mike gritted his teeth. "Don't do anything stupid. Let's just wait until dark then get what we came for and leave."

"I'm not waiting until dark or her lights go out. I want to get to the bar tonight before ten. That new barmaid is working, and I plan on being there to get her number."

John turned the truck engine over and crept up the road to the house.

Mike felt his stomach turn. He'd not signed up for rape. Theft, yes. Breaking and entering, yes, but rape; no way. The price their boss was paying them to steal a little statue was outrageous, as well as the extra pay from the Director. He was happy to commit a little larceny for the payout. He wasn't willing to go to jail for his brother's hormones. He prayed the woman wouldn't be home.

~ * ~

Glenda checked both ways at the end of the road and rolled through the stop sign.

Nasim raised an eyebrow. "A little illegal, isn't it?"

"I'd rather get a ticket than a bullet or..." she shuddered, "...worse."

She accelerated up the narrow, twisting two-lane road. "It's going to get a little crazy. These roads were designed for beauty not speed. Hold on."

He looked over his shoulder at the valley spread below them. The sun had set behind the western ridge of mountains draping everything in hues of lavender, purple and blue. A whisper of a breeze had blown away the light layer of dust that seemed to rise with the evening hours leaving the landscape crystal clear. Nasim felt a twinge of homesickness stab at his heart, and he turned forward to watch the road. It wouldn't due to lose sight of his mission to keep Ms. Nagel safe.

~ * ~

The sports car hummed along the freeway with the flow of traffic reaching speeds of 80 to 85 miles per hour. Omar smiled as he zipped around slower moving vehicles. The weight he'd felt crushing his spirit had lifted the moment he'd crossed I-5 into the Los Angeles basin. Exhaust-filled air and smog-tinted trees welcomed him home. He felt the urge to stop at his favorite bar. He might as well enjoy a well-deserved drink or two while awaiting the delivery of his treasure.

Two in the morning would arrive more quickly than he wished when he'd face the agents of the collector. Omar shuddered. *I should have listened to my cousin.*

He slid the Mercedes under the archway of the hotel. Handing the valet his keys, he watched the handsome young man ease it around the corner. *Probably an out of work actor. This area seems to be overrun with them.* Through the magnificent, expansive lobby with potted palms and Italian marble on the floor and into the understated elegance of the lounge, he strolled. He occupied one of the buttery soft leather bar stools and caught the attention of the bartender. A buxom blonde, uniformed in tuxedo shirt, black bowtie and black leather miniskirt that barely covered her tight derriere, moved in his direction.

"What can I get you, sir?" The faint fragrance of blue lotus tickled his nose.

Omar offered a wide smile and twinkling dark eyes. "An aperitif of Anise and your phone number."

"One Anise coming up." She moved away to retrieve the Anise from a high shelf, skirt hiking up to reveal a rose tattoo on her upper thigh, and grabbed a small glass from the shelf below the bottle. Returning with filled glass, she placed it on a napkin in front of him.

"That'll be $8.00, sir."

Omar pulled out his crocodile wallet and grabbed the American Express card. "Keep it open. I'm going to be here awhile."

He left the bar at 12:30 a.m. with a dent in his American Express account and the bartender's number. All in all, the evening had been a success.

~ * ~

Mike knocked on the door, furtively glancing from side to side.

John, impatient to get things moving, stomped across the front porch. He cupped his hands against the window and peered into the house. He could see no movement.

"To hell with this. Nobody's here. Let's just go in, get what we came for and get the hell out of here." John tried the front door and found the knob turning under his hand.

"If the door is open then we're not breaking and entering, are we?" John asked.

Mike pushed him into the room. "You check the office area. I'll check the bedroom."

"I want to check the bedroom." A wicked twinkle sparked in John's bruised blue eyes.

Mike turned to his brother. "We don't have time for your sick fantasies. If we want to get paid, we have one hour to find the statue. Quit thinking with your little head, and use the big one for something beside a punching bag. Move it!"

Forty-five minutes later, the house in shambles, Mike swore as he punched the door to the kitchen.

"Damn! If that thing is here, she's buried it under the house. The boss is going to be pissed. Let's get out of here."

The two men bolted out the front door to their truck. They pulled on the main road spraying sand and rocks over the pavement. By ten p.m., John sat at the bar garnering attention from the young, doe-eyed Hispanic bartender.

"Oh, John," she reached her fingertips tenderly to the sides of his eyes, "Would you like me to get you some ice? That looks *really* painful."

He pulled his mouth down allowing one corner to quiver slightly. "Thanks, Anita. It is a little sore. I'm sorry you have to see me like this. Normally, I'm a very quiet guy."

Mike, leaning his chair against the wall in the corner, pulled on his Budweiser and rolled his eyes to the ceiling. *What a crock!* He was sure within two weeks John would have bedded and broken up with the new bartender getting them banned from yet another place in town. It was time for him to start going out on his own. He glanced at the clock above the cash register and sighed. He needed to contact the boss about their failure. The big man wasn't going to be happy. They could kiss the easy money goodbye.

~ * ~

Glenda maneuvered the narrow road winding up the side of the mountain with ease. She'd traveled this way many times during ski season. The hairpin curves kept her sharp behind the wheel. One inattentive moment could send the car careening over an incline into a gorge five hundred feet deep.

As far as she knew, this road had been here forever. She remembered her grandparents taking her to ski when she was a little girl and pictures in her grandmother's album showed her mother and uncle in ski suits in front of the lodge at the top of the mountain.

At the first hairpin turn, she'd caught a glimpse of Nasim's pale face; his hands clutching the hand rest. The higher they drove, the paler his complexion. When they coasted to the stop sign at the Angeles Crest Highway, she decided to pause at the restrooms a hundred feet down the Wrightwood road. The lodge across the street was still in the process of remodeling and wasn't open to the public.

She pulled into the parking lot next to the public restroom and climbed out of the vehicle. "I've had a lot of coffee and, with the way my nerves feel, right now... well, I need this stop. I'm sorry we're in such a hurry, I think you'd like the town of Wrightwood."

Nasim took the opening offered to walk out the kinks in his legs and relieve himself. Sitting up at the house, his eyes attached to the binoculars, he'd had to forego any personal discomfort. It wasn't the first stake-out he'd done, so he knew the mission came before any personal issues; including going to the bathroom and sleep. Luckily, the time he'd spent in the empty house watching Glenda's home turned out to be one of his shorter assignments. He stretched all his muscles before climbing back into the vehicle.

"You're right. I love being around all these green trees. It's so different from my home. But right now, I think we need to put as much distance as we can between your home and us. When the men the director has engaged to find the statue realize it's not there, the situation will become extremely dangerous. He will have one thought in mind--to find the statuette at any price. Because of that, I'd like to accompany you home to ensure your safety."

"Thank you. You'll need to as I don't have my car."

Nasim grinned sheepishly. "That's right. I forgot. Shall we get going? I'd prefer not to take the chance of getting caught by Riyadh's henchmen. Most of those he chooses to assist him have no compunctions about killing to reach their goal."

They crawled into the vehicle and turned toward Los Angeles. The narrow highway was a beautiful drive in the daylight under perfect conditions but harrowing and dangerous at night. Although terrified, Nasim insisted Glenda speed down the ribbon of asphalt, tension between the pair increasing with each passing mile.

As the lights of the Los Angeles basin began to light up the horizon, Glenda felt herself relax.

"We're close to civilization--finally," she smiled in the dark at her passenger.

"I'll feel much better when we're in my office." Nasim flipped open his cellphone. "Good. I've got a signal."

He paged through his stored numbers until he located the one he wanted and hit the send button. On the second ring, the party answered.

"Hello?"

"Lydia?"

"Yes? What can I do for you Nasim?"

"How'd you…"

"Your number is in my phone."

"Oh, yeah. Listen, can you meet us at the office?"

"Now?"

"Please. It's very important, or I wouldn't ask you to come out at this hour."

"I can be there in forty five minutes."

"We're still about that much time away from the office. You won't need to break any laws."

"I'll see you when you get there."

"Thank you. Oh, one other thing…"

"What's that?"

"Would you be able to put Ms. Nagel up for the night?"

"Nasim, you dog!"

"It's not like that. The situation will be explained when we meet at the office."

"Sure."

"Goodbye, Lydia."

"Goodbye, Nasim."

Nasim heard the smirk in his partner's voice as he snapped his cell shut.

"Find the first spot you can pull over safely, and we'll change places. We're in my territory now."

Glenda saw a turn out and slid the car into the dirt viewing area. She turned to him. "We're going to your office tonight?"

"Yes. It's imperative we get the statuette verified by an expert. Director Riyadh has slipped through the cracks of too many bureaucracies because someone left out one small step."

"We have a problem."

Nasim glanced at Glenda as he maneuvered the late evening traffic on the freeway.

"What would that be?"

Glenda let loose a big sigh. "Doctor Riyadh is the only Egyptian expert currently employed by the museum."

Nasim groaned.

Glenda stared out the window. *Should I have trusted this man?*

"I'll have to call in a favor from a source I have at UCLA. Would you please dial the number I give you?"

"Sure." Glenda took his phone and input the numbers as Nasim called them out. She glanced at the sky and realized she was unable to see any stars. *Definitely not the Antelope Valley.*

Within forty-five minutes, Glenda and Lydia sat in a non-descript conference room around an oak table. They'd introduced themselves and made small talk about the situation at hand. Lydia had related a few facts about the cases she'd worked that involved international criminals stressing the point that American criminals were, by world standards, inclined to be less violent and made a shaken Glenda promise to be very careful.

Nasim entered the room trailed by a dark eyed, brunette that bore a striking resemblance to him.

"Glenda, Lydia? I'd like you to meet Professor Nahid Shabouh of the Ancient History Department at UCLA. She's an expert of the 4th Dynasty and will be able to verify the article we have."

Lydia extended a hand, rising from her seated position. "Shabouh? Any relation?"

Nahid shook her hand and nodded. "Nasim is my cousin."

"Nice to meet you."

Nahid asked. "Where's the statuette?"

He turned his attention to Glenda. "Do you have her?"

"No. I gave her to you, remember?"

He frowned slightly, gazed toward the ceiling then a look of recollection crossed his face.

"That's right. I'll be back."

Nasim darted out of the conference room returning fifteen minutes later. He handed the box containing the little princess to his cousin and placed Glenda's overnight bag on the floor next to her.

Nahid gasped when Nasim removed the top of the box.

"She's so beautiful... and ivory!"

Quickly donning a pair of gloves she'd slipped out of her pocket, she reverently held the little princess in her hands. Her eyes scanned the figurine, noting the hieroglyphics and the details on the sistrum. The trio watched the professor employ her expertise. Nahid's hands tenderly placed the centuries old statuette in her temporary resting place. She pulled a relieved breath into her lungs.

Three sets of eyes expectantly searched her face.

Nasim spoke first. "Well? Is she authentic?"

Nahid slowly allowed a smile to play over her features. "What you have here..." she pointed to the box "...is the best preserved statuette I've encountered of the goddess Bastet. Her value is priceless as a relic of the time period; not to mention what a private collector would pay for such pristine beauty."

Glenda choked. "She's real?"

Nahid nodded. "As the pyramids of Giza. How did you come to own such a relic?" A shadow of concern smoldered in the ebony eyes.

Nasim jumped to his feet, his chair falling backward to the floor.

"Cousin! Don't even insinuate what is passing through your mind. Ms. Nagel is a respected magazine editor for the Getty Museum. She and I have worked together on several articles about the demise of our heritage.

"She's the one who contacted *me* when the little princess came into her possession. I'm sure you'll recognize the name of the perpetrator when I speak it."

Nahid crossed her arms over her chest. "Well... I'm waiting."

"Dr. Omar Riyadh gave Glenda a vase she'd admired in his office saying it was a replica created by his cousin. Only when her cats, reacting with natural curiosity, shattered the imitation did the little princess emerge."

Lydia had been watching the exchange between her partner and the professor. When Nasim mentioned the museum director's name and the tanned face of the professor blanched, she couldn't help but believe the two were related. The professor faltered and clutched at the nearest chair collapsing onto the grey cushion.

"The hiya of Cairo still works and lives? I'll kill him with my bare hands." Nahid seethed the words through her clenched teeth.

"I'm afraid he will escape unless we're able to connect him to the stolen artifact. At present, it is our word against his, and you and I both know how that ends."

Nasim took a chair next to his cousin's and placed her hands into his own.

"For the honor of all our ancestors, I will see him behind bars for the remainder of his life, but cousin, I must employ the laws he feels apply to others not himself. If I do anything else… I am no better than he." Nasim watched resignation steal over the beautiful face of his favorite cousin.

She squeezed his hands and sighed. "Once again, you speak with the wisdom of our fathers. I will, of course, honor your wishes." Nahid slumped back in the chair and let her head sag to her hands.

"What do we do now?" Glenda placed her elbows on the table.

Lydia leaned forward. "There's really not much we can do. As Nasim pointed out, without proof to connect the doctor with the statue, we're stalled. Glenda, do you recall a box or wrapping paper with the doctor's address being in the room when you met him?"

"No, but the smell of wood shavings that seems to permeate every museum basement I've ever visited hung in the air. I could tell you where a package originated by smelling the packing materials. Now that I think about the fragrance, I could swear it was cedar mixed with frankincense."

Nasim nodded. "I remember seeing a single wood shaving under the doctor's desk. At the time, I didn't put much significance in it being there. He'd just recently moved into the position and would've been unpacking boxes of his personal items. But considering how clean the rest of the office appeared, the little shaving seemed very out of place."

Lydia drummed her fingers on the table for a moment then glanced at her watch.

"It's too late to go banging on anyone's door asking questions, however, first thing in the morning we can make an appearance at the director's office. I'm sure I can come up with a few questions to rattle his overconfidence. Now, I'm exhausted and ready to go to bed. Glenda, did Nasim bring in all your things?"

Glenda nodded.

"Then let's go. I've got to be back here sooner than I'd like."

Glenda hesitated. "Ms. Thompson?"

Lydia stood and turned to Glenda. "What's the matter?"

"I feel very uncomfortable with the statuette in my possession. I don't have a safe in which to lock it. Do you have a place here you could secure it until this matter is resolved? Even if the director proves he knew nothing about her, I'd prefer not to have her in my office."

Lydia thought for a moment. "I can lock her in my desk, right now, and in the morning talk with the guys in our evidence room. I'm sure we can find a safe place to put her."

The moment Lydia took the box from her, Glenda's shoulders dropped and the lines on her forehead smoothed. "Thank you. That really takes a load off my mind."

"Not a problem." Lydia gathered the container holding the priceless princess into her hands and slipped out of the conference room toward her cubicle. She locked the innocuous shoebox in her lower right hand drawer. Her desk would be safe enough until the morning. After all, this *was* supposed to be a secured government building.

Glenda folded her arms on the table and laid down her head. The excitement of the evening was beginning to wear on her nerves.

Nasim and his cousin conversed quietly in Arabic until Lydia returned. She touched Glenda on the shoulder. "You ready to go home?"

Glenda sighed as she rose from the table, grabbing her overnight bag. "Yes."

The two women moved to the exit, Lydia turning and shooting an acknowledging nod to Nahid.

"Again, a pleasure to meet you. I'll see you later, Nasim."

He watched as the two exited the room then turned to his cousin.

"I should escort you back to your car. Thank you for coming out so late. You know you can speak of this meeting to no one, right?"

Nahid nodded.

"I'll call you when the director is sitting in jail. Shall we go?"

He walked Nahid to her car and secured her door. Watching the dark Acura turn on the main street, he couldn't help but wonder if his family would ever receive justice. Walking to his vehicle, he acknowledged the night watchman at the garage exit. The temptation to drive to the director's house was strong, but as Lydia had wisely summarized; morning was close at hand, the day had been very long, and he would ruin months--no--years, of investigation if he allowed his emotions to override common sense.

Maybe a good night's rest would allow the picture of a pattern to invade his boggled mind. For the sake of his ancestors, he hoped so.

Chapter Thirteen

Omar fit his key into the lock and opened the front door. He slid his hand inside the opening to flip on the light.

"Don't." The reedy voice commanded.

Omar stopped. His stomach rolled and he felt sweat trickling down his sides beneath his silk shirt.

"Come in, for god's sake. We don't want the neighbors to think anything is out of place, do we?"

Omar slipped inside the door and shut it behind him. "I was going to call you…"

"Don't bother trying to lie. You don't have the object and won't by two a.m. You should have listened to your cousins in Cairo."

Omar stopped. "What do you mean, I don't have the object. Didn't your men do their job?"

Silence filled the air. Omar flicked on the hall light flinching as the bulb blazed away the darkness. No one appeared in the living room to his right, nor, upon quick inspection, did they sit at the formal dining table to his left. Cautiously, he slinked down the hallway, peering around corners and turning on lights in each room of his house, fear causing his skin to prickle with every night sound.

He *knew* he'd heard the voice of the man. The piercing, reedy tone was unmistakable. An allusion of expensive cigar smoke whispered through the air and, upon reflection, he realized the chairs at the kitchen table were askew.

How could they have vanished out the back door without his having heard them leave?

He trudged to the kitchen feeling an overwhelming need for water. A trickle of sweat worked its way down his cheek and Omar swiped at the moisture. He ripped a paper towel from the roll under the cupboard and dried his face.

"Water…I need a glass of water." He reached to open the cupboard.

"Ah!"

Omar staggered back until he'd shoved himself against the stove.

In the center of the cupboard, stuck firmly in place with the 8-inch ebony-handled butcher knife, was an 8 x 10 photo of his daughter, the knife protruding from the center of her face.

Omar felt the blood drain from his face and white spots began to explode in front of his eyes.

"I must get myself under control." He grit out between clenched teeth.

He sucked in a deep breath and pushed off the stove. The only way they could have gotten Khepri's picture was from his room. He grasped the knife, and gently wiggled it loose grabbing the picture as it fell. With shaking fingers, he smoothed the knife tear flat on the picture's surface. He picked up the portrait and held it to his chest. He had so hoped to keep her from this side of his work. Her mother, his ex-wife, suspected what was happening but Khepri, his precious desert flower, was unaware how she'd been able to attend Oxford and get her doctorate degree, and he didn't want her finding out this way.

Omar padded down the hallway to his room and, pushing the door with his free hand, entered his private sanctum.

Nothing appeared improper except the frame for Khepri's picture was lying on the dresser instead of standing, as was the norm.

He laid the picture on top of its frame and began to undress. Feeling in control again, habit took over and he slipped into his silk pajamas and headed to his private bathroom to complete his nightly ritual. He switched on the light and staggered against the door when he caught sight of the message scrawled across his mirror in dripping red letters.

72 hours. No cat, no daughter.

Chapter Fourteen

Nasim rinsed his cup and placed it in the dish rack to dry. He jumped at the trilling of his phone. Catching it before the call dropped to his voice mail, he answered.

"Yes?"

"Nasim? This is Lydia. Meet me and Glenda at the museum instead of our office. Let's catch Dr. Riyadh first thing this morning. We'll play good cop, bad cop same as we did last time. I think your silence unnerved him.

"See you there in forty-five minutes."

She hung up before he'd had an opportunity to respond. *Just like her.* He'd much prefer to head directly to Riyadh's house and force the answers out of him, but he knew the idea was only wishful thinking. The respected Dr. Riyadh had proven, in court, he was a formidable foe.

Nasim walked to his room and opened the closet. He stood tapping his chin with his finger, indecision etched on his face. Sighing, he reached to the far end of the shelf above his hanging clothes and pulled down a black leather briefcase that he moved to the bed. Two quick snaps of the closures opened the lid on a gleaming 9mm Glock carefully tucked into foam. He pulled the weapon from its container, checked the chamber, and wrapped his hand around the grip.

"It's been a long time, my friend; a long time. I'm afraid I must take you from your resting place."

He took out an extra clip of shells then reclosed the leather container returning it to its home in the closet. Nasim opened the top drawer of his dresser and pulled out a well-oiled, leather shoulder holster he proceeded to wiggle into, placing the Glock at his left side. Moving back to the closet, he selected a light windbreaker to wear over the weapon and its holder. He sighed. This *was* the one part of his job he disliked--weapons. He was an expert marksman, placed in that category every time he had to qualify on the range, but he didn't have to like using the weapons he was so accomplished at shooting.

He locked his apartment then drove to the museum, parking his vehicle next to a car he recognized as Lydia's company vehicle. Approaching the guard at the front door, he flashed his Interpol credentials and asked the guard to lead him to Glenda Nagel's office. As they neared the area, he spotted the women enter an office he recalled being the Director's. He glanced at his watch noting the time was 7:55.

He turned to the guard. "I see my partner. I can take it from here. Thanks."

The guard acknowledged with a nod.

Conversation floated toward him as he neared.

"Miss Showers?"

Glenda's voice.

"Actually, Miss Nagel, it's Livingston."

"I see. Is the director in his office this morning?"

"No ma'am. He usually arrives before I do, but, this morning, I haven't seen him. He probably just got stopped in traffic." Avril eyed Lydia suspiciously.

Glenda noted the closed demeanor of the young docent.

"I'd like to garner his expertise on an item I've run across before I use it in the magazine. Will you notify me once he arrives? I'll be in my office."

Avril nodded and wrote on a bright yellow pad. "I'll put a note on my calendar. As soon as the Director arrives, I'll ask him to contact you, Miss Nagel."

Glenda moved to the exit. "Thank you, Miss Livingston."

Glenda turned at the doorway, and found herself face to face with Nasim. "Did you hear?"

He nodded. "If I were a gambling man, I would say the good director is on his way to the Bahamas. Time will tell. Where is the little goddess?"

Glenda walked down the hallway to her office. Amunet was at her desk and busy setting up the office for the day.

"Morning, Glenda. I didn't realize you were coming in today."

"I didn't either, Amunet. I'd like to introduce a couple experts who've contacted me regarding this month's issue of *Archaeology Today*. Mr. Nasim Shabouh has written several articles for us although this is the first time we'll actually work face to face and Ms. Lydia Thompson is…"

Glenda hesitated.

Lydia cleared her throat and spoke up. "I'm Mr. Shabouh's photographer."

Glenda shot her a relieved look.

The dark haired beauty acknowledged the visitors. "Miss Thompson, Mr. Shabouh."

"We're going to be in a meeting. I'd prefer not to be disturbed with the exception of Director Riyadh's call. I've asked his docent to let me know the minute he arrives. Is anything else on the schedule today?"

Amunet pulled over the desk calendar and opened its pages.

"No, ma'am."

"Thanks, Amunet."

The trio entered Glenda's office, clearing paper from the chairs and desktop. Amunet popped her head through the open doorway.

"Glenda?"

She looked up.

"Would you and your guests like coffee?"

"Thanks. I think we'll need several pots before our meeting is ended." Glenda flashed a smile. *How would I survive without her?*

Amunet quietly closed the door.

Lydia leaned back in her chair. "Well, I hate to be the one to make mention of the hippo in the room but what are we to do about the absence of the good Director?"

Nasim slid forward in his chair. "I say we go to his house and search. If he left in a hurry, I'm sure he forgot evidence somewhere."

A knock on the door, followed by Amunet's entry into the room, halted their brainstorming session.

"I bring nectar of the working gods."

She carried a tray with three coffee filled mugs, sugar and milk. "Just buzz me if you need refills."

"Thanks, Amunet."

They waited until the door had snapped shut before continuing their conversation.

Glenda wrapped her hands around her cup.

"I should just take the statuette to Dr. Burkhardt, the museum director, and tell him she just showed up on my desk. I can't say I'm fond of all the suspense her being here has introduced to my life. I live in the Antelope Valley because it's as far away from the drama of Los Angeles as I can get and still be close to my work. I *like* my quiet life."

Lydia sipped her coffee. "While I applaud my partner's enthusiasm for his work and, personally, agree with his tactics, I need to remind him, Dr. Riyadh is afforded the same rights as any citizen of this country. Barging into his domicile and rummaging through his belongings without a warrant is illegal and will get the agency involved in a lawsuit. I don't know about him, but I'm rather fond of my job."

He sighed. "So where does that leave us?"

Glenda tapped her fingernails against her cup. "I've noticed several things about the Director since his arrival. One--he's painfully prompt. If I didn't know better, I'd say he was military."

Nasim was agreeing. "His grandfather served in the military with Anwar al-Sadat and, it is rumored, was part of the faction involved in Sadat's assassination. His father is still an active politician in the government."

Lydia's cell rang and she glanced at the readout. "Sorry guys, got to take this." She got up and walked through the back door to the hallway.

Glenda eyed the jacket Nasim wore. "Would you like to take off your jacket? It's quite comfortable in the office, for once."

A slow smile formed on his lips. "Not really. I still have a hard time adjusting to the coolness of Los Angeles. The only time I've felt warm, I notice the locals are complaining that it's too hot. Thank you, I'm fine."

"Okay."

Nasim and Glenda spent the remaining time before Lydia came back hashing and rehashing the facts of the previous night.

Lydia returned to the office and slumped in the chair.

Nasim raised an eyebrow. "Dare I ask?"

Lydia humphed out a reply. "My cousin picks the worst times to do business. He wants me to look at a house he thinks I need to buy--right now. I told him I actually have to work, you know, like 8 to 5?"

She shook her head and rolled her eyes. "Sorry for the interruption. Please continue."

Glenda grinned. "Okay, where were we? Oh, yeah--two-when he feels he's going to be late he calls. Why don't we wait to see if he shows up? At nine o'clock, if he's still not in his office, we can propose to Miss Livingston to call for ten or fifteen minutes to raise the Director. At that time--concerned for his welfare--we can advocate going to his home to see if all is copasetic with the Director."

A slow grin was emerging on Lydia's face. "You sure you don't want to join our organization?"

Glenda shook her head vehemently. "This week has sucked all enthusiasm for spy work out of me. I just want this to be over and have my life back."

Lydia and Glenda talked quietly sharing anecdotes about college life as Nasim sat mutely considering the situation. All jumped when Glenda's intercom buzzed. She picked up the phone.

"Yes? Really?" She leaned forward. "Call her back and tell her I'll drive over to his house and see if everything is all right."

She looked at the pair in front of her.

"It appears our plan has launched itself without our intervention. Miss Livingston has already spent the last fifteen minutes calling the Director's home phone and cell to get a response. She called Amunet in a panic wanting to know what to do. According to his secretary, 'He's *never* late.' She's worked herself into such a state of hysteria; she's convinced he's been murdered."

"Shall we venture to the Director's home and rescue him?"

With a muted scraping of chairs across carpeted floors, the trio exited Glenda's office. As she passed the desk of her secretary, Amunet handed a slip of paper to Glenda.

She raised an eyebrow. "What's this?"

"Dr. Riyadh's address."

"Remind me to give you a raise." Glenda grinned.

"Count on it."

In the hallway, they stopped.

Nasim turned to the two women. "As much as I'd like to be the first to venture into the Director's home, I think you should lead the way, Lydia."

She shot him a puzzled look. "Why?"

"My family's history with him."

"Right. I'll meet you there."

Once inside Lydia's vehicle, she turned to Glenda.

"I know you're trying to help, but, frankly, if you get out of the vehicle you could put the investigation in jeopardy. Just stay in the car when we get there. If nothing has happened to the Director, then we'll all look silly. However, if, for some reason, his house becomes a crime scene you'd probably contaminate evidence without knowing. I'd be happier if you just stay put."

"But it would be more logical if I was to come searching for him--we work together."

Lydia rolled her eyes and huffed out a breath. "Glenda, please. I'm not moving this car until you promise."

Glenda slumped in the seat. "I promise."

"Good. Let's get going." Lydia drove to the exit, checking her rear view mirror to determine Nasim's car was behind her.

Nasim considered using his GPS to locate the address of Dr. Riyadh's home and taking a shortcut since it seemed to be taking Lydia forever to leave the parking lot, but after his "you go first" speech, he realized he'd sentenced himself to following her.

Either way, he was finally going to find some retribution for his family.

Chapter Fifteen

Lydia pounded on the front door. She waited a moment then put her ear to the wooden enclosure nearly falling in the house when Dr. Riyadh opened it.

"It's about time… who the hell are you?"

Omar back stepped into his vestibule and eyed the nearly prone figure. When she stood upright, he smirked.

"Good morning, Miss Thompson. What brings you to my home," he glanced at the expensive watch on his wrist, "at this unholy hour?"

"Dr. Riyadh. Your secretary panicked when you didn't show and didn't call at your normal hour. We," she waved a hand at Nasim and Glenda, who had traipsed to the front door right behind her in spite of their conversation to the contrary, "had a scheduled meeting, this morning, and were happy to assist when Ms. Livingston asked Glenda here, to check and see if everything was all right." Lydia chuckled. "She was afraid you'd been murdered."

She watched the color drain from the man's face.

Omar cleared his throat and pasted an insincere smile on his lips.

"Well, Miss Thompson, as you can see," he waved a hand up and down, "I'm just fine, however, I know you won't be happy until you've inspected my home. So… won't you all come in for coffee?"

He stepped aside and pulled the door fully open so the trio could enter.

"Have a seat in the living room while I fetch the cups."

The three sat on the expensive brocaded divan. Lydia and Nasim's eyes scrutinized the room taking in the details of expensive furniture, and richly designed nik-naks. Nothing out of the ordinary and nothing a museum director couldn't afford.

Dr. Riyadh returned carrying a tray with an urn and four demitasse cups.

"I hope you like Egyptian coffee. I've found a wonderful outlet here in the valley that carries most of the brands from back home. It takes the sting out of being so far away."

Glenda spoke up. "I was concerned when Avril…"

The Director smiled as he poured coffee in to the small containers. "So her little secret is out, is it?"

"When Dr. Burkhardt hired me, he made sure I was fully aware of the people with whom I'd be working. As I was saying…"

Dr. Riyadh nodded his apology.

"When she said you'd not come in nor called, I was concerned. I watched you leave from my home yesterday after dinner and spotted an unfamiliar truck parked down the road. It's not unusual for kids to come up our direction to park and do whatever it is kids do these days, but there haven't been any parkers in a while."

Nasim observed the director's reaction to Glenda's statement. He was angry she'd not consulted him first before opening herself up to unknown consequences, but her statement jarred the man. His hand trembled as he passed the cups.

"I'm sorry." He gave a thin smile. "It's been a long night."

He finished serving and sat in the wingback chair placed to the left of the couch.

"You know, Miss Nagel, I saw that truck, too, and for some unknown reason when my car passed, they flashed their lights at me. I don't know who they thought I was but I continued safely on my way home." *There. Just enough information to let them know I'm aware they're watching me, but not enough to involve myself.*

Lydia and Nasim exchanged glances. This man wasn't going to make their job easy.

"The reason I didn't come in or call today is that I simply got caught up in a situation here at home."

Glenda raised an eyebrow. "I hope it's not serious."

"Well, not terribly. On my drive home, I realized yesterday was my daughter, Khepri's birthday, and I'd not sent a card, flowers, or anything. She's a doctor at a private hospital in Cairo."

Glenda looked at the glowing face of the director. "You mean she didn't want to follow in your footsteps?"

He sighed. "Yes, she did, but I told her I didn't want my grandchildren being dragged from one dig site to another while she chased ghosts from the past. She could be a weekend archaeologist if she was determined but my country needs competent women doctors and I felt she would become one of the best. She listened and now directs a private woman's hospital in the outskirts of Cairo. She's made me very proud. Now if she would just marry…"

Glenda smirked. Why was it parents were never happy?

Omar continued. "I'm afraid I indulged myself in a, what is it you Americans call it?, Pity party at my favorite bar. When I arrived home, well… let me show you. It's easier to see than try to explain."

He rose from his chair and indicated they should follow him. They traveled the length of the hallway to a modern, bright kitchen with light wood cabinets. The director led the trio to the cabinet opposite the stove and stood pointing to a spot in the center. On the marble countertop, beneath lay an 8-inch ebony handled butcher knife.

"I came into the kitchen to retrieve a glass of water, as is my part of my customary nightly routine, and I found this knife sticking out of the cabinet. I can tell you it gave me a start and, for a moment, I panicked. Once I got control of myself, I realized I'd had to unlock my door to come in the house, so, whoever visited was an expert at breaking and entering."

Lydia and Nasim started to say something when the director put up his hand.

"Before you ask, there was no note, no dead creature, nothing to indicate why someone would take such care to break in to my home and stick a knife in my cupboard. I do, however, have my suspicions."

Nasim asked, "What would those be?"

Omar, noticing the slight bulge at Nasim's left side, leaned against the counter and crossed his arms. "I've been receiving hate mail since I moved to this neighborhood. It's the usual diatribe about being Middle Eastern and why don't I go home. I think someone has taken the next step."

Lydia had pulled out her notebook and began taking down the information. "Have you saved any of the mail?"

Omar nodded. "Yes. I'm aware of the need to track these foolish people. I put each of the letters and envelopes in a shoebox in my closet. And, no, I haven't contacted the police, yet, because up until last night, it was just words on paper. I'm not sure bringing in the police at this point will do any good. I hadn't gone to work because I'm waiting for the alarm company to install a system throughout my home."

Nasim nodded. This was all too easy, too glib. Dr. Riyadh's story held the hint of rehearsal to it. He looked at the director. "Don't you think it is time to call in the local police, now?"

Omar shook his head. "It would just exacerbate a small blaze to a roaring fire."

Lydia started to object.

"I believe bringing in the local authorities would push this person, or persons, to the next step. I don't think," the director shuddered, "I wish to experience that personally. And, let us be honest, your vehicles attest to the fact you two are from some law enforcement agency."

Omar raised an eyebrow and the corner of his mouth.

Lydia pushed an exasperated sigh between her lips. "Much as I hate to admit it, the man is right."

Nasim investigated the depth of the hole created by the end of the butcher knife. He peered at the spot from the front and the side. Someone had exerted great force in pushing the large blade in the wood. The height indicated the perpetrator was either a man or very tall, muscular woman. All this would require further investigation--but not here. The director was making moves to push them to the living room.

Halfway down the hall, the doorbell pealed.

"Ah. *That* must be the alarm company." Dr. Riyadh moved around the trio and pulled open the door. A young man, who appeared no more than twenty-four, clad in the uniform of a local alarm company and clutching a clipboard, looked up at the director.

"Is this the residence of Omar--Ree-add?"

The director smiled. "Yes. Please come in, my guests were just departing."

The three filed out the front door toward their vehicles.

"Oh, Miss Thompson?" The director spoke to her retreating back.

Lydia turned. "Yes?"

"I'll bring the shoebox with those letters to work and leave them for Miss Nagel to return to you. Please inform my secretary that all is well, and I'll be in when it becomes possible."

"Thank you, director." Lydia forced a pleasant smile to her face.

Omar turned, a smirk spreading over his face as he led the young worker to the back of the house. The young Egyptian gentleman was going to bear watching.

Nasim felt the frustration building in his throat. This snake had all the answers. How was he going to clear his family name? He stomped toward his car, muttering in Arabic, plowing in to the back of Lydia.

"Geez, Nasim. Why don't you watch where you're going?"

"Sorry. Why were you stopped in the middle of the driveway?"

Lydia nodded in the direction of the house across the street.

"See that sign?"

Nasim rolled his eyes. "Lydia? I don't know about you, but I can barely afford to pay the rent for the apartment I live in now."

She turned to Glenda, standing next to her. "What do you see?"

Glenda tipped her head and shrugged her shoulders. "An overpriced white elephant?"

Lydia pushed out a sigh. "Well, you two have the question part right for Jeopardy but not the answer part."

Nasim looked to Glenda who shook her head.

"Think--think. Where are we right now in connecting the director to the little statuette?"

Both replied in unison. "Nowhere."

She continued. "Right," pointing at the house across the street she continued, "*that* is a way in. Glenda?"

"Yeah?"

"Why don't you head back with Nasim? If you don't mind, I want to mull this over on my drive back to the museum."

"No problem." Glenda walked to Nasim's car and waited.

He groaned as he slid the key into the passenger side lock.

Glenda looked at him. "What? Are you all right?"

He shook his head. "For the moment. When Lydia gets this certain look--the one she has on her face now--it usually means I'm going to be crawling under buildings, or wading in smelling things you don't even want to know about. This can only mean her idea is just barely legal. Let's go back to your office and see what trouble I'm about to enter."

Glenda giggled. She suspected Nasim liked the dirty part of his job more than he was admitting. She sat silent in the car pondering the events that had unfolded at the director's house.

As handsome as Dr. Riyadh was physically, she found herself disliking his demeanor. He reeked of pomposity. She snickered. The word conjured mental pictures of bloated men in too small suits issuing decrees to subservient underlings. Even so--his certainty that he was untouchable by the law was infuriating. She wasn't sure she could look him in the eye without glaring.

Pulling up to the museum, Nasim and Glenda watched Lydia stride purposefully up the walkway to the offices.

"Oh, boy," Nasim shook his head. "She's on a mission."

Chapter Sixteen

By the time Nasim and Glenda walked through the parking lot, Lydia had disappeared. Glenda eyed the growing foot traffic passing them in the halls but was unable to spot the agent. She walked to her offices, Nasim close on her heels. Standing in front of her secretary's desk, she surveyed the worry lines gathering above Amunet's dark eyes.

"I'm so sorry, Glenda. I couldn't stand it any longer. That other woman, Miss Thompson, was pacing circles in front of the desk and making me crazy! I sent her inside your office."

Amunet's exasperated expression started Glenda to giggling. She leaned across the desk and patted her hand.

"Don't worry. She has a lot on her mind. It's all right."

Amunet looked at Nasim who shook his head and rolled his eyes.

"She works best when she's on the move. Before I came to the agency, I heard she'd worn a path in the carpet around her cubicle. She has tile floors around her desk--the only one in the agency."

Nasim and Glenda entered and found Lydia muttering and pacing.

He cleared his throat. "What despicable, grimy, nasty task am I going to be assigned today?"

Lydia stopped mid-step and plunked down in the nearest chair.

"When we were in the field, I asked both of you what you saw across the street from the director's house. Remember?"

The two nodded as they took the remaining chairs; Glenda behind the desk, Nasim facing Lydia.

"As I recall, Nasim made some comment about barely being able to afford the apartment where he lives, and Glenda called it a white elephant. I don't know why."

Glenda explained. "Five years ago, those houses were selling for $250 to $300 hundred thousand. You probably can't touch it for less than $575 now-- same house, same problems, i.e., a white elephant."

"Okay," Lydia leaned forward in her chair. "What *I* see is a way to *get inside* the good director's home." She leaned back, a smug smile radiating over her face.

Nasim shot back. "I'm not going to jail for breaking and entering, beside that; he's having alarms installed today." *Don't want to go to jail for a weapons charge, either.* Although the agency issued handguns to their inspectors, the 9mm Glock was Nasim's own weapon chosen because of its ease of handling and the polymer frame that kept the firearm light. He didn't feel as though he had a lead growth on his side when he wore the weapon.

Glenda turned up her hands on the top of her desk. "Maybe I'm being dense, but I don't see what you mean."

Lydia slumped down in her chair. "Come on, guys. Think."

Nasim and Glenda just shook their heads.

Glenda studied Lydia. "Normally, my brain functions fairly well, but the last 24 hours have been out of the ordinary, to say the least. My little gray cells aren't working."

Lydia nodded. "You're right. You don't deal with all this intrigue on a regular basis, but Nasim, you should be able to see where I'm going with the idea."

He shrugged his shoulders.

"I think if we… bend the law a little…"

Nasim pushed out a loud groan. "Not bending."

Lydia glared at him. "…as I was saying, if we improvise the scenario I have in mind, we may beat this creep at his own game."

"How do you propose to do that?" Glenda's curiosity was stirring.

"You have to stay out of the picture. You're a civilian and as such can be sued, and spend time in prison if you attempt what I'm suggesting. On the other hand, Nasim and I have a little less vulnerability along those lines. It's, kind of--okay if we play out this scene." Lydia was choosing her words judiciously.

Nasim leaned forward in his chair and directed his dark eyes to her. "Get-to-the-point."

"I have a non-government-issue car parked in my garage at home. It was a gift from my parents for graduating so high in my college class. It wouldn't attract any attention in that neighborhood."

Glenda was intrigued. "What is it?" She watched the color creep up Lydia's cheeks, turning them a lovely shade of pink.

Coughing into her hand, she muttered, "A vintage Jaguar."

Nasim snapped his head up. "Oh?"

Lydia dropped her head to her hands. "Oh, hell." She pinned a hard stare on the other two occupants of the room. "What I'm about to admit to does *not* leave this room. Clear?"

Nasim nodded.

Glenda nodded and crossed her heart with her hand lifting a three-finger salute. "On my honor as a former Girl Scout."

A deep sigh pushed through Lydia's lips. "Thompson is my mother's maiden name." She grabbed a pencil and sticky note pad from Glenda's desk scribbling on the pad. Handing it to Nasim, she indicated he should pass it to Glenda.

Nasim whistled.

"I'll be…" was all Glenda could say.

"You can see why I didn't use that name when I applied for this job. However, as you know, Nasim, once they started the background search, the information came to the forefront. There was discussion about not hiring me due to the sensitive nature of the family name. It took a lot of pleading to get this job. For the most part, my history is fictional. If anyone looks into my records, they'll find I grew up in Redondo Beach, went to USC, and took the internship in Egypt where I worked with Dr. Riyadh.

"That, however, is off the point. My idea is to call the Realtor for the house across the street from Dr. Riyadh. I'll set up a daytime showing. If I take my own car and disguise my looks, I should be able to move freely. Once I get a viewing of the house…"

"Here it comes," muttered Nasim.

"…I can ask who does the neighborhood trash disposal as I have some issues with one of the local companies. I'll thank the agent and tell them I want to take some time to consider the purchase. This is where you come in, Nasim."

He crossed his arms over his chest, and raised an eyebrow at her.

"We'll come back on the night before trash is collected. When the director sets his can at the curb, we'll wait until he goes back into the house and the lights have been out for an hour. At that time, we take the bags from the receptacle and bring them to the lab. We can go through his trash. Maybe, we'll find something that links him to the statuette."

"And maybe, we'll just smell like garbage for a week. Dumpster diving. You know how I hate dumpster diving." Nasim's voice rose in pitch. "Isn't there any other way?"

"You tell me. You come up with something else, and I'll go along 100 percent."

"I knew it was going to be smelly, dirty, and tons of fun." Nasim was shaking his head. "When do you propose we engage this little charade and fun ride?"

"The sooner the better. If we allow the director too much time, he'll escape, again." Lydia pointed out.

"You're probably right. Well, I'm taking the rest of the day off to take a long, hot shower and sleep in my clean-smelling bed." Nasim stood and started toward the door.

"Nasim?"

He stopped to turn and look at Glenda.

"Yes?"

"I need a ride home."

His shoulders sagged.

"I'm sorry. I forgot all about that. Guess I'll need the day off, anyway. Are you in a big hurry?"

Glenda nodded. "I'm on deadline. Amunet will contact the copyeditors to read over what I've written, but I'll have to set the pages, and get the finals to the printer before tomorrow at five. I can accomplish that from the comfort of my own home. I'm just afraid of what I'll find when I get back to the house. Besides, you have most of my files and my computer in your trunk."

Lydia rose. "I've got to call a Realtor, guys. See you, later."

She headed out the door, determination in each step.

"I'm sorry, Nasim."

"Don't be. I'm the one who convinced you to drive me back. Shall we get started?"

He followed the editor as she stopped by her secretary's desk and left instructions on contacting the copyeditors.

"I'll be home within two hours if you need me. Just call and I'll get back to you. Thanks, Amunet."

She turned to Nasim. "Please take me home."

Chapter Seventeen

Omar listened patiently as the young man explained the intricate workings of the alarm system.

"...and all you need to do is push this button here, as soon as you can, and the alarm will turn off and automatically dial the police. Do you have any questions, Mr. Riyadh?"

"No, thank you, Mr. Steele. I appreciate you coming out so quickly." Omar was leading the young technician to the front door. "I shall send a note of gratitude to your boss to let him know what an outstanding job you've accomplished here today."

"Thank you. Mr. Riyadh, I'd really appreciate that. Again, if you have any questions, here's my card, please feel free to call, day or night." The young man handed Omar a business card.

"I will, thank you." Omar palmed the card, fully intending to throw it away the moment the young man left his driveway. He smiled and nodded as the technician entered his van and pulled in to the street. Shutting the door, Omar tossed the paper in the nearest trashcan. He needed to call his secretary and assure her he was on his way to work.

~ * ~

The Steele Alarm Company van turned the corner at the end of the street and slid in behind a late model Mercedes four-door with dark tinted windows.

He exited his vehicle and walked to the car, patiently standing next to the sleek auto. A window slid silently into the leather-lined, door panel.

"Is it done?" the raspy voice scratched out the question.

"Yes." Steve pulled a small remote from his pocket and handed it through the window. "Just push the green button and the gas will leak through the house. He was so busy pacing and worrying, he didn't see me install them. Give it five minutes after you push the button. You'll be able to enter undetected. The gas will wear off in an hour. If you need me, you have my number, sir."

He walked back to his van and left. This was not the first time he'd been inside the quiet, tree-lined neighborhood and that particular house.

Steve Steele's innocent, boyish looks served him well. Most people thought him to be in his twenties. The truth would surprise many. He was closer to forty and had been in more dangerous, gritty situations than he cared to count.

Turning on the main thoroughfare, Steve felt the muscles in his neck relax. He enjoyed the rush of getting in and out without detection. He *was* the best in his field.

The Egyptian wouldn't know what hit him.

~ * ~

Lydia flipped the pages of her notebook until she located the phone number listed on the real estate sign. She dialed, wading through the pre-recorded introduction and punched in the extension. A breathy voice gave a name and rattled a spiel about leaving a number.

"This is Lydia Nelson. I was cruising through the hilltop neighborhood yesterday and saw your sign on a home at Cielo Drive that I've been admiring for years. Is there any way I could set an appointment to see it? I only have today free and was so hoping we could…"

The slight hiss of recording tape that accompanied most answering machines clicked off.

"Hi. This is Trish Donnelly. I'd love to show you that home. Would 2 p.m. work with your schedule?"

"Miss Donnelly, that would be wonderful. I'll park out front. Until then."

Lydia smiled. She realized she'd need to go home and pull her other car from the garage. A quick wash would help display the image she wanted to send. She left a message for Nasim and left the office.

Two hours later Lydia stepped from the vintage, forest green Jaguar. She retrieved an alligator briefcase that matched the low heels she wore. A classic Chanel suit and simple silk blouse accented by minimal diamond jewelry mirrored the image she'd seen her mother project at many a board meeting. Lydia chuckled. People learned the real force behind the family name when her father retired, by his doctor's order. Her mother was formidable.

She felt a tug at her throat. The jet accident that killed them both still stung fresh in her memory.

"Told them just to drive to Vegas--it wasn't that far, and they could've used the company limousine. But no, Dad had to be in control just once more."

She stopped then whispered. "I sure miss you guys."

She pulled in a deep breath to steady her pounding heart and stop the possibility of tears emerging.

A functional, tan Mercedes four-door pulled behind Lydia's Jaguar and a tiny brunette on teetering heels exited. Lydia bit the inside of her mouth to keep from laughing. The woman couldn't have been more than four foot eleven inches tall. She was wobbling on three-inch heels. A recent visit to the plastic surgeon showed in the over-collagenized lips and wide-eyed expression of her face. She smiled, carefully, and offered Lydia a manicured hand.

"Hi. I'm Trish Donnelly. Are you Ms. Nelson?"

Lydia nodded and shook the extended hand. She'd had more response from the dust rag she used around the house.

114

"I've watched this home for years. My family lived in this neighborhood when I was a kid; I walked past it on my way to school for eight years. I was visiting an old friend when I saw your sign. I couldn't believe my good fortune. Please tell me the owners are serious about selling?"

Trish moved up the driveway as she searched her set of keys for the proper one.

"Yes, unfortunately. After the husband died, the wife continued to stay until six months ago. She became so frail she was unable to keep up the place. When she finally passed, the children contacted us. They'd considered living here until they learned the neighbor across the street is Middle Eastern."

Trish turned the key in the lock and swung the door open. She looked at Lydia.

"I hope that won't be a problem?"

Lydia flipped a hanging tendril of the dark wig she wore over a shoulder and smiled. "Of course not. I don't *have* to associate with my neighbors."

"How true. Everyone else around here belongs to the country club..." Trish hesitated allowing the implication of her statement to reach Lydia, "so that's really the only fly in the ointment. I guess, though, he's some kind of executive at the Getty Museum. He keeps to himself according to the other neighbors. Now, let me show you the house."

Lydia walked through the rooms of a home accessorized with a great deal of love. She felt sorry for the family who'd lived here that the children had not inherited the tolerance of the parents. They were standing in the kitchen turning to leave when she asked *the question.*

"Ms. Donnelly?"

"Yes?"

"I need to ask who the trash collection people are and what day they collect."

Trish turned to face Lydia, her brow furrowed. "May I ask why?"

"Well, as you see, today is my only day off and my husband, Bob Nelson..."

Trish's eyebrows rose. "*The* Bob Nelson?"

Lydia nodded, "…yes, *the* Bob Nelson. Anyway, he has a real issue with Skylar Sanitation. That could be a deal breaker."

Trish set her briefcase on the counter and snapped open the latches.

"Let's see here. The company who services this area is Mountain Brothers and it appears they pick up--tomorrow. I hope that will settle your concerns. Would you like to go back to the office and start paperwork?"

"Let me check with, Bob." Lydia pulled out her cell and called her own landline.

"Hi sweetie, it's me. I looked at that house I was telling you about and the good news is Mountain Brothers services this area. Do you want me to start the paperwork, now? Okay. Sure." She flipped the phone closed.

"He wants to talk about it. So, Trish, may I have your card? I'll talk with him and give you a call first thing in the morning?

Trish pulled a business card from a pocket in the briefcase. She handed it to Lydia. Her eyes held a suspicious look and her recently plumped lips pursed in disgust.

"Yes. Call me when you make a decision. Why don't you go ahead and leave, and I'll close up here?"

She thrust a hand toward Lydia, who shook it, Trish turning her back once the formalities were complete.

Lydia ambled to her Jaguar. Once inside, she flipped open her phone, and pressed speed-dial five.

"Hello?"

"Bobby?"

"Yes?"

"This is your favorite cousin. I'd like you to call a real estate broker I just had an appointment with today. Do me a favor and play along with anything she might say?"

"What have you done now, Lydia?"

"It has to do with a case I'm working on for the agency. I looked at a house today, for the case, but I really like the layout and want to buy it.

Would you arrange all the disgusting little bank details and let me know how much it's going to ding my account?"

Lydia heard the sigh from the other end of her phone.

Bobby Nelson, her cousin, was a bit infamous with the local business community. He was an investment banker with the good looks of a movie star and a client list that included many of the rich and famous. He'd lent his resources to an unknown movie director in the 70's and the film had hit box office gold setting him and the director up for life. He was also the broker bulldogging her trust fund.

"You know, Lydia, I had half a dozen places lined up for you to look at. If you've found the place you want, why did you ask me to do all this footwork for nothing?"

"Look, Bobby, I'm very grateful you and your staff put in all that work. It just worked out that this place really has caught my attention. So, please, will you call?"

Lydia knew for all his huffing and puffing her cousin hadn't lifted a finger to set up the appointments he was whining about. He had staff housed in over two floors of one of the tallest buildings in downtown Los Angeles. Some poor secretary, who was being highly compensated for her time, had put together the package.

"Sure. What's the number?"

She rattled off the number from the business card, scanning the area while she waited for him to call. Halfway up the street, parked in front of a sprawling ranch home, sat a white van. She squinted to see the name on the logo wishing she could pull out her binoculars. It appeared to be some type of plumbing company. *Hope this is not a bad sign.* Bells seem to ring in the back of her head. Earlier when she, Nasim and Glenda visited Dr. Riyadh, the alarm company van parked in the driveway had been the same style and used the magnetic signs, too. Lydia shook her head. She was just being paranoid.

Relaxing a bit, she watched the tiny real estate agent stomp precariously on her stilettoes to her vehicle. As the agent was about to enter the car, her phone must have rung because her briefcase dropped to the ground, and she frantically searched her pockets.

Lydia suspected who the caller might be and her suspicions were confirmed when the agent looked up at the Jaguar, an expression of complete surprise radiating from her face. The agent nodded then flipped the phone shut. Lydia cranked the window open on her side and turned to meet the amazed face of Ms. Donnelly.

"Ms. Nelson?"

Lydia feigned innocence. "Yes?"

"Your--husband has instructed me to give you the keys to the house. He said a cashier's check in the full amount will be delivered to me within the next two hours." Trish uncoupled the keys from her ring and let them drop into the outstretched palm of Lydia.

"He didn't even argue about the price." Confusion clouded the woman's face.

"Oh, Bobby knows better than to argue with me when I want something. I told him I wanted this house and, well, he bought it for me. Just out of curiosity… how much did this cost him?" Lydia batted her eyes.

"To be brutally honest, he--you--got a deal. The house had listed at $575 thousand but sat for the last two months; the market is very soft for sellers right now. Just last night, the owners asked me to drop the price $100,000 to move it. You got this house for $475,000."

"He still owes me a condo on the Italian Coast for that little Lear jet he bought without asking. Thank you, Ms. Donnelly. I'm sure Bobby will take care of the paperwork. You've been very helpful." Lydia watched the agent flounce back to her car, grabbing a sold sign from her back seat and slipping it in the top of the realty sign. She suspected this house was, indeed, the white elephant Glenda had called it and the agent was thrilled to escort it out of her inventory. As she drove away from her latest acquisition, her thoughts tumbled to the night ahead. She recalled the agent turning lights on and off throughout the tour but she'd have to ensure there was electricity for their campout, or was that camp in?

She still had much to do before the day was done. First was to park her car and pick up the agency vehicle. The rest would wait.

Chapter Eighteen

Glenda sighed as the veil of smog lifted through the Acton hills. The CalTrans station at the top of the climb was the landmark she used for herself to signal she was almost home. Nasim smoothly slid the government vehicle to the off ramp and navigated the serpentine section of road that would drop them on the Pearblossom Highway.

"Considering you've only been here once before, you're doing quite well." Glenda turned an admiring glance Nasim's way.

"It is one of the blessings I discovered when I was a child. The cities in my country are thousands of years old and, consequently, built with foot traffic and donkey carts in mind. The streets are a confusing maze. One has to have a good memory or a good map. My genetics blessed me with a good memory. Once I've traveled a path or road, I'll recall the way. If you have no objection, when we arrive at your house, I'd prefer to enter before you. It's been nearly 24 hours since we left, but I'll feel better knowing, for certain, there is no danger."

Glenda shuttered. "You know, I'm anxious to get home, on the one hand, but afraid of what I'll find on the other."

"That's why I'll enter first. If I think it is too--distressing, I'll let you know."

Glenda shook her head. "No. It's my home; I want to be the first inside. I promise not to do any silly girl things like faint."

She felt her stomach roll as the car turned up the road heading to Juniper Hills. She sighted her home. Trying to swallow, she discovered her throat constricted and dry. A second effort proved successful.

Nasim was keeping an eye on his passenger. She was holding up well, for a civilian, but he knew the reality of walking into a house destroyed by people searching for something could be overwhelming. He stopped the car near the garage. She walked up to the house ahead of him while he retrieved her computer from the trunk. When she opened the front door, he heard her swift intake of air.

"Are you all right?" He hesitated, monitor in his hands. Watching the back of her head, he was unable to detect her state of mind until he saw her back stiffen and a flush of crimson creep up her neck.

"Those bastards!" Glenda spit the words in the air and spun to face Nasim. "If I get my hands on them, I'll wring the life out of them." She turned and stomped to the couch under the bay window, picked the cushions from the floor, and sat. She waved her hand at the sight before her.

"You warned me they'd be brutal and I thought I was ready to face this but…" she let the thought die.

Nasim put the monitor on the dining room table and moved beside her on the couch, taking her hand.

"Believe it or not, this is not bad. Apparently, the people who were sent were professionals."

Glenda faced him and raised an eyebrow.

"I know, only too well, what amateurs can do. I had an uncle who found himself placed under investigation. He…"

Nasim hesitated. This was the second time in less than two weeks he was indulging family information to people who were all but strangers. He wasn't sure if he should continue.

"He what?" Glenda's voice shook.

He looked up at her. Her eyes burned with the need to know she wasn't alone.

He decided to plunge ahead. Clearing his throat he continued, "… worked at the Cairo museum in the warehouse. During a routine inventory, some valuable pieces had come up missing. What with him being the director of the warehouse, they jumped to the conclusion he had knowledge of the thefts or was involved. The accusations were false but didn't stop the soldiers from breaking into our home at all hours of the day and night and destroying our belongings looking for *hidden treasure that belong to the state and peoples of Egypt'*. They assumed since we were relatives he would hide things in our home as well as his own until the coast was clear.

"The first time they burst through our door was frightening. They were screaming, and waving their rifles in the air. It nearly terrified my younger brothers and sisters to death.

"After the first couple of weeks, we received a warning, from one of the few friends we had inside the government, there would be a raid sometime during the following week. My mother gathered what was left of our irreplaceable family treasures and under the dark of night placed them in safekeeping with her cousins in the country. Putting themselves at risk, her family hid our valuables and packed a bag with inexpensive, tourist trinkets my mother scattered about the house when she returned.

"The soldiers, in their arrogance, thought they were destroying valuable family heirlooms. Their plan was to humiliate and psychologically damage us into giving up my uncle. For months, we would have these night visitors until Dr. Riyadh, at that time head of the Cairo museum, produced some form of evidence the authorities felt convicted my uncle. They quit harassing us upon his incarceration.

"When we kids complained about having to clean the mess, my mother would calmly note that, we, too, could be sitting in a filthy cell next to my uncle. From that point forward, we cleaned in silence.

"What you see is surface mess. They did not break or rip apart your things. They had a specific target in mind and a general idea of where to find it. We can clean this very easily. Just let me know when you're ready. I'll bring in the rest of the computer and boxes then start wherever you need me to."

The ringing of the doorbell startled the two. Glenda, a murderous look covering her face, popped up from the couch and ripped open the door.

"What?" she stumbled backward.

Nasim leapt from the couch, reaching for his gun.

"Oh, LaVonne." Glenda's shoulders sagged.

The plump neighbor stood, hand fixed near the doorbell. Her jovial pink complexion had paled to ash gray.

"If this is a bad time, Glenda…" her eyes looked beyond the editor.

Glenda swung around to face Nasim, 9mm Glock cradled in his hand pointed waist high.

"Oh, sorry. Ma'am. Nice to see you again." Nasim lowered the gun.

"When did you start carrying that?" Glenda looked horrified.

Nasim slipped the handgun into a holster Glenda didn't remember him wearing.

"I don't often bring it with me but wanted to have it handy, just in case. That's why I wanted to enter the house before you."

Glenda swallowed. "Oh."

"I'll come back." LaVonne started to back away.

"No, no, no. Please LaVonne, come in. It appears my house was broken into and ransacked." Glenda stepped aside to let her neighbor view the chaos that was the current state of her home.

Nasim watched the blue eyes of the neighbor widen then darken to a slate color. She swept in the front room and gathered Glenda in her arms.

"Oh, baby. I'm so sorry." Placing fisted hands on her round hips, she continued. "What can LaVonne do? The sooner we get started, the better. Wait a minute; have you called the police?"

Glenda pushed a deep sigh from her lips.

"No."

"And why not?" LaVonne raised her perfectly plucked eyebrows.

"Because nothing was taken. It just looks bad. Don't you remember when Mr. Nygaard's cabin was broken into last year?"

The blonde nodded.

"He called the police. They took three hours to show up, took a quick looked around then asked for a list of things that were missing. They never did anything about the break in. I saw him about a week ago at the Farmer's Market in Littlerock. He said he hadn't heard from anybody regarding the antique silver and his wife's heritage jewelry. He was pretty disgusted. If there's no blood or a body, it seems the police can't be bothered.

"Besides," Glenda reddened, "If you've seen my office, this isn't bad at all."

Alvin, LaVonne's other half, had sauntered up the steps and faced with the jumble, emitted a low whistle.

"What happened here?"

LaVonne turned to him. "Don't be such an idiot. Somebody tossed Glenda's house, you twit. Now, roll up your sleeves and let's get started."

"What about the kitties?"

A thin worry line formed over Glenda's eyes. "My babies. Thank God, they weren't here. Would you guys mind keeping them one more night?"

LaVonne patted Glenda's arm. "Don't be silly. Of course not."

She turned and glared at her partner. "Alvin, what are you doing?"

The slender man was rummaging through his wallet. "Looking for something."

"Come on. We've got lots of work to do before Glenda can settle in tonight."

"In a minute."

The plump blonde whirled around. "In-a-minute?"

Nose buried in his wallet, he looked up at her triumphantly. "Told ya." Pulling a single piece of paper from the recesses of the leather holder, he waved it at her.

"I told ya I was looking for something."

LaVonne's face clouded, her eyes slanted, mouth pulled into a straight line.

"Alvin Merrill Prescott…"

He blinked golden brown eyes at her. "What, lambkins?"

Glenda watched all the fire drain from LaVonne's face.

"I saw a pickup truck parked about a quarter mile down the road when we came to pick up the cats yesterday. Now, that's not unusual…"

Glenda and LaVonne nodded.

"…but I noticed there were two guys in it. The way they were lounging in the cab gave me the impression they were waiting for somebody. So--I memorized the license plate, I got a look when we went past, and wrote it down when we got home."

He thrust the paper at Glenda.

LaVonne's face smoothed and her eyes twinkled. "Well, aren't you just my own James Bond?" She moved to him and wrapped her arms around his thin frame. "I think I'll keep you, handsome."

Glenda glanced at the paper. In spidery, slanted writing was a number, 7G02406. Neatly printed next to the license number was a description: 2003 Iridescent blue, Chevrolet Silverado 1500.

"Alvin, how can you be sure about the make and model?" Glenda allowed a small frown to mar her forehead.

"My Alvin is an autophile." LaVonne had started righting overturned items.

Nasim's eyes widened. "A what?"

"Autophile." Alvin answered before LaVonne. "It just means I like cars, trucks and other things that go fast with four wheels and a really big engine. That's all. I'm a little obsessed."

"A little? We own five car dealerships. Two here in the Antelope Valley and three down below." LaVonne shook her head at her husband.

"Down below?" Nasim frowned. "What's down below?"

"Here in the upper desert, we call anything in the LA basin *down below*. Since we're at 3500 feet up, 3750 meters to you," Glenda flashed him an impish grin, "we really can say LA is below us. Took me about six months before I learned to use the term with ease. It just means anywhere in the Los Angeles basin."

"Oh." Nasim shrugged and looked at Alvin with newfound respect. "So you're Prescott's Presidio?"

Alvin nodded slightly. "Yeah, that's me."

Glenda shook her head. "Gram never said anything."

LaVonne stopped and looked at Glenda.

"That's because we never told her. Why?" She shrugged her shoulders. "We moved to Juniper Hills because we like the area. It was quiet and nobody asked about our business. They just assumed we were a middle-aged couple who'd retired to the desert. For twenty years, we lived in the fast lane and all it did was give me an ulcer and nearly put my Alvin in to the hospital from fatigue. Our daughter runs the dealerships down below and each of our boys has a dealership up here. Alvin wanders in when the shipments of the new model year cars and trucks come in or someone trades in a classic, but, mostly, we hang out here gardening and doing nothing."

Nasim took the paper from Glenda. "Mr. Prescott, this is going to help tremendously. If you will excuse me for a moment, I need to contact my office."

"Not a problem. And young man?" Alvin leaned over and picked up a lamp, which he returned to the end table.

Nasim stopped and turned. "Yes, sir."

"I'm just Alvin."

"Yes, sir."

Alvin rolled his eyes at Glenda. "Least his mom raised him proper."

Glenda giggled as Nasim stepped on to the porch clutching the paper in hand. He dialed the office. A crisp voice answered at the other end requesting the extension to which the party wished to be connected. Nasim searched his memory and rattled off a four-digit number. He waited.

"Larry Kohler, here. Who's this?"

"Larry, Nasim Shabouh, International Division. I need you to process a license number for me."

"Sure. Run it by me. Any particular reason?"

"It could be instrumental in a case I'm working. Can you expedite as much as possible? Time is a factor."

"Not a problem. I can probably have it for you within the next 24 hours. Believe it or not, things are a little slow around here. I'm beginning to wonder if the bad guys have gone on vacation."

"Trust me, Larry, they haven't. Thanks." Nasim listed his cell and office number for Larry to call. "And if you don't get me, just leave a message. I'm out of the L.A. basin so there might be a problem trying to get through."

His eyes scanned the area in front of Glenda's home. He didn't want a repeat of the other night. Not seeing any loitering vehicles, Nasim sucked in a deep breath and went inside the house.

"Where do you need me?"

Glenda whisked him to her office.

"If you could bring the computer and my boxes in here, I'd appreciate it. This seems to be the worst of the mess. I don't think I can face it. Will you just pick up? Put stuff anywhere that's available and not on the floor. I'll come back and organize later but, right now, I want to get the living room back in order. The sooner I accomplish that, the sooner I can send LaVonne and Alvin home. I don't want them caught up in this, at all."

Nasim nodded. "I agree. It was quick thinking on his part to jot down the license number but, like you, I don't want to see them become involved. The people we're dealing with have no compunctions about killing anyone who gets in their way."

Glenda sighed her agreement. "I'll fix lunch then we can attack this. I think I'll feel better with something in my stomach."

As if on cue, Nasim's stomach rumbled. "Please, excuse me."

Glenda watched the Egyptian's face glow ruby.

The tips of her mouth curved up. "I'm on my way. I'll call you when it's ready." She slipped out the office door.

Nasim surveyed the room. Papers lay scattered everywhere his eye could see. However, none of the porcelain figures displayed in a corner curio cabinet appeared damaged. Moving closer to inspect the inconsistency, he noted the dust on top of the cabinet was deep enough to write his initials. The intruders didn't touch this piece of furniture. The figurines inside were valuable in an English-porcelain-collector's fashion. Had they been intent on robbing the house, this curio cabinet would be smashed, the figurines gone, and glass would litter the floor.

This office, as with the rest of the house, gave the appearance of a robbery. The intruders knew exactly where to look. He bent and began to gather the skewed paperwork on the floor. It took him ten minutes to straighten the office. As he moved to the desk, he could see the search had intensified in this area. The drawers of the desk tilted at an angle indicating the extreme force used to yank them from their spots. He feared Glenda's desk damaged beyond repair.

Here is where the search centered. Every item formerly housed in the desk now rested on the floor.

"Wow. You've been busy." Glenda entered, her face brightening. "Actually, it's cleaner than before they tossed everything. I just hope…"

Nasim held up a hand. "Don't. This appears to be the point of concentration for their search. Was this where you'd kept the little statuette?"

The glow faded from her face. Concern lines gathered around her eyes.

"Yes, it was. How could some--outsider--know this?"

Nasim allowed a small smile touch his lips.

"You've been around these archaeologic types for some time now. Where do most of them put their important papers?" He lifted a brow.

Glenda, hand on the doorknob, thought for a moment.

"In the drawer to the right of the desk."

Nasim acknowledged with a quick nod.

"Some things are consistent. It is a comfort action most people do without thinking. The lower right hand drawer would the most logical place

127

for you to place something. After all, before this abomination," Nasim waved a hand around the room, "your home was a safe, secure place. Right?"

Glenda's jaw set in a determined line.

"Yes. It's just very unsettling."

"I know."

"Lunch is ready. Come in to the dining room and eat. This disaster isn't going anywhere. It can wait for an hour."

Nasim's stomach rumbled. "Great idea."

He followed her out of the study and into the hall. He could only hope Larry would push the search on the license number. It might prove valuable and tie up at least one factor in this mess. There was nothing worse than dangling details and Nasim hated dangling details.

Chapter Nineteen

Omar smoothed unseen wrinkles from his suit as he stood and listened to the call ring through numerous time zones. A crisp, clear voice answered the other end and connected him to the office he'd requested.

A smooth baritone answered in Arabic. "Yes?"

Omar hesitated allowing the echo to die. "It is Ben. We've come across a problem. The receiving department misdirected the merchandise into hostile territory. I'm unable to retrieve the item. Will it be possible to send a facsimile? The copy must be perfect."

There was hesitation on the other end. "How soon?"

"Overnight. I must receive the shipment by noon California time tomorrow."

"Consider it done."

"Your payment will arrive the day after tomorrow."

"Pleasure doing business with you."

Omar couldn't resist smiling. He'd beat these American gangsters at their own game. He'd pass them the copy; after all, these hoodlums wouldn't know the difference, and by the time they'd discovered the truth, he'd be well tucked away on a beautiful, warm island with a lovely lady at his side.

Omar hummed as he picked up his briefcase. The installation of the alarm lifted a load from his mind. The gravel voiced man could no longer appear as if by magic. The alarm company technician had guaranteed him the system could detect the slightest movement when armed, although Omar had opted for medium sensitivity. No sense in jolting out of a deep sleep due to the movements of a cockroach. As he stepped on his front stoop, he noted the rolling rubbish bins guarding the curbsides. His brows lowered nearly meeting in the middle.

It was at these times he cursed the need for discretion. It would be *his* job to take out the disgusting receptacle to the curb this evening. Were he in Cairo, he would have household staff to accomplish these menial details.

Omar pushed a short burst of breath from his lips. "This affair needs to end quickly. I tire of this charade."

He backed out of the driveway, and drove past the Mel's Plumbing van parked in front of the ranch style home three doors down.

"I hope that's not an omen. All I need now is to have my plumbing cause problems."

Dr. Riyadh was soon zipping down the freeway lanes toward the museum, plumbing problems forgotten.

~ * ~

Headphones clasped over his ears, Steve Steele watched the Mercedes slip past. He'd dug out a magnetized plumbing sign from his collection to place over the window, just as he had done when he'd installed the alarm. The center of the sign afforded a view, albeit narrow, of passing traffic. So far, the director had no idea of the nigh-to-invisible listening bugs planted throughout his home. Steve rewound and played back the most recent phone call. He turned on the descrambling device and wrote the digits as they appeared on the screen. He then listened, without distraction, to the recorded phone call.

His uncle's reputation for compassion was legendary. He had none but, on occasion, would offer *one* chance at redemption to a business acquaintance. Dr. Omar Riyadh had just thrown away his opportunity.

Steve picked up his phone and dialed.

"Yes?"

"I have something you need to hear."

"Meet me at Il Fornao in one hour."

"Yes, sir."

Steve sighed. He looked at the shirt and tie hanging on the hook he carried for just such occasions. Normally, he could get away with jeans and a polo shirt, not with his uncle. The man insisted on shirt, tie, and jacket when conducting business--even in a restaurant.

Steve wouldn't argue. The man paid the bills.

He double-checked his recording of the call, transferred it to a CD, and slipped into the driver's seat of the van. He had a meeting in an hour in Pasadena, and traffic at this time of day was impossible. He'd best get started.

He shook his head slightly. It still amazed him that people had such a stilted view of his uncle's organization. Dr. Riyadh was clueless to the complexity and sophistication brought to this business venture. The government could take a lesson or two from the man's acumen.

Dr. Riyadh had just made the biggest blunder of his life.

Steve shuddered. He didn't know what happened to failed business associates--he didn't want to.

~ * ~

Omar slid his car into the parking spot with his name. The sky was actually peeking through the morning fog in hues of pale blue. Carrying his briefcase and box of letters, he inhaled deeply, a faint whisper of something sweet tickling his nose. He noted several types of flowers in bloom and attributed the sweet aroma to the roses. The smile, which had begun at his home, continued to grace his tanned face. Life was good right now. He glanced at his watch.

I should be able to get a few hours' of work accomplished then I think I'll visit Miss Nagel's office. I'll replace the vase her cat destroyed and leave the box of hate mail as I promised Miss Thompson. Maybe, in the comfort of her office, Miss Nagel will slip and let me know where she's hidden the little statuette. I'm certain she's found it and tucked it away somewhere. If I can pass off the forgery and keep the original for myself...well, it will definitely insure my retirement.

Smiling at his brilliance, the director entered the museum. Walking jauntily past the day guard and toward his office, he began to formulate a plan of action.

Avril jumped up from her chair. "Director, are you all right?"

He grasped her hand in his. "Yes, thank you. It was a small matter of some neighborhood kids breaking into the house. I wanted to have a security system installed before I left today and was very fortunate to find a company who came out immediately."

He watched relief wash over his docent's face and her shoulders relax.

"Thank goodness. I was afraid you'd been murdered or something."

Patting her hand, he reassured the young lady. "Avril, you have a vivid imagination. Maybe you should consider becoming a writer. I'm fine, but now, I have a mountain of paperwork awaiting my attention. Would you be so kind as to screen my calls?"

She nodded her head and sat down at her desk. "Did the --Interpol-- people find you?"

"Yes. They were as concerned as you were. I promise," he crossed his chest with a finger, "I'll not do that again. I'll buzz you if I need anything."

"Yes, sir." Avril turned to the computer and picked up typing where she'd left off when the Director arrived.

Omar closed his door and stashed his briefcase. He moved to the closet where he'd put the box of clay vases his cousin had sent and dragged them to the center of the room. A careful search uncovered one that was unblemished. Omar pulled some of the paper stuffing from inside the box and smoothed it out on the floor. He turned the little vase upside down and shook it.

A ring, tiny in size, tumbled from the jar. Omar turned the jar upright and looked inside. He jiggled it gently but could hear nothing else rattling. He set the vase on the paper and rose to grab his gloves. Carefully picking up the ring, he realized it was from the same dig as the ivory statuette with emerald eyes. He moved to his desk and rummaged through his drawer until he located the jeweler's glass. Flicking on the lamp at the corner of his desk, he examined the tiny ring through the magnifier. The small band was delicate with inscriptions on the outside surface. Two stones sat side by side--a ruby and an emerald. From his vast knowledge of the era and this particular dig, Omar knew these were the birthstones of the Pharaoh and the little princess Kia.

He slumped against his desk and muttered. "Whew. This could bring a fortune from the right bidder."

Omar ran a gloved finger slowly over the ring.

"However, if those interfering Interpol agents come up with circumstantial evidence to convince someone, just *one* someone in the right position, that I'm involved with detouring these items…"

He rose and began to pace in front of his desk. Something was nagging at the back of his mind. He needed a way to divert attention from himself and spotlight another. After the third lap in front of his desk, he stopped. His eyes lit up and a grin spread over his face.

"Of course, how could I be so stupid?"

Omar slipped on a glove and picked up the little ring from the desktop. Grabbing another glove, he stowed the ring in a cotton finger and placed the bundle inside the clay vase.

"Miss Nagel has shown an inordinate interest in my cousin's vases. After discovering a treasure in one, she's asked for another vase… I'm sure I can convince the authorities she was aware of the stolen items inside and, unbeknownst to me, is taking them and selling them to the highest bidder."

He dusted the little vase and placed it in the middle of his desk.

"It just might work."

He rummaged through his top drawer and finding the item he wanted called his secretary.

"Miss Livingston?"

"Yes sir."

"Please do me a favor and call the number I'm about to give you." He read the digits from the front of the item nestled in his palm. "Read that back to me, please."

The young secretary repeated the numbers.

"Excellent. Now if you would be so kind as to place a call, I'm trying to see if my pager still works." He waited. The little black box began to beep at him. He pressed the off button. Picking up the vase and snapping the pager on his belt, he walked into the reception area.

"Thank you. It seems to be working just fine. I'm going to take this replacement vase to Miss Nagel so I'll be there for 15 or 20 minutes. I'm expecting a very important package in the next 24 hours. If for some reason, it shows up while I'm with her, please page me. Don't allow them to leave it with you. I *must* sign for this personally."

"Yes director. Would you like me to call Miss Nagel's secretary and let her know you're on your way?"

"No, that's okay. I'll just pop in."

Omar strolled down the hallway to the magazine editor's office. His step was lighter than it had been in many a day. *I don't know why I didn't think of this sooner. If the authorities pick her up for theft of the ring, then I can convince them the statuette I have is authentic. After all, I* am *the best Egyptologist around. The authorities will come to me to authenticate the article and I'll make the switch under their very noses.* Omar chuckled. Sometimes, he amazed himself.

Entering the editor's office, he noted how quiet the room seemed. Amunet started when she looked up.

"Dr. Riyadh. Did you have an appointment today?" She frantically flipped through Glenda's appointment book.

Smiling, he put his hand on the turning pages. "No. I just dropped by to give Miss Nagel another vase to replace the one her cats destroyed. May I go in and deliver it to her?"

Amunet leaned back in her chair. "Good. I'm not losing my mind. I'm sorry but Ms. Nagel isn't here today. She's finishing the layout at home."

Omar pulled his mouth into the semblance of a frown. "I'm disappointed. Do you think she would mind if I left the vase on her desk?"

Amunet reached her hand out. "I can hold it until she comes back tomorrow."

Omar pulled the little clay pot to him. "No, I'd like to put it on her desk--myself."

Amunet eyed the director warily.

"Sure. If you can find a spot on the desk, feel free. I'll be sure to let her know to look for the vase."

Bowing slightly from the waist, Omar forced a smile on his lips. "Thank you, Amunet."

Inside the office, he closed the door and looked around. It appeared as if someone had tossed a hand grenade into a paper pile. He'd been in such a hurry last time; he'd not really looked at the mess. Turning, he couldn't believe anyone could work like this. He searched for a spot on the desk to place the vase and was unable to locate anywhere that didn't house a pile of papers. Deciding Glenda wouldn't know if he moved stuff or not, he removed a two-inch pile from her in basket. Carefully, he set the vase in the middle of the tray. Unless she was blind, she would notice the clay container. He pulled one of his cards from his shirt pocket and turned it over, leaving a hand written note.

To replace the one your cats destroyed. My cousin will be pleased. Omar

Starting to put the card under the vase, Omar glanced at the desk. If he looked in the editor's drawer, no one would be the wiser. Who could tell in this mess? He maneuvered his way around clutter and knelt to open the drawer. He tested and found it unlocked. Pulling the drawer out with as much caution as he could apply, Omar peeked inside. As messy as the office was, this drawer was neatly set up, each file folder labeled and separated. He quickly thumbed through the files and reaching the end, slid his hand to the back. He met with empty space. The rattle of the door handle alerted him someone was entering the office. He yanked back his hand and slid the drawer closed.

"Dr. Riyadh?"

Amunet looked around finally spotting the director's feet poking out from the side of the desk.

"What are you doing there, sir?"

He rose to his feet and flashed the business card at her.

"When I went to put this under the vase," he pointed to the urn resting in the top basket, "a breeze blew it out of my hand to the floor. I was retrieving it."

He slipped the card under the container and flashed Amunet a smile.

"And now, I'll be on my way." He exited the office as quickly as he could without appearing in a hurry.

Amunet looked at the vase with the card underneath it. Something didn't ring true.

"That man is up to something. As sure as I'm breathing, he's up to something." She turned off the light and, closing the door, deciding not to tell Glenda.

Omar's step had a decided spring to it as he moved through the hallway to his office. There was a need to call Interpol, anonymously of course, and help them locate a thief of artifacts.

"Miss Livingston?"

"Yes, Dr. Riyadh?"

"Do you have the business card of the agents from Interpol that visited the other day?"

The blonde docent flipped furiously through a round file. She handed the card with number printed on it to the director.

"Here you go sir. Would you like me to call?"

"No thank you. I'll handle this myself. I'm sure I don't have to tell you, no interruptions?"

"Of course."

Omar sat at his desk behind closed door, and fingered the card. He couldn't have the call traced to his phone but it wouldn't hurt the credibility of his story to have the call come from the Museum. He slipped out and walked to the pay phone in the lobby. Clearing his throat, he dialed the number on the card asking for Ms. Thompson. He'd affected a bad French accent. Luckily, Lydia's voice mail activated.

"Yesss. I wood sheck ze magazine edeetor's office at zee Getty Museum. I beleef you weel find a vas wiss a ring zat belongs to zee leetle princess. Maybe, she has zee leetle cat, too?"

Omar hung up. He smirked all the way back to his office. He'd played this game before and won. While the Interpol people checked out Miss Nagel, he'd be assuring his buyer of the authenticity of the figurine he was presenting him. Then, he'd slip through the cracks of legalities and government red tape to a sunny island that had no extradition treaty with the United States or Egypt.

Omar leaned back in his chair and chuckled. "Life is good."

Chapter Twenty

Lydia stood in her hallway staring at the open space of her linen closet. She'd grabbed her cell to call Nasim and, for the life of her, couldn't remember what she wanted to ask him. Muttering under her breath, she closed the cupboard door and started toward her living room dropping the cell from her hands when the doorbell rang. Several crude Arabic words mixed with English pushed their way through Lydia's lips, as she set her coffee cup on the dining room table and stooped to retrieve her phone.

The doorbell pealed again.

"All right, all right, I'm coming," she grumped. Peering, first through the peephole in the door, then moving her curtains slightly to see who was foolish enough to assume she'd be home during the day, Lydia eyed a familiar form on her doorstep.

"Well, call me the daughter of a camel. Mohammed has come to the mountain." Noting he was about to ring the bell again, she flung open the door.

"WHAT do you want?"

"I--I--need to speak with you." He'd withdrawn his left hand and was clutching it to his chest, his briefcase clasped tightly in his right hand.

Lydia snickered. "Come in, Bobby."

"Damn, Lydia. You scared the hell out of me."

She ushered him in the living room and dropped on the couch. With a sweep of her hand, she indicated he should have a seat.

C. L. Kraemer

"Why are you here, Bobby? You never leave the office in the middle of the day."

He blew out an exasperated breath. "You, Lydia. Your antics in buying *another* house so soon has dragged me from my comfortable haven. You always were a wild child. That's one of the reasons Aunt Dede asked me to handle your finances."

Lydia smirked.

"What?" Bobby knit his eyebrows together.

"For your information, cousin, I asked mom who she'd recommend to handle my trust fund. Your name came up."

He glared at her. "Anyway, I came over to get your signature on some paperwork for the house and see what was wrong with this place. Didn't you just buy it… what, two years ago?"

She nodded.

Bobby opened his briefcase and pulled out a sheath of papers. "Just sign where all the little red tabs are located. I'm going to show myself around." He plopped the papers on the couch next to Lydia, handing her a pen as he wandered out of the room.

She signed her legal name to every page indicated dropping the pen on top of the papers when she was finished.

"This place is amazing. Why do you want out?" Bobby took in the 1930's architecture, leaning on the fireplace with built-in bookshelf.

"It didn't look this great when I bought it," She rose from the couch and moved to one side of the bookshelf, kneeling on one knee. Locating the tome she wanted, she motioned Bobby to sit with her on the couch.

He made himself comfortable.

Lydia handed him a picture album opened to a photo of a ramshackle, building whose paint was peeling, graffiti covered portions of the walls, and the most all the windows were shattered. The foliage had overgrown the house covering the broken windows, and the surrounding fence was unstable and damaged in several places. There was trash littered over the yard and the sidewalk buckled every few inches.

139

He glanced up and looked around. "That can't be this place, can it?"

Lydia smiled. "The one and only. That's why I got it so cheaply. The current owner at the time, granddaughter of the man who'd had the place built, wanted out so badly she jumped at the price I offered."

"I wondered how you'd gotten a place with this address for so little money."

"It became my sanity. Everything done here, I did myself. I put together a pictorial diary, take a look. When things at my job would make me crazy, I'd come back here and work until late at night. I think I did a good job."

"Yes, you did. That bit of knowledge confuses me even more. I'll ask again. Why do you want to move? It's obvious you put a great deal of time into this place. Why would you leave?"

Lydia stood and turned to her cousin. "You read the news, Bobby?"

His glare was his answer.

"No, I mean really read the news. I know you probably read the business section and sports but do you read the front page and local news?"

"What's your point?"

"Do you remember about six months ago there was a huge bust at the San Pedro docks?"

"Vaguely."

"Container loads of young women from China were being smuggled into this country to work as prostitutes for several notorious organizations. Someone had called the authorities and leaked information about a shipment which led to several shipping containers and a warehouse full of young, frightened women who were being held hostage."

Bobby's bored expression changed to one of disbelief.

"You're joking, right?"

"Hardly."

"So, you're with the FBI?"

Lydia let one side of her mouth tip upward. "Something like that. I was helping a couple of other law enforcement agencies during this particular roundup. The organizers of this little importing venture got a free ride to the local police station for questioning. As I sat in the car waiting for the other agent who I was working with to help me escort one particularly nasty participant to the precinct, the sleaze in the back of my cruiser croaked out a promise that he would find my partner and me and make us both sorry we'd interfered with his enterprise. He didn't say another word--not while the agent was with me nor to the investigating officers when they questioned him. Within an hour, his slick lawyer had sprung him."

"So?"

"I made the mistake of allowing myself to get into a routine. A couple days ago, I came home from my morning jog to find some unwelcome visitors in my home. I heard them before they heard me. I crawled into my vehicle and got the hell away. They took a couple of pot shots at me but apparently, in the bad guy business they don't practice shooting their guns very often because they missed me and my car. I went to a safe place and got ready for work. When I finally came home, nothing was missing. A few of my clothing drawers were dumped, the contents spread over the floor, and they broke some old dishes in the kitchen but nothing important was damaged. I think this was their way of telling me they know where I live."

Lydia watched her cousin's face drain of color.

"Hence the need to move. I just stumbled on this place in the course of my work. It'll be perfect. The side drops sharply, and, yeah I know it's earthquake country, and the front has large picture windows so I can observe any activity going on up and down the street. The only blind spot is the garage wall. Think I'll invest in some outdoor cameras."

"What about this place, Lydia?" Bobby had been thumbing through the photo album that showed the rebuilding she'd accomplished on the bungalow.

"I'd like to keep it. Maybe somewhere down the road, when I retire, I'll be able to move back in here." She looked around and sighed. This had been her haven of sanity--she really hated to let it go. "If you have someone in your office who might be looking for a place to live then I'd consider renting to them. I trust your human resources have thoroughly checked out your staff."

The corner of Bobby's mouth twitched. "Well, yes, my HR department does, indeed, perform a thorough background search on all my employees. I'll note to my secretary to keep a lookout. What will you be asking for rent?"

"$500 a month."

Bobby dropped the album. "That's ludicrous. You could easily get $2000 a month for this place."

"Yes and have it sit for several months before it was rented. No. $500 is just right but only to someone from your organization. If anyone else asks, quote them the $2000 price.

"I have a subterfuge in mind." Lydia began to pace in front of the couch, tapping her chin with a finger. "Bobby."

"What?"

"Do you have a real estate company that you trust?"

"Several."

"I just need one that will work with you without question."

"I know of one."

"Good. I want to have a *for sale* sign put out front. Put the place on the website of the company at a ridiculously high price, run a couple of your employees over here with the agent--I'll pay for their time…"

"Damn right you will," he muttered.

Lydia threw a glare his direction and continued "…then we'll make a big production of me moving out. I'll put my things for this house in storage and take some furniture from the family house to use…"

Bobby pushed an exasperated sigh from his lips. "Why don't you just move back to the family mansion?"

Lydia stopped pacing in front of him. She dropped her voice to just above a whisper. "Too many memories. Going in there to get furniture will be difficult enough. Every time I go back, I expect Mom to come through the sitting room and Dad to pop in the door, tennis racket in hand. I couldn't take the memories."

"Well, you're going to have to do something with it soon."

"Sell it."

"What!"

"Sell it. Don't you have some famous friends who need a new place to live? I think Dad said something once about Frank Lloyd Wright designed part of the original building or maybe he just came to dinner there or something. Just sell it. I learned a new word this week that describes how I feel about the place."

"What's that?"

"White elephant. The place is a white elephant to me. Maybe someone will see it differently. Let me get furniture for the new place then sell the mansion, furniture and all."

Bobby looked stunned. He barely whispered, "What about the Bentley?"

Lydia smiled at the reverence he'd attached to the name of the car. "Bobby?"

"Yeah?"

"Consider it your commission. Have your office start the paperwork. I'll sign anything you need."

He rose from the couch and grabbed his briefcase stuffing the signed papers inside. "What about memories, Lydia? Don't you have anything you want to keep for the sentimental value?"

Lydia walked him to the front door. "As you can see by where I choose to live, I don't have the same tastes my folks did. Their memory is right here," she pointed to her heart. "That's all I need. You have my cell number, Bobby. Call if you need anything. Have to get back to work--rid the world of bad guys and tacky dressers. You know--the usual."

Bobby walked out to his vehicle shaking his head. The woman's net value had more zeros behind it than most of the people in California, including the governor's family, yet she insisted on playing cops and robbers. Go figure.

Lydia watched her cousin drive away. Her spirit felt lighter than it had in several years. She hadn't realized what a crushing sensation owning her parent's home had put on her. Knowing she would no longer have to think or deal with it, set her to whistling as she gathered the last few things she would need to stay in her new house. *Too bad tonight's stay is for business, not pleasure.* She dialed Nasim's number and found herself leaving a message.

"Mmm." *Must still be up in the Antelope Valley.* "Nasim, meet me in front of the office at 8:00 p.m."

Lydia locked her front door and headed down town. She'd finish some paperwork then drive to the house in the hills. Tonight was going to be long, boring and, with any luck, would produce something to put that smug bastard, Dr. Riyadh, behind bars.

Chapter Twenty-one

Glenda looked around the room. They'd cleaned up the mess and everything was resting in the location it had previously occupied. LaVonne and Alvin had left claiming they didn't want to leave the kitties by themselves too long. Nasim stood at the door, hand on the knob.

"You will call me if anything seems out of order. Right?"

"Look, I don't want to interrupt your day. You've already gone out of your way to help and I don't want to take advantage of your good intentions."

"Glenda," Nasim moved from the door and clasped her hand in his.

Glenda was surprised. The move was very personal, unlike his demeanor so far.

"Ms. Nagel. I know what the man we're hunting is capable of doing. Please don't hesitate to call me." The corners around his dark eyes crinkled in concern. "It is no bother to save someone else from the terror and personal agony this man can render. Promise you will call."

Glenda searched the swarthy face. Worry lines marred the perfect skin of the bronzed forehead. His set jaw and taut, thin lips confirmed his determination.

"I promise." She watched his face relax and he slipped her hand free.

"Good. I'll leave you to your work. I think I'll go home and take a shower before I find out when I'm to partake in the *garbage torture*." He bounded down the steps and to his car.

Glenda waved as he exited the driveway and headed home.

"He really *is* a handsome man." She double checked the front door and went to her office to finish the putting the magazine together.

~ * ~

Nasim drove to his apartment and performed his home-from-work routine. He slipped into the shower, allowing the hot water to sluice over his body then turning it off when the water began to cool. Padding into the bedroom, he rummaged in the drawers to locate his oldest pair of jeans and t-shirt. Dumpster diving was a guarantee to ruin whatever clothes he'd be wearing, even with the protective suits they wore. Dressed, he wandered to the kitchen to fix himself something to eat. With a stakeout, you could never be sure how long it would be between hot meals.

He sat at the table with his food and quickly perused the newspaper. His cell rang interrupting the silence of his home.

"Nasim, Larry from the lab. I've located information on that license number you gave me. You got a real winner there. The owner of the truck has a long list of petty thievery. Looks like his specialty is B and E. Don't see any major crimes here, nothing involving a weapon. Hope that helps. I left the details on your voice mail at work, gave you the file number so you could look it up yourself. If you need anything else, just give a call."

Nasim pushed a sigh between his lips. He couldn't put off going into the office any longer. Packing a clean set of clothes in his gym bag, Nasim turned on the night light in his front room and headed out. The sooner he could find a link between Dr. Riyadh and the stolen artifact, the sooner he'd see the man behind bars. He allowed a smile to emerge. That was the thought that would keep him going when he was up to his elbows in broken eggshells and used coffee filters.

~ * ~

Lydia sat at her desk, pencil between her fingers, annoyingly tapping a staccato rhythm that was setting Nasim's teeth on edge.

"Must you?"

"Sorry." She dropped the pencil on the desk. "I'm stumped."

"About what? I thought you had this all figured out?"

"So did I. But the information we got from the license number you had searched puts a monkey wrench in the works."

Nasim raised his eyebrows. "How so?"

"It lead us to a pair of low life wanna-bes, however; we have nothing to connect them to the break in at Glenda's. Yeah, it's their MO, and I'm betting if you went to their garage or storage unit you'd find a treasure trove of goodies that doesn't belong to them, but we're no closer in tying the director into the theft of the statuette today than we were two days ago. I really don't want to put too much stock in what we'll find tonight. We could be just be rooting through garbage and nothing more."

Nasim watched her rise from her chair and pace. He'd wondered how long it was going to take her to start moving.

"This is true, so why don't we just call off this venture?" He watched Lydia hopefully.

"Nice try. We're going ahead because we *could* also hit paper gold. All we need is *one* piece of evidence that links Dr. Riyadh to the break in at Glenda's or the theft of the statuette--just one."

He settled back in his chair and contemplated the unpleasant task ahead.

"How soon are we leaving?"

"Well, that's another problem."

Nasim snapped around, his eyes followed Lydia's form. "Why?"

"I've arranged to use the house across the street until it's dark enough and we're sure the good director has settled in for the night. The problem, as the good doctor was more than happy to point out, is our vehicles resemble police units. He'll be suspicious if he sees them, and we'll lose the element of surprise." Slowing her strides, she tapped her chin with her finger, eyes unfocused at a spot on the floor.

Nasim felt dread in the bottom of his stomach begin to build. He and Lydia had been partnered for a short time but he'd found she was predictable in her methods. Her current look told him she was hatching a plan that would have them filling out forms for the next three weeks.

Lydia picked up her phone and walked out of hearing range. By the drone of her voice in the quiet office, Nasim knew she was deep in plan-mode and his dread continued to mount. His fear was confirmed when she came back smiling broadly.

He hesitated but knew not asking the question would only prolong the agony.

"What's the plan?"

"It seems the house across the street from the director has been sold. The agent placed the sign on it today. If I'd just sold a 'white elephant' and wanted to be sure the new owners wouldn't complain, for a while, I'd send in a cleaning crew to do a bang up job. I do believe the realty company has done just that.

"I've requisitioned a van from the motor pool complete with cleaning company signs and we'll grab some of the white jump suits from the lab to wear. If we move fast enough, no one will notice there's no insignia on the jump suits. We can park the van in the driveway, pull out cleaning gear, and go in through the garage.

"I've arranged with the realtor to have the opener available. We can move around inside without having to skulk. After all, we'll be *cleaning*. When the time comes to leave, I'll back out and, accidentally, knock over the doctor's garbage can. We'll just do a basic snatch and grab. We take some of our own bags and switch them out so if he becomes suspicious and opens the container, there'll be garbage inside.

"What do you think?" Lydia beamed.

Nasim rose from his chair. "I think I'm glad you're on our side."

She led the way to the lab, grabbing jump suits, then to the garage where they obtained a regulation white van complete with magnetic signs--"Mighty Maid Cleaning Service."

Lydia slid behind the driver's seat and they were on their way. While she drove, Nasim struggled to get into the jump suit. He found liberal use of Arabic swear words seemed to help slip the infernal piece of clothing over his own at a faster pace. After ten minutes of profuse swearing, Lydia's explosion of laughter caught him off guard.

"I didn't know anyone could do that with a camel." Mischief twinkled in the light eyes.

Nasim blushed an intriguing color of maroon. "Sorry. I forgot you're fluent."

"That I am, but you introduced me to a whole new outlook on the relationship of a man and his camel."

Nasim continued to burn with embarrassment as Lydia chuckled the last few blocks to the house.

~ * ~

Omar glanced at his watch--again. He'd been explicit with the instructions to his cousin about sending the replica before the end of the work day on the West Coast. As it was the middle of the night in Cairo, calling would be a waste of time and energy. He was about to mutter some unkind characterizations of his uncle, the cur who fathered his cousin, when a light knock took his attention.

"Yes?"

Avril poked her head around the corner of the door. "Dr. Riyadh? There's a delivery man here who needs your signature."

"Thank you, Miss Livingston."

She disappeared pulling the door closed behind her.

Omar smiled. His right palm began to itch, a very good sign. He made his way to the vestibule of his offices. A young man with muscles bulging under his sleeves was busily entering information in his hand-held clipboard. He looked up at Omar.

"Sir. I'm going to need some identification before I release this package. The shipping party was adamant about that."

"Of course." Feeling inconvenienced, Omar tramped back to his office and retrieved his wallet with his driving license. He returned to the vestibule and flashed the card at the delivery person.

The brown clad driver noted the number on his electronic clipboard.

Omar reached for the package.

"I need your signature, sir." The delivery driver thrust the board at Omar. *I'll show him.* Omar signed in Arabic.

The act of defiance lost on him, the young man handed the package to the Director, nodded at Avril, and took off just short of a run.

"Director?"

"Yes, Miss Livingston?"

"If you have no objection, sir, I'm going to leave for the day. I have a class across town in a couple hours. I'd like to get something to eat before I go." She turned big, blue eyes on him.

Omar glanced at his watch. It was 4:30 and he knew what an abomination the traffic was at this hour.

"I see no problem in that. Drive carefully, Miss Livingston. Which class are you taking now?"

"The 3rd Dynasty of Egypt. We're finishing the last two kings this week. Thank you, sir."

"No problem." Omar took the package into his office, locking the door. He paced in front of his desk for five minutes until he heard the distinct sound of the front office door latching. Carefully, he peered into the reception office. His secretary had left. He crossed the room and locked the exit to the hallway. Ripping open the box at his desk, Omar ignored the curved cedar shavings scattering over his floor. He *had* to see the statuette. An envelope rested near the top of the shipping container. He pulled it out, laying it on his desk. He'd get to that later. Spying a flash of color, he dug his hand into the shavings and lifted out a gold-leafed box. He considered using gloves, but as this wasn't an authentic artifact, he brushed away the thought. Removing the lid, he gazed at a replica so realistic he wouldn't have known the difference had he not held the legitimate cat goddess in his own hands.

The little body was made of genuine ivory, not centuries old, but genuine just the same. He flipped the figurine over and noted there were a couple of markings on the back that resembled the original notations of the real statute. Lastly, as he turned the cat figure on its back, he sucked in a breath; his cousin had sacrificed by installing two small, genuine emeralds for the eyes. Omar grabbed his jeweler's glass from the desk and examined the stones.

"It is a wonder Fenuku allowed these stones out of his sight--they are flawless." A chuckle began to bubble deep in Omar's chest. Soon it had escaped and resounded off his office walls. He gave into the urge to laugh, the sound echoing through the nearly empty museum corridor.

He pulled the envelope to him and located his opener. Slicing the flap, he slipped out the single sheet of paper.

> *"Honorable Cousin,*
> *I put my best worker on this project. And yes, I put in real emeralds. Do not act so surprised. The businessmen you engage for this transaction are not as trustworthy as those in our own country. I hope the additional time spent to make this piece appear authentic will keep your neck in place a day longer. That should give you time to find your way to the airport. I look forward to your next visit.*
> *Fenuku."*

Omar smiled as he pulled out a book of matches. The old dog realized what was at stake here. The extra work to authenticate the little figurine *might* just give him the couple of hours he would need to flee once he sold the statuette. He didn't think his buyer was a fool; however, he was certain he *could* be fooled. Omar pulled his waste can around and placed his cousin's letter in the bottom of the metal can. Touching a lit match to the edge of the letter, he watched the paper ignite and, within seconds, vanish in a wisp of smoke.

As I thought--flash paper. When Fenuku had discovered the wonderful disappearing paper, he used nothing else for his clandestine dealings. The miracle paper evaporated away critical business information; many a time saving him from arrest.

Omar emptied the ashes into a plastic bag neatly tucked down the side of the box and tied the top. He would put the bag in front of his desk for the cleaning crew to pick up. Glancing at his watch, he was surprised at the lateness of the hour. He didn't think examining the statuette had consumed so much of the night but he was wrong. He'd been in his office for over two hours. His stomach grumbled.

"I guess I'll stop at a drive through on my way home."

Dinner handled, he gathered his briefcase and the box while closing his office for the night. His future lay in the gold leaf package clutched tightly in his hands.

The trip to his home was uneventful, despite the continued crush of traffic and terminally slow service at the drive through restaurant. The aroma of burger and fries permeated his Mercedes making his stomach complain loudly. He bobbled his briefcase with the box on top, and the bag of dinner as he fumbled to find his house keys. He stopped and looked up and down the street.

Several unkind swear words slipped from his lips, as he remembered he would need to put the rubbish container on the street.

Unlocking his door, he slipped inside and headed toward the kitchen, depositing the armful of items on the dining room table. Mumbling with each step he took, Omar went out his back door and grabbed his rubbish bin. He pushed it down the driveway and parked it curbside. Glancing up, he was struck by the notion something was different about the house across the street. The lights were blazing and there was movement inside. He peered up and down the road and started to cross. Midway, he looked at the realty sign and stopped. The sign now sported a *sold* plaque on top. *The company must just be cleaning for the new owner.* Omar shrugged his shoulders, and walked back to his house.

Since he was out all ready, he might as well put the car in the garage. Once he stored his prize possession in the pristine garage, he retired to the living room with the take out bag. His stomach was complaining in overtime. *Dinner, catch up on the news, then bed.* He was suddenly very tired.

If the Interpol people followed up on his anonymous tip, by the time they discovered the helpful hint was sending them the wrong direction, the ice in his drink on the verandah of his house in the islands would still be fresh.

He could live with that.

~ * ~

Lydia noted the plumbing van had disappeared but in its place, a cable van covered in gaudy TV characters, parked two doors closer to the director's home. She'd have to keep an eye on the van.

Parking the cleaning truck in the driveway brought attention from several fronts. Drapes opened slightly casting beams of incandescent light on the perfect lawns out front.

Lydia nodded to Nasim who'd flipped the collar of the jump suit up and jammed a baseball cap on his head to camouflage himself as best he could. They unloaded vacuums, mops, buckets and myriad cleaning supplies into the garage fussing with the props until the door slid closed.

She sighed. "And now we wait. We need to go inside and move around as if we're cleaning." She glanced at her watch. It had taken them nearly two and a half hours to pull together this charade.

Grabbing a dust rag, she headed to the living room. Slipping her hand through the curtains, she opened a small view to the director's house across the street in time to see him pull into the driveway. He got out of the vehicle, struggling with several items he carried, and glanced up and down the street. She saw his lips move and, combined with the expression on his face, figured he must be swearing. Climbing his steps, he unlocked and opened his door. Lights lit up through the house. Lydia moved the rag from one end of the picture window to the other.

The director appeared from the back of the house pushing a big green container to the street and glancing toward the house now sporting a *sold* sign.

Lydia pulled back from the window.

"Damn." She tiptoed to the side and carefully pulled back the curtain to give herself a sliver of a view. The doctor was standing with his head cocked to one side, his body language guarded. He started across the street and midway stopped.

Lydia held her breath.

"What's happening?" Nasim whispered.

"Nothing yet."

Glancing at the realty sign, then the house, Dr. Riyadh shrugged his shoulders and went toward his home. He detoured and parked his Mercedes in the garage. Lydia watched as the outside lights went dark.

She turned and slid down the wall to the floor, exhaling.

"*Now*, we wait."

~ * ~

The cleaning van across the street was unexpected. Steve uttered a curse under his breath and pulled the blanket up around his neck. He set his alarm for a couple hours after turning on the recorder, and settled in for a quick nap. He'd need to move the van and change the decals before Dr. Riyadh left in the morning. His uncle had demanded twenty-four hour surveillance on the house since he'd heard the recording of the director's plan to try and con him.

This Egyptian museum director was so cocky Steve couldn't feel sorry for him. His connections in his home country would save him there but this was the US of A and things didn't work the same. Steve and his uncle didn't really give a rat's behind about the theft of ancient artifacts but they did object to someone ripping them off. The Egyptian had overstepped his boundaries once again. He was living on borrowed time--he just didn't know it.

~ * ~

Nasim started when Lydia touched his shoulder.

"It's almost time."

She'd watched the cable van move down the lane and drive out of the neighborhood. Something about it didn't feel right to her. First, what cable company worked past six o'clock at night and second, there seemed to be too many problems on this one street. An alarm company, then a plumbing company, and now cable issues within the last couple of days--too convenient or surveillance?

Gathering the cleaning equipment, Nasim and Lydia put everything back in the van. They secured the house and, as planned, Lydia accidentally knocked over the garbage container in front of Dr. Riyadh's house as she backed out the van. Quietly, the two swapped out garbage bags, and left the neighborhood. They didn't see the other pair of eyes watching their operation.

"Just don't get in my way. By the time you've found a link to whatever it is you're looking to find, the Egyptian will no longer be a problem."

Chapter Twenty-two

Glenda sat at her home desk giving one last look through the articles her staff had emailed, catching a couple of style and format errors. Outside of that, the magazine was ready to print. She picked up the phone and called the printer. Arranging to send the work and get the process started, she pushed the send button on her computer and slumped in her chair a deep sigh pushing through her lips.

"Done--for this month."

She pulled up solitaire and dealt herself a hand, promptly winning on her first try. Bored and not wanting to start anything so soon, she went online and pulled up the English version of the Cairo daily paper. There was the usual litany of politico and finance problems. Several articles noted the decline of tourism due to the problems in Iraq, but, for the most part, it could have been any daily paper in the world.

Glenda was ready to search for something else when a small article on page seven, at the bottom, caught her attention. It was datelined Yemen and briefly stated that the recently discovered sarcophagus of an obscure princess of the Third Dynasty era was being plundered according to local authorities. Several items, most notably, an ivory statuette of the cat goddess, Bastet, and a ring with two stones, one emerald and one ruby, had gone missing from the inventory of the crypt. The government was urging all collectors to be aware that anyone caught with these items in their collection would be prosecuted to the full extent of the law.

She tried to swallow and found her throat dry.

"I need to let Lydia and Nasim see this."

She started to panic then realized the article must be a plant. Lydia and Nasim were with Interpol, an international organization solving international crimes. She bet the agency placed the piece in the paper to warn dealers throughout the region. Feeling a bit foolish she'd allowed her imagination to get the better of her, *not cut out for this spy business*, Glenda took a different tack. She put Dr. Omar Riyadh in the search engine and let the machine do its stuff.

The response was overwhelming. There were over a million notations to the name Omar Riyadh. She read the first twenty-five then got up and made tea. She needed a break from the computer. Her eyes ached and had started to blur. From the information so far, Riyadh was highly respected in the field of archaeology and in his country, however, the further afield she got from the first entries, the less shining the good doctor appeared. His name started appearing in news articles where the rate of antiquity thefts rose right after his arrival.

"I think I'll snoop some more but from a different angle," she carried her hot cup of tea back to her office. She sat the tea on the desk and entered another name in the search engine. When the engine returned the response, Glenda sat back in her chair and began to read. This was going to take some time.

Chapter Twenty-three

Lydia pulled the agency van into the garage. She jumped from the driver's seat and grabbed a dolly so she could move the trash bags. Nasim descended and rounded the back of the van in time to help unload. The two walked in silence to the lab where Lydia had reserved a room to continue their investigation.

He unloaded the green plastic containers onto a long, metal table pushing the dolly to the corner. Testing the air, he noted there was only an insignificant aroma of rotting food.

"I think I need coffee before we get started on this. How about you, Lydia?"

"Sounds good."

The two detoured to their desks, stripped out of the disposable cleaning garb, and grabbed their coffee cups.

"I'm going to look at that file records sent me on the license plate I had them research." Nasim leaned down and turned on his computer.

"I should check my emails and messages. I haven't been in long enough today to knock any of that stuff down. Would you get me coffee, too? Black." Lydia shoved her cup his direction.

"I'll be expecting a big tip."

She shot him a dirty look. "Don't hold your breath."

Lydia fired up her computer and noticed the message light on her phone was blinking.

She got into the system-answering center and retrieved the message left a few hours earlier. She listened to it once, rewound and listened again. Something about the barely audible French accented voice was familiar; the guttural intonations nagged at Lydia. It was so… so… Egyptian. That was it!

"Well, well."

"What?" Nasim placed the full coffee cup on her desk.

"Listen to this." Lydia replayed the message on the speaker.

"Glenda is not a thief. This fool is a liar."

Lydia shook her head. "Nasim, listen. It's not the content of the call; listen to the *way* the caller speaks the words. I'll play it again and, this time, listen to the *words* not the message."

Nasim tuned his ear to the inflection of the words the caller spoke.

"He's Egyptian."

"Yes! Get it?" Lydia's eyes lit up.

"The good Dr. Riyadh is trying to redirect our efforts. How… predictable. What angers me is he is willing to let another innocent person go to jail for his greed."

"Come on, Nasim. If it looks like a jackal, smells like a jackal, and howls like a jackal, then we can conclude we are dealing with a jackal."

"You're right."

"Of course, I am. That's why I'm the senior partner." She flashed him an insincere smile while batting her eyelashes. "That and I'm so darn beautiful."

Nasim rolled his eyes. "Please. It's going to be a long time until we eat. Don't upset my stomach now."

Lydia stopped the antics. The twinkle in her eye had stopped and her mouth set in a determined line. "We have a bigger problem."

Nasim raised an eyebrow.

"The stakes have just ratcheted up a notch. The director wants us to take Glenda out of the picture for a while. Why? What's he up to?" She got up and moved to the five-drawer filing cabinet that anchored one corner of her cubicle. She slid open and shut two drawers and on the third try, starting thumbing through manila folders. "I know it's here somewhere." She looked up at Nasim.

"Didn't we get a detailed listing of the items missing from the crypt when the Yemen government called us in on this case?"

He nodded his head. "I have it readily available if you want me to get mine."

She frowned at him.

Taking the hint, he grabbed a chair and sat blowing across the top of his mug to cool the tasteless dark brew the government types tried to pass off for coffee.

"I know I have it--somewhere. Ah, here it is." Withdrawing a folder nearly two inches thick, she brought the file to her desk, and opened the front page. Sorting through the paperwork, she slipped out two pages stapled together.

"Here." Humphing with each item she ticked off the list, Lydia lifted her cup and sipped. She flipped the paper to the second page. "Ha! I knew it was here." She set her cup on the desk and tapped the item on the page with a finger.

Nasim moved to her side from his chair. "Which one?"

There were listings for several rings but only one stated the jewelry belonged to the princess.

"That SOB has just handed us a clue for a second stolen item. Bastard's pillaged the sarcophagus."

Nasim shook his head. "He wouldn't get his hands dirty. He had someone do it for him--probably a cousin or brother. Some relative a few times removed."

"We need to contact Glenda. As trite as it sounds, she could be taking her life in her hands to go to her office. Let me have her number and I'll call."

Nasim checked the clock hanging on the office wall. "Lydia, no. Look at the time. It's nearly midnight. Even if she's awake, calls this late in the evening are never good news. This can wait until tomorrow morning."

He watched his partner's face cloud.

"After all, we have such a fun night planned for ourselves. I can look at the file from the records department later. Now... well, now we get to play in garbage! Don't want to miss that."

Nasim rose slowly from his chair, his mind a jumble. He found himself concerned about Ms. Nagel – more than just professionally. *What is happening to me? I've maintained distance from everyone until now. Then, in the space of one week, I tell my life story to two people. I must be losing my edge.*

Lydia stomped behind him to the lab. They turned the overhead fluorescent lights on, and suited up in biohazard gear. There were two green garbage bags. Lydia opened the first bag. The overpowering smell of cut grass permeated the room.

Nasim sneezed.

She dumped the contents on the table. Quickly digging through the pile with Nasim sneezing every thirty seconds, they discovered the bag was nothing more than grass clippings left by someone, presumably a hired gardener. They put the cuttings back in the bag, and set it out for the cleaning crew to dispose of.

Nasim pulled open the top of the second bag. Piece by piece, they placed each item on the metal table. It took the better part of two hours but they finally emptied the contents.

Standing back, they eyed their project.

"You notice something?" Lydia's blue eyes darkened over her mask.

"Yes. There is no food here – no eggshells, leftover meat, nothing. The only things I see are old coffee leavings and take out containers." Nasim smiled.

Even behind the mask, Lydia could see the crinkle of his eyes and twinkle in the darkness. She walked along the ten foot table eyeing the contents.

"It also appears the director feels no need to shred any of his paperwork. We're not going to have to put together paper puzzles."

"I think I'm beginning to like Dr. Riyadh's arrogance." Nasim grabbed a clipboard and pen from his shirt pocket. He started listing the items at his end of the table. When he'd noted how many restaurant to-go cartons were present, he put them back in the bag.

At her end, Lydia was progressing on the same task. They met in the middle.

"There is very little here to indict him." Nasim felt his stomach sour. "The hiya will get away again."

"Not so fast, kimo sabe."

He frowned. "Kimo sabe?"

"Old American TV phrase. Never mind. Do you have anything interesting on your list?"

Nasim went down the items he'd put on his paper. "Not really. Dr. Riyadh doesn't cook for himself. There's enough take out cartons here for nearly a week."

Lydia rechecked her own clipboard. "What you don't have in cartons, I do, except… wait a minute."

"What?"

"I think we may have stumbled onto something. As you keep pointing out, the good director is very arrogant and extremely sure of himself. I do believe he may have slipped up."

Nasim looked at the spot where Lydia had pointed her pencil.

"What are you showing me? All I see listed is an envelope."

She blew out an exasperated breath and rolled her eyes. "Of course it's an envelope. Come here." She led him toward the far end of the table, the smell of mixed variations of rotting food beginning to scent the air.

Nasim wrinkled his nose. Eight years of digging in garbage cans, and the discards of people's lives, and he still had to fight the urge to throw up. Would he ever get over it?

Lydia took a forefinger and a thumb and extracted an inexpensive looking envelope stained on one corner with coffee. She flattened it on the table.

"There. Now what do you see?"

Nasim stared at her. "It's still just an envelope. It's what people send letters in, and bill collectors put their money demands in. So?"

"What was that last thing you said?"

"About bill collectors?"

A slow grin emerged. "Yes… bill collectors. Look at the envelope and tell me what is written on the front. Who is it addressed to?"

Nasim moved to the table and picked up the envelope. "To Khepri Riyadh? Isn't that the director's…"

"…daughter."

"Didn't he say she was…"

"…practicing medicine in Cairo."

"If she's a doctor in Cairo, why is she getting mail here?"

"Read the business name on the return address."

"Alpha Storage Facility, San Pedro. Why would she need a storage unit in America?"

"Precisely. There's one other slip of paper here…," Lydia moved to a spot midway on the table and inched out a torn piece of lined paper. "…that I think could be important. It has a phone number written with no name. It's a 661 area code."

Nasim's head snapped up. "That's Glenda's area code."

Lydia nodded her head. "I know." She slipped the torn piece of paper and envelope into separate evidence bags, dating and initialing each one. A quick glance at the clock on the wall convinced her the exhaustion she was feeling wasn't her imagination. She and her partner had been in this stifling, stinky room for nearly four hours.

"Let's go look at the file Research sent you. Maybe, just maybe, we can connect a couple of dots here." Lydia looked up at her partner's confused face. "Never mind. Let's go look at that file."

They stripped off jumpsuits and disposed of them in the hazardous waste basket.

This time they sat at Nasim's desk while he opened his email and the attached file sent to him by Larry in the research unit. The computer worked at rapid speed since there were very few agents in the office at 4:00 a.m. He opened the file and concentrated as his computer loaded a booking form and picture to his monitor.

The face in the picture was average -- no distinguishing marks, no scars, and in this photo looking scared.

"He doesn't look the sort to commit murder." Nasim scanned the information on the booking sheet. "Mike Killian; born in Lancaster about thirty-four years ago, raised in a place called, Pearblossom, went to the local community college, got an associates' degree in auto mechanics, then opened his own garage." He sat back in his chair. "Sounds like the American Dream. Why would anyone risk that for a couple bucks?"

Lydia leaned over Nasim's shoulder. "Looks like this isn't his first brush with the local law." She pointed a finger at the list of charges going back five years; assault, drunk and disorderly, and disturbing the peace. "Our boy likes to drink and fight and, wait a minute, seems he has a partner in crime. Pull up that other rap sheet."

Nasim minimized Mike Killian's booking sheet and clicked on the second attachment. In the few minutes it took to download the information, he leaned back in his chair and stretched his muscles.

"I have an idea how we can keep Glenda out of trouble and draw in Dr. Riyadh."

Lydia had stretched her legs in front of her, clasped her hands behind her head letting her eyes drift shut. "I'm listening."

"We'll call later this morning and let her know about the anonymous call we received. I don't believe she's planning to visit her office today but, as the magazine's editor, there is always some emergency that needs her personal attention."

"Um-hum, go on."

"We'll have her call and leave a message on my phone about canceling a lunch date or something, and we'll visit her under the guise of following a lead. We'll make a big show of discovering the ring and bring her to the office along with the vase and its contents. I suppose handcuffs will make a better show of things. We'll have to go through the whole routine of booking her. I think, if we brief the lieutenant beforehand, we can get her in here under the subterfuge of arrest and provide her protective custody until we have Dr. Riyadh in custody."

Lydia opened her eyes and jumped.

"Whoa. He won't win any beauty contests, will he?"

The booking form and photo of the second attachment had downloaded and a glaring, hateful face peered out from the screen. One eye was blackened and swollen nearly shut. The nose also appeared swollen, but they couldn't be certain because it was so crooked they weren't sure which direction it pointed. The split lip was on the opposite side of the blackened eye and the person appeared to be sneering. Lydia leaned toward the screen reading over Nasim's shoulder.

"Well, well. Looks as if there are *two* Mr. Killians. I'd say this one is the reason the other has been in so much trouble. Bring up the other form and put them side by side."

Nasim enlarged the first booking form and used his computer's split screen view to set them next to each other on the monitor.

Lydia continued. "Mr. Mike is the older of the two. I bet he's been bailing baby brother's ass out of trouble all his life. Mikey here was married at one time. I'm sure the ex could tell us stories that would turn our hair gray."

Nasim sighed and slumped in his chair. "Probably but as you pointed out before, just because these guys parked near Glenda's house, doesn't mean they've committed a crime. We're still nowhere near connecting the director to the statuette. Maybe Glenda did steal it. She does have an affinity for cats and Egyptian history."

Lydia stood. "That's it. You're too tired to be making any sense. We both know Ms. Nagel is incapable of committing this crime. She's so squeaky clean it's nauseating. I want to check one more thing on these booking forms then we'll call it a very long night and go home. After a couple hours of good sleep, I'm sure you'll kick yourself for that last comment."

She pulled the evidence bag with the phone number off the file cabinet she'd set it on.

"Looks like we have a match. The last time these two were picked up was only six months ago. The sheriffs confiscated their cellphones as well as everything else when they threw them in the drunk tank and, thank you very much guys, wrote down the numbers. Our phone number belongs to, drum roll please, contestant number one! Mike Killian.

"We have at least one lead. Now if we can just get this guy to talk... in the meantime, let's go home. I'm exhausted and I need a shower."

Nasim agreed. He was sure he didn't want to see the inside of this office for eight hours, at least.

Lydia turned to him. "Need a ride?"

"No thank you. I'll make it okay. I'm going to set my alarm to call Glenda, then I'm going back to sleep. I'm turning off my phone so don't bother trying to call me."

"You know the policy..."

"I know, I know. It just feels good to say it."

The two shut down their computers. Lydia opened her lower right hand drawer and realized she still had the statuette inside.

"I've got to get these items to the evidence room--tomorrow, I mean later today. Now--home, shower, bed."

Waving at each other in the parking lot, the two parted ways to their own vehicles.

Lydia noted the sky was shedding the inkiness of night and beginning to bask in the glow of morning heralding yet another sunshiny day in the Los Angeles basin.

"Another beautiful day in paradise. It *will* be perfect if we can nail that camel dung, Dr. Riyadh to the wall. Oh, well, I can always dream."

She headed home, parking her vehicle in the driveway, and reconnoitering the house before entering. No sense in being careless just

166

because she was tired. Certain there were no unwelcome visitors, she went in, and leaving a trail of clothes on the hallway floor, headed to the shower. Taking more than her usual five minutes, she let the hot water beat away the stress of the last twenty-four hours. Within five minutes, Lydia was in a deep sleep. Everything would have to wait until later.

Nasim drove on autopilot. His mind filing and refiling pieces of information that pointed to the director but just missed indicting him. He swore as he slammed the heel of his hand on his steering wheel.

"He will escape again! I am so sorry, father. I've failed you and the family."

Wallowing in his misery, Nasim dragged himself to his apartment. Lydia was right. Maybe a good night's sleep would shed new light on the information and trigger some solution to this conundrum.

~ * ~

Omar Riyadh was basking in the adulation of a very beautiful, amply endowed, young woman as he consented to enlighten her in the dark mysteries of the ancient Egyptians--in his dream.

"Does he know we're here?" the dark figure leaned over the museum's antiquities director.

"No. He suddenly felt really tired and opted to go to bed early. He has no idea what's happening. I'm showing the boss the system works as well as he wished." The second figure motioned for them to leave.

Outside in the van, the first man pulled off his mask and turned to the second. "How did we get in and out without the alarm going off?"

The second man wretched the mask from his face and smiled. "Because I installed it."

Chapter Twenty-four

Glenda stretched under her covers. She was surprised her feet had missed being attacked by Scat and lifted her head to see where her three roommates were.

"They're still at LaVonne's. I'll need to get the little monsters today. This place doesn't feel right without them underfoot."

Her eyes, feeling dry and sand blasted from the reading she'd done last night, ached. She reached for the glass of water she kept on the night table and rummaged in the single drawer for some aspirin and eye drops. After she washed the aspirin down with the water, she applied the eye drops, wondering if she would be as patient as Nasim given the same circumstances.

His family had a long and revered history until the incident in Cairo. The Egyptian newspapers had exploited the family's misfortune for nearly a year. When Nasim's father left his post under a cloud of suspicion, the press rehashed the story of the uncle's dishonorable demise and insinuated the family had jumped sides joining with the tomb robbers instead of upholding the family job of tomb protectors. With the death of the uncle, the paper wrote one final article about the downfall of honor among the ancient bloodlines. They ignored the death of his father.

Glenda now understood Nasim's vehemence in wanting to see Dr. Riyadh in jail. Throughout the entire Cairo ordeal, the papers had deified the museum director. They threw light on his longsuffering of the situation and overplayed his generous forgiving nature. Glenda found herself disgusted at the fawning the press had afforded the man.

Maybe her own brush with him was jading her opinion but she regarded every move he made with suspicion. What she had seen as a charming, engaging smile she now viewed with distrust.

Starting at the sound of her phone, Glenda put off her ruminations and went to answer it.

"Hello?"

"Hello, Glenda. It's Nasim."

"Nasim, it's awfully early. What can I do for you at 8:00 in the morning?"

"I was curious if you planned to go to your office today?"

"Nope. Magazine has gone to press, and I have three days to catch up around the house with my critters. Why?"

Nasim explained the anonymous phone call left for Lydia and the conclusion the partners made regarding the caller. He went on to lay out the scenario he'd cooked up.

"This is all voluntary on your part. It sounds as though Dr. Riyadh has more than just the little cat statuette hidden away somewhere. While having your help would be instrumental, you need to know this is dangerous. None of us, least of all me, can predict what the doctor will do. This could just be an embarrassing episode to cause the museum to have second thoughts about your employment. We'll have to get Dr. Burkhardt aside and explain the situation. Do you think he'll play along?"

Glenda thought for a moment. "I don't know, Nasim. Dr. Burkhardt was instrumental in getting the museum to hire Dr. Riyadh. He comes highly recommended, at least on paper. Telling the head of the museum his golden child is a thief and possibly a murderer is attacking his judgment."

"What if my agency director speaks with Dr. Burkhardt? Do you think he would be more receptive to helping us then?"

Glenda searched her feelings. "It could work. It would be one high level executive talking to another high level executive. His judgment wouldn't be in question, just his cooperation. I believe that would work."

"Let me call Lydia."

Nasim cringed. He had tried to sleep but with little success. His mind was alive with possibilities; the most vivid was seeing the director, the untouchable Dr. Omar Riyadh led off in handcuffs and locked up forever. He could only hope Lydia had been restless as well. "As soon as I iron out the details with her, I'll call you back and we can set up a plan. And, Glenda?"

"Yes?"

"Words cannot express my thanks. Please know if this works out the way I envision, I will be forever in your debt."

Glenda let the thought hang in the air, responses forming and reforming in her mind.

"Let's hope it works, Nasim. I'll wait for your call. Goodbye." She stood, her hand resting on the phone, and contemplated the conversation. She could lose her job if this fell through and the governing board took a dim view of the cloak and dagger antics she was about to engage in.

On the other hand, there had been a bit of a scandal a few years earlier about art pieces disappearing into private collections without the museum's or board's knowledge. She was sure they wouldn't want to face the scrutiny from their contributors again. Art donors were notoriously fickle about attaching themselves to the proper organizations. It wouldn't be prudent to back a scandal-ridden museum.

She wouldn't be able to live with herself if she could help stop the theft and didn't. Nasim's phone call would be the determining factor. Glenda sluffed back to her room and grabbed her casual clothes, and cowboy boots then headed for the bathroom. Might as well shower and get the day moving. Either way, she wasn't going to have the luxury of lazing in bed--besides, lazing in bed without the kitties wasn't any fun.

~ * ~

Lydia grabbed the phone before the offensive thing screeched again. "What?"

"Sorry, partner. I need to talk to you."

She sighed and swung her legs over the edge of the bed. "Hold on. I'm going to the kitchen and grab the extension in there while I make coffee."

Nasim could understand as he was doing the same thing. A minute later, he heard a distinctive click.

"You still there?"

"Yeah."

"Hold on. Sorry about that. Now, what is it we need to discuss?"

"The idea I had last night, or early this morning if you will, about Glenda helping us out by allowing us to arrest her."

"What's the problem?"

"I wasn't thinking clearly about the repercussions it could have on her job."

"What repercussions?"

"If we go barging in there and arrest her without including the museum's director in the plan, she could lose her job. Glenda mentioned the director was instrumental in getting Riyadh hired so telling him he screwed up isn't going to sit well. We need to have our agency director speak with Dr. Burkhardt, one agency director to another. If he induces him to cooperate, maybe we can pull this off without any problems."

Lydia poured coffee into her cup and caught her English muffin as it popped out of the toaster. She spread marmalade on the two slices and moved the dish with her breakfast to the nook. Retrieving her coffee, she sat down.

"I hadn't thought about that. I'll contact the Captain and have him bring in our local agency director. Once we brief him, he can talk to the museum director, one on one, and secure his collaboration. I wouldn't want Glenda to lose her job in the course of helping us.

"Have her come into work but stress to her *not* to touch the vase. I'm sure the two of you can cook up some reason for us to visit."

Nasim would tackle that while he got ready for work. He could nap later if he got tired.

"Sounds good. I'll get back to you with the details."

Nasim scrubbed his hand over his face. So much of this plan depended on other people falling into line. *Should* he involve Glenda? Others were forcing the issue. If he didn't implement his idea, Dr. Riyadh wouldn't hesitate to call the local police and have her dragged away in handcuffs. This way, he and Lydia could guarantee Glenda's safety without official intervention. Yes, it would look as though they were placing her under arrest, but the reality of the scheme was to protect her from Dr. Riyadh and keep her *out* of the jail system.

He called Glenda back.

"Hi. Nasim, again. I've talked with Lydia and we'll be pulling in the director of the Los Angeles division to explain the situation. He's going to contact your Dr. Burkhardt and they'll have a business meeting to discuss the progress of the antiquity theft case. I believe your job will still be waiting for you.

"You need to call your secretary and make some excuse for coming to the office today. When you get there, ask about the vase, but don't touch it. Do you trust your secretary?"

"Implicitly."

"Have her call me and say you're canceling dinner tonight because something came up. Lydia and I will leave the office and get to the museum in about forty minutes. We're going to come barging in and do some shouting about the vase and theft and what not. Please remember this is for show. Do your best to act angry, shout back and get belligerent so the handcuffs won't seem out of place."

"Do you have to use them?"

"I think it will add to the authenticity of the situation. Remember, we've just discovered that you, supposedly, have stolen items from an Egyptian crypt. They're priceless. International relations could crumble and the museum could face prosecution. I'm sorry we're going to have to take you through the lobby but, that way, the director will be sure to hear about it."

"I wish we could do this differently."

Nasim sighed. "So do I but if we don't play into Dr. Riyadh's hands a little, he'll make things happen himself, and I'm afraid you might be injured."

"Yeah, there's always that possibility. Well, let me give Amunet a call and get the ball rolling. See you later, Nasim. And thanks."

A frown passed over his face. "For what?"

"For caring enough to keep me safe."

He felt the heat rush to his face. "Sure. See you later, Glenda."

"Later."

He hung up the phone and cursed. He hated Dr. Riyadh controlling the situation. His manipulation of events had killed Nasim's uncle and eventually his father. Maybe being ahead of him, this time, would keep someone he cared for safe. Nasim started. He realized he'd admitted his growing affection for the magazine editor.

No one can know about this. It could put Glenda in more danger than she already faces.

Nasim trudged to the shower to start his day. Fatigue from the previous night seeped through his bones. Several cups of coffee and rolling down his car window on the way to work should shake off his weariness and the growing sense of dread building in his stomach.

Today was shaping up to be an enormous challenge. *Might as well get started and hope the plan will work to our advantage. If not, the consequences will be dire.*

Chapter Twenty-five

Lydia pulled herself together and arrived at the office before Nasim. She would brief the Captain and, hopefully, the agency director after she secured the evidence. Strolling through the din of the office, she decided she liked it better at 4:00 a.m.

Phones were ringing, people talked over cubicle walls and gathered in the hallways; there was a mail person delivering letters and paperwork to each desk and, in some cases, feeling the need to strike up a conversation. The cacophony of noise was distracting. She needed to find a place to concentrate on the unfolding events.

Pulling forms from her desk drawer, she filled in all the spaces, crossing the t's and dotting the i's, then called the evidence room to verify someone would be around to take her evidence packages. She walked the length of the building and headed into the basement. That was the key in these older buildings--half the space was underground. A sign at the top of the doorframe sticking out in the hallway declared the office within was "Evidence." Lydia entered and walked to the counter. It divided the room reaching from one wall to the other forming a barrier. Behind the counter, a desk sat shoved against a wall, several paper trays covering the surface. The agent sitting at the desk looked up when she walked in.

"Can I help you?"

"Yes. I called about forty minutes ago. I'm Officer Thompson and I have some evidence I need checked in for safe keeping."

He pushed his chair away from the desk and trundled to the counter. According to the nametag pinned to his uniform shirt, his last name was Cruz. He reached his hand out and Lydia obliged by sliding the papers across the top of the counter.

"What ya got?"

Lydia pulled a pair of gloves from her slacks pocket and gloved up.

Officer Cruz raised an eyebrow. "There something here that's gonna make me sick?"

She shook her head. "No. The statuette in the shoebox is nearly three thousand years old. I'm being exceptionally careful. Once we're through with our investigation, it will go back to the museum where it belongs. If you don't mind, I'll hold it and put it back in the box."

He shook his head. "No problem."

Lydia opened the lid of the box and cradled the statuette in her hands. She pulled it up far enough for the evidence curator to identify the markings as she had described on the paperwork. She replaced the cat goddess in her cardboard sarcophagus and closed the lid. She then pulled the two pieces of paper evidence from her jacket and put them on the counter.

"Could you make a copy of these for me? I want to start working on them today."

Cruz took the baggies and, one by one, placed them on the copy machine, handing the copies to Lydia.

"I'm putting these items in a separate, stand-up locker. I had a small one open up yesterday. Your paperwork is in order so I'll sign off on it. If you need to retrieve any of these items, fill out a form, and get it to me twenty-four hours prior to the time you'll need them. Here you go." He slid the papers back to Lydia with his signature at the bottom.

"Three thousand years old, you say? Whew."

Lydia watched him hold the box in front of him and walk very carefully to the back. Once he'd nestled the items in their locker, he shut the door and slumped against the row, blowing out a deep breath.

"Thanks, Officer Cruz."

He waved her off. "Yeah."

Lydia dragged her feet going back to her cubicle. Something about today's plan wasn't jelling. She couldn't put her finger on the exact problem but she felt uneasy about their arrangement. She sat at her desk and stared blankly at the wall in front of her running through the steps they were setting in motion.

Nasim poked his head around the corner. Lydia appeared lost in thought.

"Oh. I'll come back later."

"No, no." She waved him in and indicated for him to sit. "There's something not quite right about this idea. I've gone over every step in my mind and I can't put my finger on what's missing. Humor me and go through the plan again."

Nasim settled in the chair.

"Okay. Glenda will call when she gets to work. That's our sign to head to the museum. Once we get there, we'll go to her office pushing past her secretary and making a big fuss about the vase on her desk. We say we've received information indicating she has knowledge of the cat statuette and a ring from the crypt. One of us will grab the vase and empty it finding the ring. We slap handcuffs on her and walk her through the lobby to the car. We'll make sure we announce we're booking her at our offices. What isn't working for you?"

"When does Dr. Riyadh find out? How can we be sure he'll be in his office? This is all show for him, isn't it?"

Nasim tapped his chin with his forefinger. She had a point. How were they going to guarantee the doctor would buy their one act play?

Lydia rose from the desk. "I have a meeting with the Captain and the director in fifteen minutes in the penthouse. Figure out this wrinkle and let me know when I get back."

Nasim headed for his cubicle. He needed to call Glenda and see if she might offer a solution. Much as she hated this spy business, she was pretty good at it.

~ * ~

Glenda paced in her kitchen. She'd called LaVonne and received her assurance that keeping the kitties for the day wasn't a problem.

I'm going to have to get her something really nice for hanging on to my monsters for so long. What can I tell Amunet? Just showing up will arouse her suspicions. She was walking past the stove for the umpteenth time when the kitchen phone rang. Setting her coffee on the counter, she answered.

"Yes?"

"Glenda, this is Amunet and I really hate to bother you but something has come up on the magazine."

"What?"

"Well, the printer says there's a problem with the front article layout. One of the inside information boxes is longer than you designed. We need a quick fix to go to print on time. Do you want me to try to get hold of one of the copy editors? He said if he crops the picture, you'd lose the integrity of the shot, or something like that. Can you call him?"

Glenda let Amunet hear her sigh. "Actually, it would probably be better if I came down and handled it from the office. That way, if I have to, I can go to the printer's and fix it myself."

"I'm so sorry."

"Don't worry about it, Amunet. That's why I get paid the big bucks. I'll make them take us both to lunch. How's that sound?"

"Like a date. See you in a couple hours. Bye."

Glenda finished her coffee and put the empty cup in the dishwasher. *Might as well get moving.* She was packing things in her briefcase when her phone rang again. Picking up the office extension, she answered.

"What's up now, Amunet?"

"I'll ask her when I see her."

Glenda coughed in surprise. "Nasim. Same question, what's up?"

"We need to guarantee Dr. Riyadh sees you being taken away in handcuffs. Any ideas how we can involve him?"

Glenda tapped her chin with a finger. "Well, he's certain I have the cat, which I did but I don't now, so--hmmm. How about this--when you and Lydia burst into my office and discover the ring, I'll deny knowing about it. My secretary will probably confirm our suspicion that Dr. Riyadh left the vase, and she'll tell you he's the one you need to talk to. You harangue me for a minute, and I'll yell to Amunet to call Dr. Burkhardt who will not be there. I can tell her to call Dr. Riyadh to verify he left the vase. I'll swear up and down I have no idea where this came from any more than I knew how the cat showed up.

"That will tell him I did have the cat. If he sends those goons to the house again, I'll be ready."

"No. I don't like the idea of you putting yourself in the line of fire. That's why we're dragging you to the station so we can arrange to protect you. I wouldn't put it past the good director to have his associates recheck your house. He has a lot riding on finding that statuette. His security and future depend on keeping his activities covert. We can't take the chance he'll try to quiet you permanently."

"Thanks, I think."

"I like most of your plan; except the part about telling him about the cat."

"Nasim, it will push him to be careless."

"Or it may push him to be dangerous and deadly. Please don't say anything."

"I won't promise."

He pushed an exasperated breath between his lips. "Fine. I can't force you to protect yourself. I'll attack the stack of papers piling up in my in-box until we hear from you. And Glenda?"

"What?" she was fractious that he'd nixed her plan.

"Be careful. Goodbye."

178

Caught off guard, she was speechless. He'd hung up before she could respond. Her stomach reacted by flipping. She looked down. "Knock it off. He's just a nice guy worried about an innocent bystander."

A voice in the back of her mind whispered, "Think again."

One hour later, Glenda sat twenty miles away on Highway 38 facing the one light in Littlerock waiting for the blasted thing to turn green. She was feeling peckish and grumpy. Her skin itched and she clenched and unclenched her hands.

"I need to get myself under control." She sucked in a deep cleansing breath and moved forward with the traffic. It wouldn't do any good to snipe at the rest of the world because she was out of sorts. She needed her wits around her for the next twelve hours, at least.

~ * ~

Omar woke with a pounding headache. He squinted his eyes at the clock on his nightstand. He realized his alarm had failed to sound. *Oh, well.* A long, luxuriant stretch and Dr. Riyadh started his day. His first stop was the bathroom for a handful of aspirin. He couldn't fathom the reason for his throbbing head. He hadn't had any wine last evening, in fact, he'd felt so tired, he went to bed an hour early. Moving through his morning routine, Omar got ready and left for work.

If Lydia was still the over achiever he remembered from her college days, she'd bite on the anonymous message left on her voice mail.

Omar smiled. His headache was receding and the thought of having the little statuette in his hands was warming.

By the weekend--the Bahamas.

~ * ~

Lydia tapped her finger on the evidence bag containing the phone number now sitting in the center of her desk. Should she call? She glanced at the clock on her phone display. It was 10:00 and Nasim had his head buried in paperwork. It couldn't hurt and she could always say she'd dialed a wrong number. She sat and tapped. An idea was forming and, as she pulled the booking sheet from her top tray, it exploded into action.

Lydia dialed the number.

"Yeah?"

She hesitated.

"Who the hell is this? You got two seconds and I hang up."

"Mike?"

There was silence on the other end. Lydia thought she might have lost the connection.

"Yeah. Who's this?"

"This is Brenda. We met about..." Lydia checked the date on the booking form, "...ten months ago at the Ten West bar."

"I don't remember. You've got the wrong guy."

"I'm the redhead with long legs."

The hesitation told Lydia she'd guessed pretty well considering she was improvising on the fly.

"Oh, yeah, Brenda. Why has it taken you so long to call?"

"I've been a little busy what with the pregnancy and new baby."

The phone went dead.

"Gotcha." The phone number Dr. Riyadh had crumpled and dumped in the waste can belonged to the oldest of the brothers. But it still didn't connect them to the director.

Lydia wasn't sure how she was going to accomplish that feat.

~ * ~

Glenda slowed her Lexus and guided it between two vehicles into her parking space. She looked around the lot. Spotting the director's Mercedes, she pulled her cellphone from her cup holder and dialed.

"He's here and so am I; just heading in to my office. See you soon."

She had decided to wear casual slacks that would hold up under rough conditions. The butterflies in her stomach fluttered. Glenda carried her briefcase with her as she sauntered up the steps. A nod at the front door guard and she made her way down the corridor to her office. She stepped inside and stopped at Amunet's desk.

"Hi. Do you have any more information from the printer?"

Amunet shook her head.

"Well, give me what you have and I'll get started fixing this problem. And Amunet?"

"Yes, Glenda?"

"Good morning." Glenda smiled and received one in return.

She read the email Amunet had printed out and set her briefcase next to her desk. When she looked up a vase was sitting in her tray. The size, shape, and color were a match to the one Pandora had destroyed. She remembered Nasim's admonition not to touch it. She picked up her phone and buzzed her secretary.

"Yes?"

"Could you come in to my office?"

"Sure."

Amunet poked her head around the doorsill. "What do you need?"

"What is this in my in tray?"

"Oh, that."

Glenda slowly nodded her head. "Yeah, that."

"Dr. Riyadh came in yesterday, I think, and insisted on dropping it off. He said it was to replace the damaged one. I think there's a note under it." Amunet started to cross the office and lift the vase to show Glenda the note.

"That's okay. I'll look at it later. I need to fix this layout snafu before noon. Thanks, Amunet."

"No problem. Oh, and one more thing."

"What?"

"I kind of waved him through cause I was finishing up my typing. When I realized how long he'd been here, I poked my head in and found him on all fours on the floor. It just didn't seem right. He said he dropped the card but, frankly, I didn't believe him."

"Thanks. He probably *did* just drop his card. I'll investigate later. Since I'm going to be tied up on this magazine deadline I appreciate if you held all calls and visitors."

"Sure thing."

Glenda watched her secretary close the door. *Now fix the article, get the printer moving, and wait.*

Chapter Twenty-six

Nasim's phone rang and Lydia popped up from her desk. It had been conspicuously quiet all morning. She peeked over the top of the cubicle and caught his eye. He nodded then hung up.

"It's time."

Lydia opened the center drawer of the desk retrieving her handcuffs. The right side drawer where she'd put the little statuette held her gun and holster. She pulled out the agency-issue .38 and double-checked to be certain there was no bullet in the chamber then switched on the safety. This time was strictly for show, nothing more. She leaned over and dialed the phone.

"Hi. This is Officer Lydia Thompson. Please tell him we're leaving now. Yes, thank you."

Nasim poked his head around the corner. "Ready?"

"Yep."

"My car or yours?"

"Let's take yours. Mine needs a tune-up. It's running like crap."

They started toward the parking lot when Lydia stopped in the middle of the hallway.

"Hold on. I forgot something."

Nasim turned, gazing at the pictures of agency directors displayed on the wall. Five minutes later, Lydia panted up. He lifted a brow.

"Got it. Let's go."

The two agents were quiet on the forty-minute trip through the concrete maze to the museum. They climbed from the parked car and marched to the front door. The guard at the door watched them walk through then scurried to catch up.

"Hold it."

Nasim looked at Lydia and rolled his eyes.

She turned and faced the guard.

"What's the problem?"

"Your weapons." He had his hand resting on the butt of his own gun.

Lydia and Nasim held one hand up while they put the other in their pockets and retrieved their badges. The guard grabbed each badge and examined the shield and identification against the person.

He lowered his hand from his weapon and handed the black wallets back to them. "Sorry, guys. You just can't be too careful these days."

Lydia shook her head. "You're doing your job. And, if I might add, very well. We'll be certain to let your supervisor know how diligent you've been."

The young man beamed. "Thanks, guys." He strutted back to the front podium by the entry doors.

Nasim shot Lydia a questioning look.

She muttered lowly. "Hey, can't hurt to have him on our side."

The duo strolled through the museum to Glenda's office hesitating at the door.

He pulled in a deep breath. "You ready?"

She nodded.

They walked in and found Glenda's door closed, Amunet glaring at her computer.

Nasim cleared his throat. "Ma'am. We need to see Ms. Nagel."

Amunet scowled and saved the information on her screen. "I'm sorry but she isn't seeing anyone right now, Mr. Shabouh. Can I take a message and have her contact you once she's free?"

He glanced at Lydia who narrowed her eyes and lifted her eyebrow.

"We need to see her--now."

The set of the young secretary's jaw told the pair they'd hit a nerve.

"She's not seeing *anyone*. If you don't have a message, I would suggest you leave before I call security." The crossed arms over her chest, fingers tapping against her arm, emphasized her point.

Lydia pulled out her black badge holder and flipped it open revealing her identity as an Interpol agent as Nasim opened the office door and entered.

"Ms. Nagel."

Glenda rose from her chair. "What is…"

He put up a hand. "Don't blame your secretary. She tried to stop us."

Lydia came around him and moved to the in-tray. Sitting in the center of the tray was a clay vase. Lydia pulled a baggie from her hip pocket and pulled out a pair of gloves. Donning the latex, she slipped two fingers in the opening of the vase and a finger on the bottom. She proceeded to examine it closely.

Nasim looked at Glenda, the tiniest twinkle appearing in the dark eyes. "Is this yours?"

Amunet had appeared in the doorway and was frantically waving her hands at Glenda. She was shaking her head and drawing her finger across her throat.

"I suppose. It's a gift from a friend. Why?"

Nasim looked at Lydia and she nodded. "We've received a call from a source that described this vase and said there is an antiquity hidden inside. Would you know anything about that?"

Glenda narrowed her eyes and set her mouth in a thin line. "I would not. Feel free to check out the vase. You'll find nothing but dirt from the Egyptian desert inside." She leaned back in her chair and glared at the agents.

Lydia set the vase back on the tray. With one hand, she barely touched the sides of the vase as she slipped two fingers of the other hand inside. She tugged and a latex glove fell out. Peering at the glove, she poked an item settled in the middle.

"Well, Ms. Nagel. Can you tell me about this item?"

Glenda rolled her eyes. "How can I tell you about something I don't know?"

Lydia worked the piece out the end of the glove. A tiny ring with two stones lay next to the vase. The three leaned forward and looked at the small ring. The workmanship was the finest Lydia had seen in her years as a student on archeological digs. The two stones, while not polished as the modern ones, were nearly flawless and deeply colored.

They looked at each other.

"Ms. Nagel, I think you need to come downtown with us to answer questions." Nasim stepped back and pointed toward the door.

"I'm not going anywhere with you. I haven't done anything wrong and I won't be taken downtown and disappear into some government building."

Glenda turned to Amunet. "Please call Dr. Burkhardt and Dr. Riyadh."

She looked at Nasim. "I'm sure there's a simple explanation."

Amunet left the doorway and Lydia leaned back to see if she'd gone to her desk to phone.

Nasim leaned to Glenda. "Look, Dr. Riyadh will come in and deny everything. At that point, I'll come around and handcuff you. Don't fight too hard because I'm putting the clasp on the loosest connection I can. If you struggle too much, they'll fall off." He let a thin smile play over his lips. "We need to make this seem as real as possible." Straightening up, he glowered.

"Ms. Nagel. I'm going to ask you again where you got the little ring."

She leaned forward, her hands placed against the desk rim. "And I'll tell you again I have no idea how that got there. I-don't-know."

They heard the door of the outer office open. Dr. Riyadh appeared followed by Amunet her eyebrows knit together, eyes hooded in concern.

"What is going on here?" His voice rumbled with the appropriate amount of umbrage.

"Dr. Riyadh." Nasim acknowledged his presence. "We have reason to believe Ms. Nagel, here, might have knowledge of the thefts we've been investigating."

"I don't believe it. From where are you getting your information?"

"We have a source." Nasim watched the corner of the doctor's mouth flicker.

"Ms. Nagel and her secretary tell me you provided this," Nasim pointed to the clay urn, "vase to her. Is this the case?"

Omar nodded. "I did."

Lydia stood back mutely watching the director.

"Did you place anything inside the vase as a surprise for Ms. Nagel?"

"I did not. I brought the vase to Miss Nagel because she admired it and seemed so distressed when her animals destroyed the other one. You saw, didn't you, Miss Amunet? There was nothing inside."

Amunet's eyes lost their concerned look and took on a dangerous hue of black. "I saw very little as I was busy at my desk. I couldn't verify that you didn't bring in a jarful of diamonds."

The director shrugged. "I can only tell you the truth; I didn't place a surprise inside the container."

Nasim turned to Glenda. "Then I am left with the conclusion that you stuffed the ring," out of the corner of his eye, he caught the director straining to see the ring in the tray, "inside the vase to smuggle it out of the museum and take it for yourself or sell it to another."

He moved around the desk and gently lifted Glenda up from the chair.

"I didn't put that ring in there. I don't know anything about it!" Glenda's eyes took on a wild look and she threw her shoulder back to dislodge Nasim's hand.

"Let go of me!" Glenda wretched herself back and forth as Nasim placed the handcuffs on her wrists. "Dr. Riyadh!"

Lydia gathered up the ring and glove placing them back in the vase, and took hold of Glenda's other arm. They walked her to the hallway.

Glenda wriggled around and shouted at the director.

"You know you put that ring in the vase, just like you put the cat statue in the other one."

Lydia twisted her head and watched the expression on the director's face. His skin tone blanched and his eyes flinted. She watched his jaw flex and he clinched his fist. It was a fleeting picture because he realized she was watching. He forced himself to soften and take on an expression of pity.

Amunet dashed to her phone. "I'll call the company lawyer, Ms. Nagel."

The trio walked through the halls, people stopping to gawk at the scene. Nodding at the front door guard, they marched Glenda to the car, and held her head as she climbed in the back.

When they cleared the parking lot and were barreling down the freeway, Nasim looked in the review mirror at Glenda.

"I thought you promised not to mention that."

"Mention, what?" Lydia frowned.

"That bit about the cat." Glenda squirmed free of the handcuffs and rubbed her wrists. "I thought you said you left these things loose."

"I did. If I had tightened them, you'd have permanent dents on your wrists. I asked you not to say anything about the statuette. Omar Riyadh is a very dangerous man. What were you hoping to accomplish?"

Glenda could see anger flash in his eyes. "Sometimes you have to tease the tiger. All of this charade would have been for naught if I hadn't mentioned the cat. Didn't you see him? He was standing there looking officious and smug. He had no problem with you arresting me."

Nasim sighed and settled in the driver's seat. "What did you expect him to do? Jump up, raise his hand and say '*no, no, it was me, take me.*' Come on, Glenda. That's how the good, honest director works. He finds the antiquities, someone else steals them, and some innocent hard-working soul goes to jail for something he didn't do."

"The rich just get richer," he spit out.

"What happens to me next?" Glenda watched the changing scenery from the window.

"You need to let Lydia cuff you again then we'll take you through the booking procedure and secure you in an interrogation room. After an hour of interrogation, you'll be released on your own recognizance. Lydia will accompany you home and we'll keep a watch on you round the clock until the director makes his move."

"You seem determined he's going to try something," Glenda snapped on one side of the handcuffs holding her hands up so Lydia could reattach the other side.

Nasim hesitated. Should he tell her the truth of what he knew?

"Not personally but his history shows he leaves no stone unturned when he is on the trail of a lucrative possibility. After all, you just admitted you knew the cat was in the vase."

Glenda groaned. He was right.

"That's why I'm coming along. If they show up, they're going to get a nasty welcome." Lydia pulled the .38 from her holster and took bead on the bumper of the car in front of them.

"We've arrived. I'm really sorry about this, Glenda. In a few hours, you should be home with your cats."

Glenda closed her eyes and took a deep breath. "Let's get this over with."

~ * ~

Amunet glared at the director. "Please leave. I have a lot of work to do."

Omar tipped his head and walked out the door watching the two Interpol agents escort the magazine editor through the building. He ducked into the men's room and leaned over the sink as he washed his hands. The rumble of laughter echoed around the ceramic walls of the lavatory. Once again, the execution of his plan was unfolding through the naivety of others.

Omar stared in the mirror. One issue he needed to clarify. Miss Nagel had mentioned the little cat. The thugs his buyer had sent to find the cat relayed the information that her house hadn't yielded the statuette. The only other explanation of its absence was they had kept it for themselves and were going to cheat him out of his money. He needed to find them and make them talk.

He yanked a paper towel from the dispenser to wipe his hands and tossed the paper into the rubbish receptacle. Omar walked quickly to his office. His secretary wasn't at her desk, a quick glance at his watch verified it was lunchtime. He scribbled a note saying he was taking paperwork home and she could leave at her own discretion. He would see her the next day.

He locked his office. Omar's mind was calculating all the way to his car how he was going to approach this bump in his plan. He had the home number of the two thugs. A call threatening to expose their plot to their distasteful boss would have them talking in no time. Omar was certain of it. He shuddered at the thought of crossing the raspy voiced man.

"It would make me talk."

He stopped at an electronics store and purchased a disposable cell, angry for not thinking of this earlier. "A wise man knows where all the exits lie," he grumbled.

He shed his suit and opted, instead, for his time worn jeans and soft leather loafers. Although a bit early, Omar decided to indulge in a glass of wine. He poured his finest merlot and sipped. The warmth of the elixir soothed his trepidation about calling the hoodlums. He wandered to his study and sat at the desk. A quick scan of the desktop didn't reveal the torn piece of paper with the number on it. He searched the drawers and cubbyholes unsuccessfully.

"Damn it!" he threw himself back in his chair. A deep pull of the ruby contents from his wineglass helped chase the tension from his shoulders. Glaring at nothing in particular, Omar felt the chill of desperation beginning to creep up his spine. Then, the idea struck him so hard; he nearly fell out of his chair.

"Of course. What a nattering fool I've been." He rose from the chair, grasped his wineglass in hand, and went in search of his briefcase. Once found, he popped the latches open and grabbed his phone. Scrolling through the numbers-called feature, he found what he needed. On the kitchen counter was the disposable cell he'd just purchased. He transferred the number from his cell to the throwaway. Feeling pleased with himself, he poured another glass of wine. He'd do paperwork later. Right now, he was relaxing before his big scene. He would have the little cat statuette and the forgery before the week's end.

190

~ * ~

Glenda sat in the dreary white room clutching the tepid coffee in the Styrofoam cup. She sincerely hoped she would never go through this humiliation again in her lifetime. After her entrance into the system-- fingerprinting, mug photo, and having her possessions placed in an envelope until her release, Lydia and Nasim had led her to an interrogation room to wait for an hour while someone called her lawyer. The truth of the matter was she was cooling her heels until the proper time span had passed. Her boss, Dr. Burkhardt, had been by, congratulated her on her cooperation with the Interpol people, and guaranteed her position with the Getty was secure. Glenda could tell he was contrite about having misjudged Dr. Riyadh so badly.

Well, weren't they all? The antiquities director was a smooth talking snake in an expensive suit. She felt her neck heat up and made a mental bet she was glowing red, not from embarrassment but from the anger she felt at the man who could rob a country of its heritage without the slightest twinge of conscience. If she ever got her hands on him...

Lydia and Nasim came through the door, Nasim holding a cup steaming with dark, black liquid.

"You guys are a lifesaver. I was just going through the ways I'm going to..."

Nasim held up a hand. "Everything said in this room is recorded. You should know that before we go any further." He placed the cup in front of her.

Glenda bit the side of her lip. "I see."

Lydia glanced at the watch on her wrist and held up five fingers. She lowered one, then another, and another until they were all down. She got up and exited the room.

Glenda frowned. This was all too covert for her. She started, "Wha.."

Again, Nasim held up his hand. Lydia opened the door and motioned them out.

Nasim held Glenda's elbow as they walked down the busy hallway to the elevator. Entering, Lydia pushed the button to the basement. They rode in silence. Once the doors opened, Nasim took the lead and the trio journeyed to a conference room. Comfortable chairs surrounded an oak table covered in paperwork. When the three were inside the room, Nasim closed the door and latched it.

"Now, we're in a safe room. There's no recording going on here. Most of the building is set up to tape all conversation in all the rooms, and yes, it seems like an invasion of privacy. However, it's a precaution the latest director felt necessary in this day and age of terrorism. Nobody knows what a terrorist looks like and with the amount of international agents here, it would be easy to slip one into our ranks."

Glenda sighed clutching the hot mug in her hand and slumped into the comfortable seat.

"Oh, yes. This beats those ugly, uncomfortable orange chairs upstairs. So why all the secrecy?"

Lydia spoke. "Technically, you're a suspect. But that's to outside eyes. I wanted to show you what a roomful of eager probies, probationary agents, can do. All of this," she waved a hand over the sea of paper covering the table, "came from two pieces of paper."

"Shouldn't have left them alone to multiply," Glenda muttered.

Lydia narrowed her eyes and clenched her jaw.

"Sorry. Couldn't resist," Glenda shrugged her shoulders and took a sip of coffee.

"To continue," Lydia moved to the far end of the table, "I came down and took a look while Nasim was interrogating you, Glenda. Last night, our little foray into the work of rubbish reclamation produced two usable items. One, a number with the 661 area code; and two, an envelope from a storage company in San Pedro made out to Khepri Riyadh."

Glenda sat up and leaned forward. "Isn't she in…"

"...Egypt. Exactly. Tell me, how long has the director been at the museum?"

Glenda's eyes took on a faraway look as she thought. "I just met him not too long ago but I recall some mention of his arrival in the newsletter last month, so, two months, maybe?"

"Okay. To your knowledge, Dr. Riyadh has been in LA for, let's say, three months. He'd need time to find a place to live and move in, right?"

Nasim and Glenda nodded.

Lydia picked up a sheaf of papers and held them up. "Then why would he need a storage warehouse starting six months ago?"

Glenda spoke up. "To store his household items? Maybe he shipped a car?"

Lydia smiled. "Thanks for playing devil's advocate but," she put down the one stack of papers and picked up a thin folder, "he bought his Mercedes here three months ago, just about the time he moved into his house with the garage. There would be no need to store the car and since his daughter practices medicine and lives in Cairo, why would she have need of a warehouse in San Pedro?"

Glenda leaned back in her chair and considered all the information.

"Maybe he's going to ship vehicles back to Egypt. Are they cheaper here?"

Nasim stood and began to look at the work on the table. "No. Actually, it's cheaper to buy a Mercedes in Egypt than here. The shipping charge is minimal and, if you know the right official," he rubbed a thumb and forefinger together, "there are no import taxes. No, this warehouse is to store items coming in. It looks," he picked up a sheet of paper, "as if the director has been receiving shipments from outside the country starting immediately after he engaged the warehouse space."

"That's how I read it," Lydia picked up another sheet. "The second piece of information gave us the two thugs that tossed your house. Let's see, a John and Mike Killian. Mike owns a garage and John works in a nursery in

Littlerock." She pushed the mug shots toward Glenda and frowned. "Why would anybody come all the way from Arkansas to break into your house?"

Glenda and Nasim shook their heads saying in unison. "Littlerock, California."

Lydia squinted at the sheet of paper. "Oh."

Glenda, mug shots in hand, paled, and began to shake.

"You okay?"

Glenda shook her head. "No. He," she put the picture of John on the table, "came to my house last summer and helped put in the garden out back. Made my skin crawl the whole time. I felt like the main course for dinner. I've never been so glad to see someone leave my property, as I was when he left at the end of each day. He creeped me out so badly, I changed the locks."

"Well, it looks like he used the knowledge of your house to break in and ransack it. Your comment about the cat statuette may push the director to contact these goons again. We just can't be sure. That's *why* I'll be accompanying you home. If they decide to revisit you, well…" Lydia let the idea hang.

Nasim had been examining the paperwork spread over the table. "I think I'll make some inquiries about warehouse rental. I believe I feel a large shipment of Egyptian pottery from my family in Aswan coming on. I'm going to need somewhere to store it until I can locate a buyer." He pulled a slip of paper with the information he needed from the pile. "Might as well get started while you two lounge about in the desert."

Lydia rolled her eyes. Personal protection assignments were the worst. As an agent, when you were responsible for your own life that was one thing, but to have the responsibility to keep someone else alive? She'd rather be forced to go through her *introduction-to-society* ball again.

"Well, just don't have too much fun." She glanced at her watch and back to Glenda. "I think it's time to take you home. We'll pick up your personal property and swing by the museum so you can get anything you need from there and your car. Please don't try to lose me."

Glenda sighed. "Lydia?"

"Yes?"

"I'm too tired and thankful to try and ditch you. Can we go home, now?"

Lydia smirked. "Yeah. Let's go. Nasim?"

He looked up from the form he was reading. "Yes?"

"Keep me posted."

Chapter Twenty-seven

He had his head under the hood of a 1964 Lincoln Continental with suicide doors. Unscrewing the nut on the air filter, he gave it one last twirl and removed it. He grabbed the regular screwdriver from his back pocket and gently shimmied beneath the edge of the filter cover. A little wiggle and the cover snapped open. He took off the top and set it on the rag he had draped over the fender. With two fingers, he pulled out the blackened filter and wrinkled his nose. Sliding from under the hood, he turned to face the slim, silver haired woman looking expectantly his way.

Her big blue eyes creased slightly at the edges, a small line appearing on the otherwise smooth forehead. "John said the problem was with the… um… air intake valve. He said I'd have to leave the car for three days and it would probably cost about six hundred dollars. Now, Michael, I don't mind the cost but I hate being without my car." She fisted a tiny hand on her hip.

"Mrs. Englewood? There is nothing wrong with your car. I hate to say this, but my brother would rob the Pope if he thought he could. You have a dirty air filter that will cost fifteen dollars to replace. That's all. In fact, I have one I'll put in right now, and we'll call it even. Please remember to talk to me when you need something for the car--not John."

"Michael Ignatius Killian."

He scrunched his shoulders and cringed at the use of his full name. "Yes. Ma'am?"

"My Daryl told me you get what you pay for. I'll be paying you forty dollars to install a new filter and you can bet I'll be talking with you when the Lincoln needs work." She walked up and pecked a kiss on his cheek. A smile lit up her face. "Your grandfather would be so proud. You've made such a success of your life. Now John," she sighed and turned up her hands, "well, there's always one bad apple." She slipped two twenties into his hand and raised her eyebrows when he started to complain.

He was watching her drive away when his cell rang. He didn't recognize the number on the readout but answered anyway.

"Mike the Mechanic. How can I help you?"

"You can give me what's mine."

Mike walked inside the garage office and took a seat behind his desk. "I beg your pardon?"

"I have it on good authority you are in possession of a rare antiquity--a cat statuette--that belongs to me."

The museum guy.

"I think you've been drinking your lunch. When we finished the job you asked us to do, which we never got paid for, we had nothing. There was no statue, no computer, no TV, nothing of value in the house. I don't know who told you we had your statue but they're full of it and so are you. Don't call back or I'll go to the police. Get it?"

"It's a move you would regret."

"So sue me." He ended the call and switched off the phone. He couldn't believe the size of that guy's balls. They had hung their asses on the line for him and he stiffed them. Now he was accusing them of finding the statue and keeping it for themselves? Let him swing in the wind.

~ * ~

Omar sat back on the sofa and touched the volume control on his television. He was certain those thugs had his statuette.

197

That's all right. I'll sell the fake and set some of my *people on the task of relieving those Neanderthals of my property.*

He grabbed his wine glass and noted it was empty; time for a refill. He stood up intending to wander to the kitchen. Peering through the sheer curtains at his front window, he spied a white van with lettering on the side parked at the house across the street. *What's going on now?* A glance at his watch reminded him the mail should have arrived by this time. He'd investigate the van as he retrieved his mail.

He combed his fingers through his hair, and ventured to his mailbox. The sign on the side of the van touted some carpet-cleaning firm.

Ah, for the new owners. He promptly forgot the vehicle and started to sort through the letters, smiling when he recognized the elegant turn of his daughter's writing. He held the envelope to his nose and pulled in deeply. She always sprinkled the paper with his favorite fragrance from home. He'd refill his wine glass after reading his mail. He wanted to share his daughter's news with a clear head. He turned and gave the van one last look and disappeared into his home.

~ * ~

Steve Steele directed the camera at the front door the moment he saw movement. The Egyptian was staring right at him but not moving. It had been a stroke of sheer luck to park right across the street with a carpet cleaning sign on his van thanks to those government types who'd come in as a cleaning crew a couple days ago.

The director stopped, pulling one particular letter to his nose, and smiled. Must be a woman. Steve rewound the audiotape from the director's recent call and listened again to the conversation. It was time to call his uncle.

"Sir. I'm sorry to interrupt but there has been a development in our foreign situation."

"Go on."

"The target contacted our northern contingent…"

"Steve?"

"Sir?"

"In English."

"Yes, sir. The Egyptian contacted the boys in the Antelope Valley and accused them of stealing the statuette and keeping it for themselves."

The wheezy, hacking response from the other end of the phone took Steve off guard. It had been a long time since he'd heard his uncle laugh.

"He's desperate. Those two combined don't have the brain cells of a senile pigeon."

"What's your recommendation, sir?"

"I think it's time to set up a face-to-face to buy my artifact. If he continues in this vein and tries to sell me the fake, we'll, uhm, send the Egyptian back home. Am I clear?"

"Crystal, sir. Do you want me to arrange a confab?"

"Steve, you're talking jargon again. No. I think I'd better initiate the meeting. I want to make it clear that no one crosses me--ever. He'll be a good example to anyone else who might entertain the idea."

"What about the artifact, sir?"

"I've gotten over it. I think I'm beginning to like things from China now, you know, Ming vases, and things like that. I'll send out feelers in that direction."

"Yes, sir. Do I need to contact you again, sir?"

"No. If things go the way I plan, two of my business associates will visit you at your location around, let's see, twelve plus seven equals, around 19:30 to use your terminology. Contact me when you've completed your assignment."

"Yes, sir."

Steve stretched his legs and pressed the heels of his hands together exerting immense pressure. Now, he needed to wait until 19:30 and keep an eye open and ear tuned.

~ * ~

Nasim looked up the number of the warehouse on the internet. He checked the company's Web page, did a background check through his records, the local police, and the Better Business Bureau. The storage warehouse Dr. Riyadh appeared to be using was under surveillance by every law enforcement agency in the land. A raid, six months before when he was on vacation, had spotlighted the extent of the activities happening inside the units but legal mumbo-jumbo by the company's lawyers freed them to conduct business as usual.

He was certain he could get close enough to the director's unit to estimate the size but beyond that, he was at a loss at how to get inside and see if the Dr. Riyadh was dealing in stolen antiquities in America. It irked Nasim how the director could stay *just* under the radar.

He called the warehouse.

"Alpha Storage Facility. This is Shania, how can I help you?"

Nasim felt his nerves assaulted with the irritating snap of gum.

"Yes. I'm needing to find, uhm, how do you say, a big houseware to store my pots. I heard you have very big rooms to store, yes?"

He figured sounding too American would bring out suspicion. This way, the management would see dollar signs--a foreigner with money--and not ask him too many questions.

Shania, snapping her gum, giggled. "Yes. We have large storage spaces available. What do you want it for? Pot? We don't do anything illegal here."

"No, no, for my pots. I sell dishes, vases, uhm, uhm, what is word, pottery. I sell many, many pots to stores in Los Angeles. I need a big space to hold them when the ship comes from Egypt. Do you have big spaces? Could I see?"

More gum snapping. "Uhm, let me check with the boss. Hold on, please."

Nasim doodled on the sticky note pad in front of him listening to the piped in advertising that filled the hold void.

He knew the secretary had returned to the line by the irritating pop of gum.

"Uh, Big Jimmy said you'll have to come by tomorrow. It's too late today to show you anything and, uh, well, just come by tomorrow at ten in the morning. What's your name?"

Nasim hadn't thought that far in advance. "Oh, ah, it is Jones. I am Bill Jones."

"From Egypt?" Even the secretary wasn't buying this.

"My father was American. My mother let him name me. What can I say?"

"Whatever. Just be here at ten tomorrow." Click.

Nasim gritted his teeth. There was that American habit of hanging up without saying goodbye. He couldn't move any further on this lead until tomorrow. Leaning back, arms behind his head, he closed his eyes. He jolted awake. A glance at the clock told him he'd been sleeping for ten minutes. Maybe going home early wasn't a bad idea.

With a good night's sleep, he would be more apt to come up with a way to get a look inside the director's storage unit. Nasim struggled out of his chair and left the office. There was nothing on his desk that couldn't wait for one more day.

Chapter Twenty-eight

Lydia watched the scenery change from wall-to-wall houses and brown air to brown mountains and open skies. She thought about the fact she hadn't been this way since coming back to Los Angeles. She vaguely recalled a camping trip when she was very young to a place called Red Rocks Canyon. Something in her brain niggled at her that the fact was the trip abruptly ended when her mother spotted a rattlesnake slithering across the road. So much for outdoor education. Following Glenda, she wound her way up the side of the mountain and parked behind the Lexus in a comfortable looking house with attached garage. She opened her car door and stepped out, turning to take in the view.

She was amazed at how much like the Middle East this valley looked: sparse vegetation, jutting jagged mountains, and Joshua Trees. Lydia smiled. She'd forgotten the incredible tree that could be burned and still live. She closed her driver door and wrestled her overnight bag from the back seat. This might not be such a bad assignment after all.

Once inside, Lydia put her things in the guest room and reconnoitered the property. The location so beautiful in scenery was a nightmare for logistics. There were so many accessible windows; Lydia started to feel a headache building.

Glenda put together a quick lunch and the two women sat on the porch overlooking the valley.

"If I didn't like my job so much I could be real happy here," Lydia sipped her coffee.

"Yeah. There are some down sides to the isolation but not enough enticements to get me to move closer to town. You can't put a price on this." Glenda swept her hand at the vista.

"I've got my fingers crossed that tonight will be quiet," Lydia shot Glenda a glance.

"Let's hope."

~ * ~

Omar let the answering machine take his calls most of the afternoon. Around 5:00 p.m., he received a call that brought him to his feet. He was online looking at the most recent photos sent to him by his realtor in the islands. His patience was wearing thin. Maybe, he'd go without this last sale to plump his bank account. The phone rang and he allowed the machine to catch the message.

"Unless you want one of my associates to relocate your liver, I'd pick up the phone." The raspy voice held a hint of irritation.

Omar grabbed the office extension. "Hello, I'm sorry. I've been screening sales calls. I wasn't expecting to hear from you for another twenty-four hours."

"I decided I wanted to see the merchandise tonight."

"I told you…"

"Don't lie, doctor. It's very unattractive. I have it on good authority that you have the cat."

"I--I--do. What time and where do you want to meet?"

"I'll come to your house at 7:30 tonight."

The phone went dead. Omar leaned back in his chair and closed his eyes. With a great deal of luck, this would be over tonight. He could get a good night's sleep and fly out of Los Angeles first thing in the morning. A glance at his watch told him, there was still time to go out for one last dinner at the Egyptian restaurant he so enjoyed.

The carpet cleaning crew was pulling out of the driveway as Omar locked his front door on the way to the garage. He calculated they had spent nearly four hours, that he knew of in, the house across the street.

"They must be very thorough. I'll have to remember their name and have them clean my house. I don't think the Realtor who sold me this house was as meticulous. Then again, I'll be in my new home in the islands and it won't matter." The thought cheered him up and dampened the dread he felt building about the buyer's visit.

~ * ~

Steve dropped the van another car length behind the Mercedes. One thing he could safely conclude about this target is the man was obsessed with his vehicle. At no point in this operation had he left the car vulnerable to having a tracking devise put on it. When he was home, he garaged the car. When he was at the museum, he parked in his designated spot near the front door where the guards could watch it. His obsession had made Steve revive some of his basic tailing techniques. He kept an eye on the Mercedes as it pulled into the parking lot next to a restaurant. Once around the block and to a side street that gave a straight view of the front door, Steve slid the van into the treed parking spot. After five minutes, he got out and began to pull the plastic paint covering from his van. What had appeared as a white working van was now burgundy with gray accents. Taking the magnetized signs from the sides, revealed deeply tinted windows and, for effect, Steve popped open the sunroof. He crawled into the side, retrieved a soda from the small refrigerator, warmed a burrito in the microwave, and settled in the driver's seat to have his dinner. If the plan went as expected, tomorrow he'd hop on his Harley and drive up to the wine country. He deserved a holiday.

~ * ~

Glenda and Lydia were cleaning up after dinner and chitchatting when the knock sounded on the front door.

Tossing a worried glance Lydia's way, Glenda wiped her hands on the dishtowel and started to the door.

"Wait a minute." Lydia pulled her gun from the holster and flattened herself against the wall by the front door. She'd have full view of the party on the other side and a clear shot if needed when Glenda opened the door.

Glenda pulled in a deep breath and opened the door.

"Can I interest you in some cats today?" LaVonne held up two carriers whose occupants were complaining loudly.

"LaVonne! Scat! I Ching! Come in, come in." Glenda stepped back and shook her head at Lydia.

When LaVonne had maneuvered the entry, she turned and glanced behind the door having noted Glenda's actions. She nearly dropped the carriers.

"What is it with you people and guns? You okay, Glenda?" The blonde woman gently set the animals on the floor.

"I'm fine, LaVonne. This is Nasim's partner, Lydia." Lydia and LaVonne nodded at each other. "They seem to think those thugs from the other night might be back and Lydia is here to guard me."

"Ooooo. A bodyguard. How exciting! Let me go get the royal pain and I'll be right back. I will take a cup of coffee if you have it. My Alvin is in town tonight with one of his buddies. They're over in Quartz Hill at a car show. He'll be gone for hours. You can fill me in on the details"

Lydia reholstered her weapon and moved to the kitchen. She had been at Glenda's for a couple hours now and the two had established a rapport that Lydia felt free to put drinks together for the three and set it on the coffee table in the living room.

LaVonne set the last carrier on the floor then made a beeline for the couch. Once the door closed, the three women opened the carriers. All three cats while complaining long and loudly were tentative about stepping out.

"Let's just sit and have coffee. They'll come out in their own time." Glenda slid onto the love seat in front of the window.

LaVonne took a deep draught of her beverage and sat back. "Okay. Tell all. You know, LaVonne won't say a thing."

Glenda backed up LaVonne's trustworthiness with a nod to Lydia.

Lydia sipped her drink wondering how much should she safely indulge to this woman Glenda seemed to trust.

"Well, do you have time?"

LaVonne resettled herself on the couch and held her coffee cup close to her. "Hours."

"Okay. Let me tell you from the beginning. About fifteen years ago, I was a student in Egypt working on the most recently uncovered tomb…"

~ * ~

Omar pushed his plate away. He always ate too much when he came to the restaurant. Masood, his waiter, smiled and, as was their ritual, brought the small demitasse cup of rich Egyptian coffee.

"Here you go director."

"Thank you, Masood. How is your family?"

"Doing well, sir. Thank you for asking."

"Please give my regards to them."

"Thank you, sir, I will."

The waiter moved away and allowed Omar the peace to drink his coffee. Zahra was about to start dancing and most nights he would have stayed to watch. She was the best belly dancer he'd seen outside of Cairo. Tonight, though, he had a meeting in, he looked at his watch, an hour that he couldn't miss. It was the final installment in his retirement plan.

He sighed and signaled the waiter for his bill and, after paying and leaving his usual hefty tip, left. There was still enough traffic on the streets that he would make it home with maybe ten minutes to spare. He argued with himself whether he should play the host or simply conduct the sale and encourage the buyer to leave as soon as possible.

He gave the rear view mirror a fleeting look and looked again. He could swear the red van a couple cars back was following him. He checked his side mirrors and caught the flash of color as the van turned off the street.

"I'm getting paranoid in my old age," Omar chuckled.

Steve Steele had seen Dr. Riyadh checking his mirror. He turned off the main road and took the back streets to the director's home. Parking a couple blocks away, he watched the Mercedes glide past him and turn on the right street. He dialed the number and left the message. "Everything is a go."

Ten minutes passed and the Mercedes limo slowed to a crawl past the street where Steve sat. There was a knock on the window of his van and he peered into a frightening face looking at him. His phone rang.

"Yes, sir."

"I've let the boys out and they're to sit with you. My transaction will conclude within the half hour at which time I will engage the green button when I pass you. By your own instructions, you and the gentlemen waiting by your vehicle need to wait five minutes before you go inside and accomplish the task. Call me when you've finished."

Steve had rarely heard his uncle speak so much. "Yes, sir."

He opened the side door to the van and nodded at the two bruisers who stood waiting outside. They snuffed out cigarettes on the street, picking up the butts and field stripping the remainder scattering the bits along the gutter.

Steve looked at the inside of the van. It was going to be a tight squeeze for the next twenty minutes. As one started to crawl inside he held up his hand.

"Just a minute."

Opening a cabinet under the bench seat located against the driver sidewall, he pulled out three military-issue gas masks.

"What's this for?" Bruiser number one asked.

"Nitrous oxide."

"What?" Bruiser number two looked confused. "Isn't that laughing gas?"

Steve nodded. "Yes, and it will put most people to sleep within five minutes. We have that much time to get two blocks over, three houses up, and inside to complete our mission. Will that be a problem?"

The two shook their heads.

"Good. Get inside now. We have about half an hour to wait."

Steve sat in the driver's seat, his uncle's men in the back. None of them spoke.

~ * ~

Omar parked his car in the garage and went in the house. He'd decided it was best to be gracious with his buyer. The man's influence could be international and he didn't want to get on his bad side before he fled the country. He pulled out the bottle of merlot and two crystal wine glasses. The little sarcophagus of the cat goddess rested innocuously upon the coffee table.

At precisely, 7:30 the doorbell pealed. Omar opened the door and looked up. A very large man in a chauffeur's uniform blocked his view of the street.

"He's here."

The wall-of-a-man moved aside and held the door for a thin businessman in a tailored suit to enter. The businessman turned to his driver.

"Wait in the car. I won't be long."

Omar had to curb the reflex to scrunch his shoulders at the reedy sound of the man's voice.

"Yes, sir." Moving with surprising speed and agility, the driver trotted to the limousine parked at the curb.

Omar escort his guest to the living room.

"Wine?"

His guest nodded and accepted the glass. A sip of the blood red liquid and his eyebrows shot up.

"It's quite good."

"I have it imported from France."

A dip of the head, "I see. Shall we dispense with the usual formalities? Where is the item in question?"

Omar leaned forward and pulled off the top of the gilded box. He carefully extracted the little figurine and cradling it in one hand presented the cat goddess statuette to his guest.

The man took the statue, and examined the front turning the figurine over to check the back.

"Are you sure this is authentic?"

"You have my word as the most notable authority in the field, this is the cat goddess Bastet."

The businessman shot him a glance and put the figure in the gold sarcophagus. "Your payment will be made before the end of the night." He stood.

Omar escorted his guest to the front door. Neither said goodbye as their relationship had ended with the transfer of the relic.

He watched the limousine pull away from the curb, keeping his expression neutral. Closing the door, he let out a hoop.

"How very American I'm becoming." Grinning from ear to ear, he rushed to his bedroom and pulled his luggage from the shelf in the closet. He started shoving clothes into the opened bags and, suddenly, stopped mid-toss.

"What am I doing? I have enough money to buy anything I need. I'll just leave the Mercedes at the airport and have my cousin send one of his associates to pick it up--reward for a job well done. I'd better call the storage company and tell them someone will be by to take over the supervision of my merchandise. I can start shipping it when I'm settled and established."

He stopped and dropped on the bed. "This almost didn't happen. I'm glad it's done."

Rousing himself, he wandered to the living room and picked up the glasses, holding the businessman's goblet with two fingers and rinsing it the first thing when he got to the kitchen. He replaced the merlot in its spot, and put away the cleaned glasses.

In a call to the warehouse, he left a message one of his assistants would be coming by to check out things and taking over while he was out of the country. His next call was to his cousin.

The phone rang with a hint of an echo in the background.

"Good morning."

"Feneku?"

"Omar? What fortunate circumstance causes you to call me twice in the same week? Your business deal was successful?"

"Yes, cousin, it was thanks to you. I need your assistance."

"Whatever I can do."

"Do you have an associate in the Los Angeles area who has gone above and beyond your requests of them?"

"Yes."

"As I have concluded my business here, I will be leaving on the next flight out to my island retreat. I'll be driving my Mercedes sportster…"

"The one we saw at the dealer?"

"The same model and color."

"I thought you were keeping a quiet front."

"I couldn't resist just this one extravagance. Anyway, I'll leave the keys in a box under the front fender and sign over the title. Have your associate pick up the car and go to this address…"

Omar searched his wallet for the warehouse business card and rattled off the address.

"…and talk with the manager. I've told him I'll be out of the country for a few weeks and my associate would be watching over the merchandise and completing an inventory. Let your person keep the car. It could ensure a measure of silence. Don't do anything until I call you from the island. You should hear from me within the next twenty-four hours."

"I will see to it the situation is handled. Your buyer found no problems with the merchandise?"

"He did not even look twice. The workmanship was exquisite. You have surpassed yourself."

"It was a challenge and a thrill. Until your call, cousin."

He hung up the phone and stretched his back. It had been a long day of waiting and he was feeling the tension knot up along his spine.

He blinked his eyes several times suddenly feeling the overwhelming urge to sleep. Stumbling, he tried to make his way to the bedroom, passing out and slumping to the floor in the hallway near the front door.

~ * ~

The limousine slid up to the curb. Steve's phone chirped.

"Send one of the boys over to the car. I have something I want to leave at the scene. The boys will know what to do. I'm pushing the green button."

Bruiser number one returned with a gold box. Steve looked at it and shrugged. His job was to terminate with prejudice a problem. Any messages his uncle wanted to leave were his own business.

He looked at the two standing outside the van. "You ready?"

They nodded.

"Got your masks?"

They each held up a mask.

"Let's go."

At a quick step, Steve, dark rucksack held close to his body, and the two large shadows skulked the streets to Dr. Riyadh's house. They slipped up the driveway and around the back. Steve pulled a palm-sized control box out of his jacket pocket and checked the light. The color was glowing green.

"Don your mask and let's go."

With military precision, the three slipped the masks over their faces, the two larger men following Steve in the back door. He pulled a pin light from his other pocket and quickly located the slumped body of the director in the middle of the hallway.

"He dead?" the first bruiser asked.

"No. Not yet." Steve replied. A metallic sneeze finalized his reply; the muzzle flash hidden by the expensive closed drapes.

One of the bruisers pulled the gold box from his jacket. He opened the top and pulled out the figurine, which he stuffed into the still warm mouth of the antiquities director. He dropped the box on his chest.

Two sets of footsteps, avoiding the spreading lake of dark fluid expanding around the head of Dr. Dabir Omar Ben Rashid Yacoub Riyadh, echoed through the empty house to the back door.

"Aren't you coming?" one of the pair asked.

"I've got some cleaning up to do. I'll be out of here in twenty minutes. You'd best go."

The two disappeared out the back door and slinked down the street, entering the limousine a few blocks away. It moved from the curb, lights off, and within two blocks was moving from the area in normal fashion.

Steve completed his task and quietly exited the back door. He pushed a button on the control box. The light changed from green to red. Silently, he stole down the street, entered his van, and removed the bulging backpack. No one would know of his presence at the home of Dr. Omar Riyadh. Starting the van, Steve left the neighborhood.

This morning there would be no large deposit in the private Bahamian account of Ben Rashid aka Omar Riyadh.

Chapter Twenty-nine

Nasim wasn't sure what he was going to tell the girl at the warehouse. The story he'd concocted yesterday sounded lame to his own ears and he knew he couldn't pull it off with a straight face. He was not a good liar.

He'd had to consult his GPS system to find the warehouse by the San Pedro docks, as he'd never had the occasion to be in the area. He got out of the car, an hour early hoping to catch them off guard, and practiced going over his story to himself when he reached the office door. It swung open and a man with enormously muscled arms stepped out.

"You that guy the museum director sent over?"

Nasim stopped. For a moment, he was speechless. Should he tell the truth? He thought better of it and figured if the director showed up he would worry about his position then.

"Uh, yeah."

"About damn time. I don't have all day to wait on your pansy asses. Come on then. Follow me." The man was rifling through a large silver ring holding countless keys as he strode down the driveway at a pace that pushed Nasim to break into a trot. He seemed to find one he liked and stopped in front of a large metal door with a padlock. He put the key to the padlock and opened it, muscling the metal sliding door aside.

Nasim gasped. The warehouse was large enough to hold a plane, which it did--a small private jet, and an acre of priceless objects. All the items were boxes and marked *pottery*.

"The director left a message saying you'd be handling this stuff while he was away. Rent's due on the first. No grace period. You don't pay, this stuff's mine." He eyed the jet. "I could make use of that."

With a jangling of keys, he hung the open padlock on the door and started back to the office.

"Lock up before you go," he yelled over a shoulder.

Nasim moved to the first box he spied that appeared unsealed. He swung open the wooden door and staggered back. Inside was a six-foot tall, golden statue of the cat goddess Bastet. The form glowed in the diffused light streaming through the grimy windows high above the metal sliding doors.

"Your gods shine on me today, father." This was the treasure from the little princess Kia's tomb. He dialed Lydia's cell and got her voice mail.

"We've hit gold. I think we can nail Dr. Riyadh to the wall. I'm inside the warehouse and it is stuffed to the rafters with treasures. I'm sure his fingerprints will be all over this stuff. I'm going to do as much of an inventory as I can right now. The manager made the comment that the director was leaving town. We need to verify it before he escapes again. Call me when you get this message."

Nasim stepped back and looked over the tightly packed warehouse. He pulled a notebook and pen from his pocket and started taking down serial numbers from the boxes. The numbers and the shipper's names on each of the crates would help lead them to who and how the treasures were being spirited away from their homeland.

For the first time in more years than he could remember, the weight of shame was lifted from his shoulders. Nasim allowed his gaze to caress the cat goddess.

"This one is for you, father... and you, too, Uncle."

Minutes before, when he was rehearsing his story, he would not have bargained on the feeling of exultation he was currently experiencing. "It is good to be alive and be a Shabouh."

Nasim continued his work whistling a tune his mother sang to him as a child.

~ * ~

Lydia felt the vibration of her cell but couldn't risk answering in the traffic sludge that passed for early morning rush hour. When her phone rang the second time, she swore and pulled to the right side of the road taking the nearest off ramp. Even leaving at some ungodly hour, upon Glenda's recommendation, Lydia was going to be late getting to the office.

She listened to her messages. The first was from Nasim who had, somehow, wrangled his way inside Dr. Riyadh's storage unit. The second call was from the director's secretary.

"Ms. Thompson. This is Avril Livingstone and I need you to check on Dr. Riyadh, please. He hasn't shown up for work and I've been calling for the last half hour. I'm worried. Please call my personal number, 909-459-3218, and let me know I'm just being silly – again."

Lydia checked the time on her radio. It was nine thirty. The director was indeed late. Well, if she was going to his house, she was dragging Nasim with her. She checked the signal on her cell and was pleased to see she could make a call.

Nasim answered on the second ring.

"Hello?"

"Nasim, it's Lydia. I got your message and am surprised, to say the least. We have a situation with the director. His secretary called and says she can't raise him. Meet me at his house as soon as possible. I'm crawling my way over the mountains from the Antelope Valley. I'll be there as soon as I can."

Nasim cleared his throat. "How's Glenda?"

Lydia smiled. Her partner had a crush. How cute. "She's fine. I don't know what's worse--having something happen or being awake all night thinking something is *going* to happen."

"Did something happen?" Panic oozed through the phone.

"No. That's just it. It was absolutely the quietest night I've spent in a long time."

Nasim blew out his breath. "That's good."

"Yes. Ms. Nagel and all her kitties are doing fine. I'll see you at the director's house."

Rolling her neck and shoulders to release the tension, Lydia sighed and started her car. The sooner she got through this automotive maze the better. The hair on the back of her neck was prickling and she had a sinking sensation in the pit of her stomach that this time the director's secretary might not be crying wolf.

~ * ~

Lydia pulled to the front of the house and saw Nasim's vehicle in the driveway. She parked and got out to locate her partner. He strolled from the back of the house and nodded at her.

"Looks like the car is tucked away." He tipped his head in the direction of the garage.

"You try the door yet?"

He shook his head. "Thought I'd wait until we were both here."

They walked up to the porch and listened for a moment. When they couldn't hear any noise from inside, Lydia pushed the bell and stood listening to the sound of the doorbell echoing hollowly. Her stomach began tightening.

I have a bad feeling about this.

Nasim crept up the driveway to the back of the house. Nothing appeared out of order. The lawn was lush, green, and manicured drops of morning dew glistened on the perfect blades. White wicker lawn furniture provided a comfortable conversation area in the genteel backyard oasis. He moved stealthily around the outside of the house checking in the soft dirt of the flowerbeds. The doorbell sounded through the house forlornly.

Nasim activated his two-way radio.

"Lydia."

"What?"

"I'm not finding any evidence of activity back here. You?"

The muted hiss of white noise met his question.

"Nasim."

"Yes?"

"Can you see into the house from where you are?"

He moved across the decking, the scent of freshly cut, damp cedar assaulting his senses. Looking to the porch, he realized it was a recent addition. The morning dew rested on the planks in perfect crystal domes. If anyone had been here, it was late last night before the ever-present dampness of marine air had settled over the valley.

"I'll try. The curtains don't meet over the sliding glass door."

He was ill-at-ease with the actions he was taking. He was, after all, a law enforcement officer. Should this become a crime scene, every action he took from this moment forward could disturb important evidence. Yes, he wanted Omar Riyadh to go to jail, but he wanted to be sure there would be no legal loopholes through which this cobra could slither.

Placing each foot carefully down, Nasim moved to the glass wall and squint his eyes, focusing on the room beyond the drapes. The shuttered illumination of morning sun through the closed draperies was casting a feeble light in the front entryway. He could make out a briefcase, a small table next to the front door with keys on the top and…

Lydia heard the string of Egyptian spit through the two-way radio.

"Nasim? Nasim! What is it?"

She started to leave the front porch when her radio crackled to life.

"Don't come round back. Call the local authorities. Dr. Riyadh's body is in the hallway."

He retraced his footsteps and trudged to the front of the house. His shoulders were sagging, mouth turned down at the edges.

"This is not how I wanted to capture this snake. From what I can see, this doesn't appear to be an accident. There's a lot of blood on the floor."

Nasim and Lydia walked to their vehicles. She called the emergency number, letting the operator know she was with law enforcement.

Within half an hour, there were several police cars, and EMT's from the local fire station. The police questioned Lydia and Nasim for an hour before letting them go inside and view the scene.

The two stood looking down at the body, bullet through the forehead. The director appeared relaxed, almost asleep, except for the statue wedged in his mouth.

"I'm not sure who he tried to sell this to but I have a good idea." Lydia shook her head. "He was so far out of his league; I don't understand how he could think he'd get away with ripping these people off."

Nasim sighed. "Because in Egypt, no one was more devious or had more officials in their pocket than Omar Riyadh. He met his match here."

Lydia regarded her partner. "What does this do for you?"

"Well, at least some other family won't go through the hell we tolerated but it leaves my family name without vindication. I'm not sure what I'll do now."

She touched his shoulder. "Let's get out of here. This place smells like death."

Walking to their cars, the partners maintained a contemplative silence.

"We need to go back to the office and grab the artifacts from the evidence locker. I'll contact the Yemen government and arrange to return the items. Too bad we couldn't have found the other relics on that list. See ya there."

Nasim nodded and walked to his car in a fog. His mind swirled with the realization that his ten-year search had ended. Not in the manner he would have liked, but it was over. Now, he needed to find a way to let go of his anger. If only there was something he could do to show the government of his country how wrong they were about his father and uncle.

He pulled into his parking spot and trudged to his desk. He was sitting with his head bent over the pages of paperwork he and Lydia had to fill out when his phone rang.

"Yes?"

"Listen, bud. I need to know if you and your boss are going to keep this space. I just heard something on the news that some guy with the same name was murdered this morning."

Nasim snapped his head up. *Of course!* "Yeah, we're keeping the space. Just a coincidence about the name. You know how news people are with foreign names. I'm coming back with my secretary at three o'clock. Leave the key at the front desk. I'll lock up and return it when I'm finished."

Lydia peeked around the corner. "What's up?"

"We're going to check out the warehouse."

"The warehouse."

"Yeah. When I got there this morning, they thought I was someone else sent over to take care of the cargo inside while the director was out of town. Looks as though the director was about to leave again."

"Nasim. If these are the items stolen from the little princess' crypt, we could endanger a case against Dr. Riyadh and any of his family that might be involved."

"Well, we won't know unless we take the list we got from the Yemen government and check it against what is stored in that warehouse. I'll bet if we verify the tag numbers from the dig on at least two items, we can get a warrant to search legally. *And,* when we get into the manager's background a little further, we'll find he can't afford to be involved in anything illegal."

Nasim sat back in his chair and folded his arms across his chest.

Lydia rolled her eyes. "Why are we waiting?"

Armed with the two-page list sent by the Yemen government, Lydia and Nasim returned to the warehouse in San Pedro. Nasim noted the muscled manager was nowhere in sight and the gum popping secretary had been replaced with a middle-aged woman typing furiously at the computer when they retrieved the keys.

Trudging along the dock, Nasim stopped in front of the metal door he remembered from the morning. The key slipped easily into the lock and, together, Lydia and Nasim opened the door. His stomach had been flipping since the moment he'd seen the new receptionist.

The boxes piled to the ceiling were still in place but the jet had disappeared.

Nasim moved to the box he'd opened previously and found the six-foot guardian cat resting inside.

Lydia walked to the statue, mouth open, and stared.

"This is worth more money than I'll see in my lifetime."

"Yeah. Everything is here except the jet. I've got a feeling we won't be able to find Big Jim or Shania anywhere. Let's get busy. I think we might be able to lock this place down tonight if we work fast enough."

"For once partner, I think you might be right."

An hour later, the list in Lydia's hands had checkmarks on more than twenty items.

"It's time to call the boss and have him start the wheels." Lydia called and laid out the situation. "He says to stay put. If the secretary gets pushy, we're to flash our badges. Let's just continue opening these boxes."

It was well past five o'clock when they heard a vehicle pull up outside. Lydia stepped to the door and peeked through.

Captain O'Sullivan shoved aside the heavy metal door and gaped at the filled space.

"All this is stolen antiquities?"

Nasim and Lydia nodded.

"Much of it from the Yemen dig." Lydia said.

"How far have you gotten on that list of yours?"

They handed him the paper populated with checkmarks. He ran his finger down the page.

"Son of a bitch. Well, I've got the warrant here," he waved the form, "and we've got half a dozen young, eager officers coming out to take over for you. You two go home. This doesn't get you out of paperwork; just have the start of it to me by end of day tomorrow."

Nasim opened his mouth to speak, and Lydia jabbed him in the ribs.

"Thanks, Captain." She smiled.

Turning to Nasim, she muttered as she grabbed his arm and steered him to the door, "Just go. Captain O'Sullivan doesn't have a generous nature. If he tells us to go, we need to get the heck out. This may end the story for Dr. Riyadh but for us it's just the beginning of a mountain of paperwork. An undisturbed afternoon to lounge around sounds good to me."

Nasim blew an exasperated breath threw his lips. "Yeah, me too."

Chapter Thirty

Antelope Valley, three months later

Nasim stood and watched the heat undulate toward the sky in waves distorting the distant view and highlighting the brown, scorched earth below a denim-washed blue sky.

Glenda placed the iced tea with no ice cubes on the coffee table.

"You sure you don't want ice cubes?" she looked up to the profile of the handsome young man who'd become a regular visitor at her home.

He turned and smiled. "I know you Americans don't understand but some of us don't like our drinks icy cold. Thank you." He touched the back of her hand marveling at the soft skin.

Glenda felt the heat rush to her cheeks. She hated that about herself.

"Why don't we sit? You mentioned something about a surprise."

He settled in the love seat. As if on cue, three furry sets of paws thundered down the hallway. Scat, rubbed against his legs and he reached down to scratch her ears. I Ching took up guard on the back of the love seat, her tail draping over his shoulder the minute he sat back. It was Pandora who'd surprised Nasim and Glenda with her immediate possession of the frequent visitor. She claimed her usual spot in the middle of Nasim's lap. He began to stroke her fur.

"So what's happening now? We discussed how you guys were able to track Dr. Riyadh's cousin through the warehouse records. I hadn't thought about this before, but, why were they so suddenly helpful? Didn't you tell me Lydia said there was a prostitution ring that used space next to the Dr.'s to hold captives?"

Nasim sipped his tea and replaced it on the little coaster on the coffee table.

"Yes. Last year when I went home to visit, Lydia volunteered for a combined task force that was watching the docks. They received an anonymous call about activity occurring around a certain pier and certain warehouse unit. When the curs were apprehended at the same warehouse the Dr. was using, the businessman who appeared to be giving the orders threatened her. Lydia thinks it was the mobster as she calls him who ordered a couple guys to break into her house one morning. That's why she moved."

"Oh. But what about the owners? Weren't they being watched?"

"Yes. The husband of the actual owner managed the warehouse units. He wasn't immune to slipping money in his own pocket to ignore illegal happenings within the business. The raid Lydia helped pull off wasn't his first brush with the law. He was looking at spending a long time in jail under your three strikes provision. When it became clear there would be law enforcement problems, he took off with the receptionist, a gum popping slip of a girl. His wife, the named owner on the business title, was the middle-aged woman who I met the second time I opened Dr. Riyadh's unit. She helped in every way she could; opening the books to us so she could hang on to the family business."

"So what did you find out about Dr. Riyadh?" Glenda chased I Ching from her choice spot and moved next to Nasim.

"He has a cousin in Cairo who was the operations manager of this business enterprise. We've tried to locate the man but at this point, he's disappeared into the dust of the desert. The cousin had a network of people who kept him up to date on all the digs happening in and around Egypt. If there was a major find and security was lax, he employed several known tomb raider families…"

Glenda raised an eyebrow.

Nasim smiled at her and ran his finger down her delicate cheek. "There are still people in my country who make a living stealing from the dead."

She shook her head and sipped her tea.

"… as I was saying, he employed people to sneak into the dig under the darkness of night. He would have a list of the items he desired and the thieves would go shopping. As with his cousin, Dr. Riyadh, Feneku has often slithered out of the hands of the law leaving lowly thieves and their families to suffer for his greed."

"What we uncovered at the warehouse were items from the Yemen dig--the little princess' sarcophagus, items from several digs in the Valley of the Kings, and items from the museums where the director oversaw the antiquities departments. The warehouse owner's husband tried to steal the jet but authorities apprehended him and his girlfriend at the John Wayne airport trying to hire a pilot.

"Dr. Riyadh had rented and moved the items in right under the noses of the Coast Guard, Harbor Patrol, and local law enforcement. His reputation covered him.

"I only wish my father were alive to reap the benefits of this operation. There were items from the museum in Riyadh and Cairo that the government accused my family of stealing. This sets the name of Shabouh back in the rightful annals of the pharaohs. He would be proud."

Glenda heard the catch in his voice and slid her hand over his. He turned to gaze at her with those chocolate brown eyes she'd come to love. She leaned forward and initiated a kiss. Her eyes closed as she allowed the sensation of his velvety lips stir her hormones into a rage. Pulling back, she caught her breath.

"Whew. You still haven't told me what my surprise is."

His eyes twinkled as he leaned forward, provoking a plaintiff yeowl from Pandora. He pulled his wallet from his back pocket and opened the leather container. Extracting two creased envelopes, he handed one to Glenda.

She unfolded the white envelope and opened the flap, slipping her fingers in to retrieve the paperwork. As she began to yank it out, she recognized the insignia.

"What is this?" her eyes glowed.

"It is with the deepest thanks and gratitude, the government of Yemen has asked me to convey to you their desire for you to see the tomb of the little princess first hand. *We* have tickets to visit." He flashed her one of his rare smiles.

"When, how, what about my kitties?"

Nasim held up a hand. "They would like us to arrive within the month to help them celebrate the find of the little princess' tomb. They're hosting a celebration at the University in Ta'izz and we'll be guests of honor."

"Why?"

"We helped to bring back the relics to their rightful owners. Your perception and keen eye spotted the cat goddess for her true self. The government and people of Yemen are grateful. Is that so hard to believe?"

Glenda shook her head as she drew circles on the top of Nasim's hand.

"As for the monsters here," he waved his hand at Glenda's three furry roommates, "LaVonne and Alvin have agreed to take them for the month we'll be gone."

"A month?... We?" Glenda cast a suspicious eye on him.

"Yes. Lydia has entwined herself with a beau and won't be coming with us but all three of us were invited. When I talked with Dr. Burkhardt about the trip…"

"Why am I the last to know?" Glenda pretended a pout.

"…he thought it would be a wonderful opportunity for the magazine's editor to capture the flavor of the land she so often waxes poetic about."

"Oh."

"The reason you weren't included is because I wanted to be the one to give you the news. We're going to take a side trip so you can meet my relatives. They want to thank you for helping to restore the family name. We'll be in Cairo for a week before we leave for Yemen."

"Well, you've thought of everything, haven't you?"

It was Nasim's turn to blush. "Uh, no. I'm sorry ...if you don't wish to meet my relatives, I'll understand..." He dropped his gaze to the Persian in his lap and continued to pet her.

Glenda tucked a finger under his chin and raised it so his eyes met hers.

"You're going to have to learn that I like to tease you. It would be an honor to meet your family and find out how they put up with you all these years. Thank you for talking with LaVonne about the kitties and Dr. Burkhardt about my job--now and before. I don't think I'd be able to find anything I loved quite so much." Glenda's eyes twinkled. "Well, on second thought, maybe I could."

Glenda felt the need to switch gears. She noted Nasim always got uncomfortable when she expressed how she was beginning to feel about him.

"What would you like for lunch?"

He rose from the love seat amid loud complaints from Pandora and moved to Glenda's side.

"How about you tell me again what you love?" He pulled her into his arms and tilted her head. Dropping his lips to meet hers, he snugged her to him, and kissed her with a passion she'd not recalled. When he broke the kiss, Glenda was breathless.

"I want my family to meet the woman I hope to marry."

"Hope? How about will?"

They stood in the middle of the living room kissing, oblivious to the three cats winding themselves in and about the couples' legs.

Plans for lunch and the trip could wait until later.

About the Author

C. L. Kraemer is a multi-published author whose books run the gamut from romance to mystery and fantasy. A love of all things desert and cats brought Cats in the Cradle of Civilization to life. Other interests include riding her Harley and spending time with family and friends at the Coast.

Other books by Christie L. Kraemer
Available at Rogue Phoenix Press

Healthy Homicide

Two murders have occurred at the Barrel Springs Day Spa. Police hurry to find the method and reason before anyone else is murdered.

MANIC READER REVIEWS says: Healthy Homicide by C.L. Kraemer is an intriguing plot driven mystery. The plot is well written and pretty much carries the whole story...

Dragons Among Us

In a world full of anomalies such as the platypus and self reproducing Komodo dragon, is the human race willing to accept that dragons may be real?

Sapien Draconi-human-dragon shape shifters-all over the world face this dilemma every day. The question has become life and death as their species is plagued with unexpected and unwanted shifting in the most unlikely of places.

The Ancient Ones-full-blooded dragons-can offer advice, but few seem to put forward workable solutions to the problem.

The fate of the shape shifters hangs in the balance, and an answer must be found before the Homo Sapiens find, dissect, and hunt Sapien Draconi to extinction.

Dragons Among The Eagles

Aleda Sable faces the toughest decision of her life--to stay in dragon form, live as a two-legged or put one foot in the human world and one talon in the dragon world.

An urgent call from her newspaper editor sends Aleda to report on an accident whose driver appears to be a dragon. Authorities have the scene locked down and aren't allowing access to anyone. Television broadcasts flash pictures of scaly legs hanging from a crashed car. However, the bodies disappear into thin air. When the stations try follow-up reports, all they find are state highway workers busily tearing up the roads.

In determining the truth of the shifter disappearances, Aleda finds the truth of her own dilemma.

Shattered Tomorrows

Lucy Daniels has a secret--a deeply guarded secret.

Her life was going along just fine until she accompanied her best friend, Cassie, to her attorney's suite on top of the Equitable Building in downtown Salem, Oregon.

Once inside the lawyer's office, the world turned upside down and Lucy was forced to face a demon from her past. Thirty years ago, life had been different. Lucy had discovered Prince Charming and was headed to her happily ever after.

That's when the devil intervened and because of her brush with the devil, innocent people died.

Joker's Wild

Four brothers raised in the Northwest.

Two choose to stay and pursue life in Oregon. Two are seduced by the promise of Hollywood.

Life throws the Palmer brothers an ugly curve when two are killed in preventable accidents. Even more upsetting is the lack of justice in the trials of the perpetrators.

The remaining brothers will find justice using a shared passion of all the participants--motorcycle poker runs.

C. L. Kraemer
is also featured in these anthologies available at
Rogue Phoenix Press

A Different Kind of Valentine

A collection of four short stories:

Witness by k. J. Dahlen

When Colten finds an injured woman the police are looking for her, should he trust his own judgment about keeping her hidden from the law even if it means she might kill him?

The Prize by C. L. Kraemer

A computer geek learns valuable life lessons when he is given his dream car as well as a condo and the perfect job.

Crazy 'bout You by Clay Renick

Can a psychologist and a romance writer find true love in time for Valentines Day?

Time Changes by Nicolette Zamora

Laurie is just about ready to give up on love when she spies Rob Hender, her high school sweetheart's older brother.

A St. Patrick's Day Tale
by
Christine Young, C. L. Kraemer, Genene Valleau

Tumble through time…

…to Ireland in 1817, when tensions are high between Protestants and Catholics and fae people guide the fate of villagers. A lovely Catholic lass stumbles upon the weakly ritual fisticuffing between Irish lads. She falls into the lap of a handsome young Protestant. Family ties, grudges, and two conniving faeries threaten their budding love. But the faeries outsmart themselves when they hijack a time machine that has mysteriously appeared in their forest and are whisked to…

…Eugene, Oregon in the 20th century, amid a property feud between the local faeries and night elves. The conniving faeries from Olde Ireland try to stir up more mischief. However, a warrior gnome convinces the magic folk to control their own destiny, and forces the intruding faeries to take refuge in the time machine again, spinning their way toward…

…A modern day castle in western Oregon. An eccentric inventor is determined to reclaim his wayward time machine and save his beloved wife from her latest misadventure. If only they can travel safely past the black hole…

A Valentine's Anthology

The Lending Library-a fantasy by C. L. Kraemer

Faeries try to fit into the human world when the forest where they make their home is destroyed by a mysterious enemy.

Chasing Rainbows-a contemporary romance by Genene Valleau

An eccentric aunt, an inventive uncle, a mother who wears poodle skirts, and a brother who wears pearls provide a hilarious backdrop for the courtship of a young woman who yearns for a "normal" family.

The Gift-an historical romance by Christine Young

A man and a woman on opposite sides of the Civil War get a second chance at love after one final battle returns soldiers to their war-torn homes to rebuild their lives.

VISIT OUR WEBSITE
FOR THE FULL INVENTORY
OF QUALITY BOOKS:

http://www.roguephoenixpress.com

Rogue Phoenix Press

Representing Excellence in Publishing

Quality trade paperbacks and downloads
in multiple formats,
in genres ranging from historical
to contemporary romance,
mystery and science fiction.
Visit the website then bookmark it.
We add new titles each month!

www.ingramcontent.com/pod-product-compliance
Lightning Source LLC
Chambersburg PA
CBHW051946220626
47052CB00004B/821

* 9 7 8 1 6 2 4 2 0 1 2 8 8 *